A Swiftly Tilting Planet

OTHER YEARLING BOOKS YOU WILL ENJOY:

A Swiftly

A YEARLING BOOK

Madeleine L'Engle

Tilting Planet

Published by
Bantam Doubleday Dell Books for Young Readers
a division of
Bantam Doubleday Dell Publishing Group, Inc.
1540 Broadway
New York, New York 10036

Grateful acknowledgment is made for "a swiftly tilting planet" from the poem entitled "Senlin: A Biography" by Conrad Aiken, published by Oxford University Press in *Collected Poems*.

ISBN: 0-440-40158-5

Reprinted by arrangement with Farrar, Straus & Giroux, Inc.
Printed in the United States of America

January 1981

26   25

OPM

for Hal Vursell

Contents

A Swiftly Tilting Planet

1

In this fateful hour

The big kitchen of the Murrys' house was bright and warm, curtains drawn against the dark outside, against the rain driving past the house from the northeast. Meg Murry O'Keefe had made an arrangement of chrysanthemums for the dining table, and the yellow, bronze, and pale-gold blossoms seemed to add light to the room. A delectable smell of roasting turkey came from the oven, and her mother stood by the stove, stirring the giblet gravy.

It was good to be home for Thanksgiving, she thought, to be with the reunited family, catching up on what each one had been doing. The twins, Sandy and Dennys, home

3

from law and medical schools, were eager to hear about Calvin, her husband, and the conference he was attending in London, where he was—perhaps at this very minute—giving a paper on the immunological system of chordates.

"It's a tremendous honor for him, isn't it, Sis?" Sandy asked.

"Enormous."

"And how about you, Mrs. O'Keefe?" Dennys smiled at her. "Still seems strange to call you Mrs. O'Keefe."

"Strange to me, too." Meg looked over at the rocker by the fireplace, where her mother-in-law was sitting, staring into the flames; she was the one who was Mrs. O'Keefe to Meg. "I'm fine," she replied to Sandy. "Absolutely fine."

Dennys, already very much the doctor, had taken his stethoscope, of which he was enormously proud, and put it against Meg's burgeoning belly, beaming with pleasure as he heard the strong heartbeat of the baby within. "You are fine, indeed."

She returned the smile, then looked across the room to her youngest brother, Charles Wallace, and to their father, who were deep in concentration, bent over the model they were building of a tesseract: the square squared, and squared again: a construction of the dimension of time. It was a beautiful and complicated creation of steel wires and ball bearings and Lucite, parts of it revolving, parts swinging like pendulums.

Charles Wallace was small for his fifteen years; a stranger might have guessed him to be no more than twelve; but the expression in his light blue eyes as he watched his father alter one small rod on the model was mature and highly intelligent. He had been silent all day, she thought. He seldom talked much, but his silence on this Thanksgiving day, as the approaching storm moaned around the house and clapped the shingles on the roof, was different from his usual lack of chatter.

Meg's mother-in-law was also silent, but that was not surprising. What was surprising was that she had agreed to come to them for Thanksgiving dinner. Mrs. O'Keefe must have been no more than a few years older than Mrs. Murry, but she looked like an old woman. She had lost most of her teeth, and her hair was yellowish and unkempt, and looked as if it had been cut with a blunt knife. Her habitual expression was one of resentment. Life had not been kind to her, and she was angry with the world, especially with the Murrys. They had not expected her to accept the invitation, particularly with Calvin in London. None of Calvin's family responded to the Murrys' friendly overtures. Calvin was, as he had explained to Meg at their first meeting, a biological sport, totally different from the rest of his family, and when he received his M.D./Ph.D. they took that as a sign that he had joined the ranks of the enemy. And Mrs. O'Keefe shared the attitude of many of the villagers that Mrs. Murry's two earned Ph.D.s, and her experiments in the stone lab which adjoined the kitchen, did not constitute proper *work*. Because she had achieved considerable recognition, her puttering was tolerated, but it was not work, in the sense that keeping a clean house was work, or having a nine-to-five job in factory or office was work.

—How could that woman have produced my husband? Meg wondered for the hundredth time, and imaged Calvin's alert expression and open smile. —Mother says there's more to her than meets the eye, but I haven't seen it yet. All I know is that she doesn't like me, or any of the family. I don't know why she came for dinner. I wish she hadn't.

The twins had automatically taken over their old job of setting the table. Sandy paused, a handful of forks in his hand, to grin at their mother. "Thanksgiving dinner is practically the only meal Mother cooks in the kitchen—"

"—instead of out in the lab on her Bunsen burner," Dennys concluded.

Sandy patted her shoulder affectionately. "Not that we're criticizing, Mother."

"After all, those Bunsen-burner stews did lead directly to the Nobel Prize. We're really very proud of you, Mother, although you and Father give us a heck of a lot to live up to."

"Keeps our standards high." Sandy took a pile of plates from the kitchen dresser, counted them, and set them in front of the big platter which would hold the turkey.

—Home, Meg thought comfortably, and regarded her parents and brothers with affectionate gratitude. They had put up with her all through her prickly adolescence, and she still did not feel very grown up. It seemed only a few months ago that she had had braces on her teeth, crooked spectacles that constantly slipped down her nose, unruly mouse-brown hair, and a wistful certainty that she would never grow up to be a beautiful and self-confident woman like her mother. Her inner vision of herself was still more the adolescent Meg than the attractive young woman she had become. The braces were gone, the spectacles replaced by contact lenses, and though her chestnut hair might not quite rival her mother's rich auburn, it was thick and lustrous and became her perfectly, pulled softly back from her face into a knot at the nape of her slender neck. When she looked at herself objectively in the mirror she knew that she was lovely, but she was not yet accustomed to the fact. It was hard to believe that her mother had once gone through the same transition.

She wondered if Charles Wallace would change physically as much as she had. All his outward development had been slow. Their parents thought he might make a sudden spurt in growth.

She missed Charles Wallace more than she missed the twins or her parents. The eldest and the youngest in the family, their rapport had always been deep, and Charles Wallace had an intuitive sense of Meg's needs which could not be accounted for logically; if something in Meg's world was wrong, he knew, and was there to be with her, to help her if only by assuring her of his love and trust. She felt a deep sense of comfort in being with him for this Thanksgiving weekend, in being home. Her parents' house was still home, because she and Calvin spent many weekends there, and their apartment near Calvin's hospital was a small, furnished one, with a large sign saying NO PETS, and an aura that indicated that children would not be welcomed, either. They hoped to be able to look for a place of their own soon. Meanwhile, she was home for Thanksgiving, and it was good to see the gathered family and to be surrounded by their love, which helped ease her loneliness at being separated from Calvin for the first time since their marriage.

"I miss Fortinbras," she said suddenly.

Her mother turned from the stove. "Yes. The house feels empty without a dog. But Fort died of honorable old age."

"Aren't you going to get another dog?"

"Eventually. The right one hasn't turned up yet."

"Couldn't you go look for a dog?"

Mr. Murry looked up from the tesseract. "Our dogs usually come to us. If one doesn't, in good time, then we'll do something about it."

"Meg," her mother suggested, "how about making the hard sauce for the plum pudding?"

"Oh—of course." She opened the refrigerator and got out half a pound of butter.

The phone rang.

"I'll get it." Dropping the butter into a small mixing bowl en route, she went to the telephone. "Father, it's for you. I think it's the White House."

Mr. Murry went quickly to the phone. "Mr. President, hello!" He was smiling, and Meg watched as the smile was wiped from his face and replaced with an expression of—what? Nothingness, she thought.

The twins stopped talking. Mrs. Murry stood, her wooden spoon resting against the lip of the saucepan. Mrs. O'Keefe continued to stare morosely into the fire.

Charles Wallace appeared to be concentrating on the tesseract.

—Father is just listening, Meg thought. —The President is doing the talking.

She gave an involuntary shudder. One minute the room had been noisy with eager conversation, and suddenly they were all silent, their movements arrested. She listened, intently, while her father continued to hold the phone to his ear. His face looked grim, all the laughter lines deepening to sternness. Rain lashed against the windows. It ought to snow at this time of year, Meg thought. —There's something wrong with the weather. There's something wrong.

Mr. Murry continued to listen silently, and his silence spread across the room. Sandy had been opening the oven door to baste the turkey and snitch a spoonful of stuffing, and he stood still, partly bent over, looking at his father. Mrs. Murry turned slightly from the stove and brushed one hand across her hair, which was beginning to be touched with silver at the temples. Meg had opened the drawer for the beater, which she held tightly.

It was not unusual for Mr. Murry to receive a call from the President. Over the years he had been consulted by the White House on matters of physics and space travel; other conversations had been serious, many disturbing, but this, Meg felt, was different, was causing the warm room to feel colder, look less bright.

"Yes, Mr. President, I understand," Mr. Murry said at last. "Thank you for calling." He put the receiver down slowly, as though it were heavy.

Dennys, his hands still full of silver for the table, asked, "What did he say?"

Their father shook his head. He did not speak.

Sandy closed the oven door. "Father?"

Meg cried, "Father, we know something's happened. You have to tell us—please."

His voice was cold and distant. "War."

Meg put her hand protectively over her belly. "Do you mean nuclear war?"

The family seemed to draw together, and Mrs. Murry reached out a hand to include Calvin's mother. But Mrs. O'Keefe closed her eyes and excluded herself.

"Is it Mad Dog Branzillo?" asked Meg.

"Yes. The President feels that this time Branzillo is going to carry out his threat, and then we'll have no choice but to use our antiballistic missiles."

"How would a country that small get a missile?" Sandy asked.

"Vespugia is no smaller than Israel, and Branzillo has powerful friends."

"He really can carry out this threat?"

Mr. Murry assented.

"Is there a red alert?" Sandy asked.

"Yes. The President says we have twenty-four hours in which to try to avert tragedy, but I have never heard him sound so hopeless. And he does not give up easily."

The blood drained from Meg's face. "That means the end of everything, the end of the world." She looked toward Charles Wallace, but he appeared almost as withdrawn as Mrs. O'Keefe. Charles Wallace, who was always there for her, was not there now. And Calvin was an ocean away. With a feeling of terror she turned back to her father.

He did not deny her words.

The old woman by the fireplace opened her eyes and twisted her thin lips scornfully. "What's all this? Why would the President of the United States call here? You playing some kind of joke on me?" The fear in her eyes belied her words.

"It's no joke, Mrs. O'Keefe," Mrs. Murry explained. "For a number of years the White House has been in the habit of consulting my husband."

"I didn't know he"—Mrs. O'Keefe darted a dark glance at Mr. Murry—"was a politician."

"He's not. He's a physicist. But the President needs scientific information and needs it from someone he can trust, someone who has no pet projects to fund or political positions to support. My husband has become especially close to the new President." She stirred the gravy, then stretched her hands out to her husband in supplication. "But why? Why? When we all know that no one can win a nuclear war."

Charles Wallace turned from the tesseract. "El Rabioso. That's his nickname. Mad Dog Branzillo."

"El Rabioso seems singularly appropriate for a man who overthrew the democratic government with a wild and bloody coup d'état. He is mad, indeed, and there is no reason in him."

"One madman in Vespugia," Dennys said bitterly, "can push a button and it will destroy civilization, and everything Mother and Father have worked for will go up in a mushroom cloud. Why couldn't the President make him see reason?"

Sandy fed a fresh log onto the fire, as though taking hope from the warmth and light.

Dennys continued, "If Branzillo does this, sends missiles, it could destroy the entire human race—"

Sandy scowled ferociously. "—which might not be so bad—"

"—and even if a few people survive in sparsely inhabited mountains and deserts, there'd be so much fallout all over the planet that their children would be mutants. Why couldn't the President make him see? Nobody wants war at that price."

"It's not for lack of trying," Mr. Murry said, "but El Rabioso deserves his nickname. If he has to fall, he'd just as soon take the human race with him."

"So they send missiles from Vespugia, and we return ours to them, and all for what?" Sandy's voice cracked with anger.

"El Rabioso sees this as an act of punishment, of just retribution. The Western world has used up more than our share of the world's energy, the world's resources, and we must be punished," Mr. Murry said. "We are responsible for the acutely serious oil and coal shortage, the defoliation of trees, the grave damage to the atmosphere, and he is going to make us pay."

"We stand accused," Sandy said, "but if he makes us pay, Vespugia will pay just as high a price."

Mrs. O'Keefe stretched her wrinkled hands out to the

flames. "At Tara in this fateful hour . . ." she mumbled.

Meg looked at her mother-in-law questioningly, but the old woman turned away. Meg said to the room at large, "I know it's selfish, but I wish Calvin weren't in London giving that paper. I wish I'd gone with him."

"I know, love," Mrs. Murry replied, "but Dr. Louise thought you should stay here."

"I wish I could at least phone him . . ."

Charles Wallace moved out of his withdrawn silence to say, "It hasn't happened yet, nuclear war. No missiles have been sent. As long as it hasn't happened, there's a chance that it may not happen."

A faint flicker of hope moved across Meg's face. —Would it be better, she wondered, —if we were like the rest of the world and didn't know the horrible possibility of our lives being snuffed out before another sun rises? How do we prepare?

". . . in this fateful hour," the old woman mumbled again, but turned her head away when the Murrys looked at her.

Charles Wallace spoke calmly to the whole family, but looked at Meg. "It's Thanksgiving, and except for Calvin, we're all together, and Calvin's mother is with us, and that's important, and we all know where Calvin's heart is; it's right here."

"England doesn't observe Thanksgiving," Sandy remarked.

"But we do." His father's voice was resolute. "Finish setting the table, please. Dennys, will you fill the glasses?"

While Mr. Murry carved, and Mrs. Murry thickened the gravy, Meg finished beating the hard sauce, and the twins and Charles Wallace carried bowls of rice, stuffing, vegetables, cranberry sauce, to the table. Mrs. O'Keefe did not move to help. She looked at her work-worn hands, then dropped them into her lap. "At Tara in this fateful hour . . ."

This time nobody heard her.

Sandy, trying to joke, said, "Remember the time Mother tried to make oatmeal cookies over the Bunsen burner, in a frying pan?"

"They were edible," Dennys said.

"Almost anything is, to your appetite."

"Which, despite everything, is enormous."

"And it's time to go to the table," Mrs. Murry said.

When they were in their places she automatically held out her hands, and then the family, with Mrs. O'Keefe between Mr. Murry and Meg, was linked around the table.

Charles Wallace suggested, "Let's sing *Dona nobis pacem*. It's what we're all praying for."

"Sandy'd better start then," Meg said. "He's got the best voice. And then Dennys and Mother, and then Father and you and I."

They raised their voices in the old round, singing over and over, *Give us peace, give us peace, give us peace.*

Meg's voice trembled, but she managed to sing through to the end.

There was silence as the plates were served, silence instead of the usual happy noise of conversation.

"Strange," Mr. Murry said, "that the ultimate threat should come from a South American dictator in an almost unknown little country. White meat for you, Meg?"

"Dark, too, please. Isn't it ironic that all this should be happening on Thanksgiving?"

Mrs. Murry said, "I remember my mother telling me about one spring, many years ago now, when relations between the United States and the Soviet Union were so tense that all the experts predicted nuclear war before the summer was over. They weren't alarmists or pessimists; it was a considered, sober judgment. And Mother said that she walked along the lane wondering if the pussy willows would ever bud again. After that, she waited each spring for the pussy willows, remembering, and never took their budding for granted again."

Her husband nodded. "There was a reprieve then. There may be again."

"But is it likely?" Sandy's brown eyes were sober.

"It wasn't likely then. The pussy willows, nevertheless, have budded for a good many springs." He passed cranberry sauce to Mrs. O'Keefe.

"In this fateful hour," she mumbled, and waved the sauce away.

He bent toward her. "What was that?"

"At Tara in this fateful hour," she said irritably. "Can't remember. Important. Don't you know it?"

"I'm afraid not. What is it?"

"Rune. Rune. Patrick's rune. Need it now."

Calvin's mother had always been taciturn. At home she had communicated largely in grunts. Her children, with the exception of Calvin, had been slow to speak, because they seldom heard a complete sentence until they went to school. "My grandmother from Ireland." Mrs. O'Keefe pointed at Charles Wallace and knocked over her glass.

Dennys fetched paper towels and mopped up the spilled liquid. "I suppose, cosmically speaking, it doesn't make much difference whether or not our second-rate little planet blows itself up."

"Dennys!" Meg cried, then turned to her mother. "Excuse me for using this as an example, but Den, remember when Mother isolated farandolae within a mitochondrion?"

He interrupted, "Of course I remember. That's what she got the Nobel Prize for."

Mrs. Murry held up her hand. "Let Meg speak."

"Okay then: farandolae are so minuscule and insignificant it doesn't seem they could possibly have any importance, and yet they live in a symbiotic relationship with mitochondria—"

"Okay, gotcha. And mitochondria provide us with our energy, so if anything affects our farandolae, that can affect our mitochondria—"

"And," Meg concluded, "if that happens, we could die from energy loss, as you well know."

"Go on," Sandy said.

"So if we blow up our planet it would certainly have some small effect on our solar system, and that could affect our galaxy, and that could . . ."

"The old chain-reaction theory?" Sandy asked.

"More than that. Interdependence. Not just one thing leading to another in a straight line, but everything and everyone everywhere interreacting."

Dennys threw out the wet paper towels, put a clean napkin over the soiled tablecloth, and refilled Mrs. O'Keefe's glass. Despite storm windows, the drawn curtains stirred and a draft moved across the room. Heavy drops of rain spattered down the chimney, making the fire hiss. "I still think," he said, "that you're overestimating the importance of this planet. We've made a mess of things. Maybe it's best we get blown up."

"Dennys, you're a doctor," Meg reprimanded.

"Not yet," Sandy said.

"But he's going to be! He's supposed to care about and guard life."

"Sorry, Sis," Dennys said swiftly.

"It's just his way of whistling in the dark." Sandy helped himself to rice and gravy, then raised his glass to his sister. "Might as well go out on a full stomach."

"I mean it and I don't mean it," Dennys said. "I do think we've got our priorities wrong, we human beings. We've forgotten what's worth saving and what's not, or we wouldn't be in this mess."

"Mean, don't mean," Mrs. O'Keefe grunted. "Never understand what you people are going on about. Even you." And again she pointed at Charles Wallace, though this time she did not overturn her glass.

Sandy glanced across the table at his baby brother, who looked pale and small. "Charles, you've eaten hardly anything, and you're not talking."

Charles Wallace replied, looking not at Sandy but at his sister, "I'm listening."

She pricked up her ears. "To what?"

He shook his head so slightly that only she saw; and stopped questioning.

"At Tara in this fateful hour I place all Heaven with its power!" Mrs. O'Keefe pointed at Charles and knocked over her glass again.

This time nobody moved to mop up.

"My grandma from Ireland. She taught me. Set great store on it. I place all Heaven with its power . . ." Her words dribbled off.

Mrs. O'Keefe's children called her Mom. From everybody except Calvin it sounded like an insult. Meg found it difficult to call her mother-in-law anything, but now she pushed her chair away from the table and knelt by the old woman. "Mom," she said gently, "what did your grandmother teach you?"

"Set great store on it to ward off the dark."

"But what?"

" . . . *All Heaven with its power,*"

Mrs. O'Keefe said in a singsong way,

> "And the sun with its brightness,
> And the snow with its whiteness,
> And the fire with all the strength it hath—"

At that moment it seemed as though a bucketful of water had been dumped down the chimney onto the fire. The flames flickered wildly, and gusts of smoke blew into the room.

"The fire with all the strength it hath," Charles Wallace repeated firmly.

The applewood logs sizzled but the flames gathered strength and began to burn brightly again.

Mrs. O'Keefe put a gnarled hand on Meg's shoulder and pressed down heavily as though it helped her to remember.

"And the—the lightning with its rapid wrath,
And the winds with their swiftness along their path—"

The wind gave a tremendous gust, and the house shook under the impact, but stood steady.

Mrs. O'Keefe pressed until Meg could barely stand the weight.

"And the sea with its deepness,
And the rocks with their steepness,
And the earth with its starkness—"

Using Meg's shoulder as a lever, she pushed herself up and stood facing the bright flames in the fireplace.

"All these I place
By God's almighty help and grace
Between myself and the powers of darkness."

Her voice rose triumphantly. "That'll teach Mad Dog Bran-what's-his name."

The twins looked at each other as though embarrassed. Mr. Murry carved some more turkey. Mrs. Murry's face was serene and uncommunicative. Charles Wallace looked thoughtfully at Mrs. O'Keefe. Meg rose from her knees and returned to her chair, escaping the unbelievably heavy pressure of her mother-in-law's hand. She was sure that her shoulder was going to hold black and blue finger marks.

As Meg moved away, Mrs. O'Keefe seemed to crumple. She collapsed into her chair. "Set high store on that, my grandma did. Haven't thought of it in years. Tried not to think. So why'd it come to me tonight?" She gasped, as though exhausted.

"It's something like *Patrick's Breastplate*," Sandy said. "We sang that in glee club in college. It was one of my favorites. Marvelous harmonies."

"Not a song," Mrs. O'Keefe contradicted. "A rune. Patrick's rune. To hold up against danger. In this fateful hour I place all Heaven with its power—"

Without warning, the lights went out. A gust of wind dashed across the table, blowing out the candles. The humming of the refrigerator ceased. There was no purring from the furnace in the cellar. A cold dampness clutched the room, filling their nostrils with a stench of decay. The flames in the fireplace dwindled.

"Say it, Mom!" Charles Wallace called. "Say it all!"

Mrs. O'Keefe's voice was weak. "I forget—"

The lightning outside was so brilliant that light penetrated the closed curtains. A tremendous crash of thunder followed immediately.

"I'll say it with you." Charles Wallace's voice was urgent. "But you'll have to help me. Come on. In this fateful hour I place all Heaven with its power . . ."

Lightning and thunder were almost simultaneous. Then they heard a gigantic crackling noise.

"One of the trees has been struck," Mr. Murry said.

"All Heaven with its power," Charles Wallace repeated.

The old woman's voice took up the words. "And the sun with its brightness . . ."

Dennys struck a match and lit the candles. At first the flames flickered and guttered wildly, but then steadied and burned straight and bright.

> *"And the snow with its whiteness,*
> *And the fire with all the strength it hath*
> *And the lightning with its rapid wrath . . ."*

Meg waited for the lightning to flash again, for the house itself to be struck. Instead, the power came back on as abruptly as it had gone off. The furnace began to hum. The room was filled with light and warmth.

> *". . . And the sea with its deepness,*
> *And the rocks with their steepness,*
> *And the earth with its starkness,*
> *All these I place*
> *By God's almighty help and grace*
> *Between myself and the powers of darkness."*

Charles Wallace lifted the curtains away from one corner of the window. "The rain's turned to snow. The ground's all white and beautiful."

"All right—" Sandy looked around the room. "What's this all about? I know something's happened, but what?"

For a moment no one spoke. Then Meg said, "Maybe there's hope."

Sandy waved her words away. "Really, Meg, be reasonable."

"Why? We don't live in a reasonable world. Nuclear war is not reasonable. Reason hasn't got us anywhere."

"But you can't throw it out. Branzillo is mad and there's no reason in him."

Dennys said, "Okay, Sandy, I agree with you. But what happened?"

Meg glanced at Charles Wallace, but he had his withdrawn, listening look.

Sandy replied, "Much as we'd like it to, a freak of weather here in the Northeastern United States isn't going to have anything to do with whether or not a South American madman pushes that button to start the war that very likely *will* be the war to end wars."

The baby moved within Meg, a strong affirmation of life. "Father, is the President going to call again?"

"He said he would when—when there's any news. One way or other."

"Within twenty-four hours?"

"Yes. I would not want to be in his position at the moment."

"Or in ours," Dennys said. "It strikes me the whole world is in it together."

Charles Wallace continued to look out the window. "The snow's stopping. The wind has shifted to the northwest. The clouds are moving. I see a star." He let the curtain drop.

Mrs. O'Keefe jerked her chin toward him. "You. Chuck. I come because of you."

"Why, Mom?" he asked gently.

"You know."

He shook his head.

"Stop him, Chuck. Stop Mad Dog Bran . . . Stop him." She looked old and small and Meg wondered how she could have pressed down so heavily on her shoulder. And twice Mrs. O'Keefe had called Charles Wallace *Chuck*. Nobody ever called him Chuck. Occasionally plain Charles, but never Charlie or Chuck.

Mrs. Murry asked, "Mrs. O'Keefe, would you like some tea? or coffee?"

Mrs. O'Keefe cackled without mirth. "That's right. Don't hear. Think I'm crackers. Not such a fool as all that. Chuck knows." She nodded toward Charles Wallace. "Woke up this morning, and wasn't going to come. Then something told me I was to come, like it or not, and didn't know why till I saw you with them big ancient eyes and the rune started to come back to me, and I knowed once more Chuck's no idiot. Haven't thought of the rune since my grandma and Chuck, till now. You've got it, Chuck. Use it." Her breath ran out. It was the longest speech they had ever heard her give. Panting, she finished. "I want to go home." And, as no one spoke: "Someone take me home."

"But, Mrs. O'Keefe," Dennys wheedled, "we haven't had salad, and it's got lots of avocado and tomato in it, and then there's flaming plum pudding."

"Flame yourself. I done what I come for. Someone take me home."

"Very well, Mrs. O'Keefe." Mr. Murry rose. "Den or Sandy, will you drive Mrs. O'Keefe home?"

"I will," Dennys said. "I'll get your coat, ma'am."

When the car had driven off, Sandy said, "One could almost take her seriously."

The Murry parents exchanged glances, and Mrs. Murry replied, "I do."

"Oh, come on, Mother, all that rune stuff, and Charles Wallace stopping Mad Dog Branzillo singlehanded?"

"Not necessarily that. But I take Mrs. O'Keefe seriously."

Meg looked anxiously at Charles Wallace, spoke to her mother. "You've always said there was more to her than meets the eye. I guess we've just seen some of that more."

"I rather think we have," her father said.

"All right, then, what was it all about? It was all—all unnatural."

"What's natural?" Charles Wallace asked.

Sandy raised his eyebrows. "Okay, little brother, what do you make of it, then? How do you plan to stop Branzillo?"

"I don't know," Charles Wallace replied seriously. "I'll use the rune."

"Do you remember it?" Meg asked.

"I remember it."

"Did you hear her call you Chuck?"

"I heard."

"But nobody ever calls you Chuck. Where did she get it?"

"I'm not sure. Out of the past, maybe."

The phone rang, and they all jumped. Mr. Murry hurried to the phone table, then drew back an instant before picking up the receiver.

But it was not the President. It was Calvin, calling from London. He spoke briefly to everybody, was sorry to miss his mother and Dennys; but he was delighted that his mother had come; his paper had gone extremely well; the conference was interesting. At the last he asked to speak to Meg again, and said only, "I love you," and hung up.

"I always fall apart on overseas calls," she said, "so I don't think he noticed anything. There isn't any point telling him when he can't do anything about it, and it would just make it awful for him . . . " She turned away as Dennys came in, blowing on his fingers.

"Calvin called from London." She swallowed her tears. "He sends you his best."

"Sorry to have missed him. How about some salad, now, and then that plum pudding?"

—Why are we trying to act normal? Meg wondered, but did not speak her thought aloud.

But Charles Wallace replied, "It's sort of like the string holding the package together, Meg. We'd all fall apart otherwise."

Her father said, "You know, my dears, the world has been abnormal for so long that we've forgotten what it's like to live in a peaceful and reasonable climate. If there is to be any peace or reason, we have to create it in our own hearts and homes."

"Even at a time like this?" Meg asked. The call from Calvin, the sound of her husband's voice, had nearly broken her control.

"Especially at a time like this," her mother said gently. "We don't know what the next twenty-four hours are going to bring, and if it should be what we fear, then the peace and quiet within us will come to our aid."

"Will it?" Meg's voice faltered again.

"Remember," Mr. Murry said, "your mother and I take Mrs. O'Keefe seriously."

"Father," Sandy chided, "you're a pure scientist. You can't take that old woman seriously."

"I take the response of the elements to her rune seriously."

"Coincidence," Dennys said without much assurance.

"My training in physics has taught me that there is no such thing as coincidence."

"Charles Wallace still hasn't said anything." Meg looked to her small brother.

Dennys asked, "What about it, Charles?"

He shook his head slowly. He looked bewildered. "I don't know. I think I'm supposed to do something, but I don't know what. But if I'm meant to do something, I'll be told."

"By some little men from outer space?" Sandy asked.

"Something in me will tell me. I don't think any of us

wants more salad. Let's turn out the lights and let Father flame the pudding."

"I'm not sure I want the lights out," Meg said. "Maybe there isn't going to be any more electricity, ever. Let's enjoy it while we have it."

"I'd rather enjoy the light of the plum pudding," Charles Wallace said.

Mrs. Murry took the pudding from the double boiler where it had been steaming, and turned it out onto a plate. Dennys took a sprig of holly and stuck it on the top. Mr. Murry got a bottle of brandy and poured it liberally over the pudding. As he lit the match, Charles Wallace turned out the lights and Sandy blew out the candles. The brandy burned with a brilliant blue flame; it seemed brighter than Meg remembered from other Thanksgivings. It had always been their traditional holiday dessert because, as Mrs. Murry remarked, you can't make pie crust over a Bunsen burner, and her attempts at mince or pumpkin pie had not been successes.

Mr. Murry tilted the dish so that all the brandy would burn. The flames continued, bright and clear and blue, a blue that held in it the warmth of a summer sky rather than the chill of winter.

"And the fire with all the strength it hath," Charles Wallace said softly.

"But what kind of strength?" Meg asked. She looked at the logs crackling merrily in the fireplace. "It can keep you warm, but if it gets out of hand it can burn your house down. It can destroy forests. It can burn whole cities."

"Strength can always be used to destroy as well as create," Charles Wallace said. "This fire is to help and heal."

"I hope," Meg said. "Oh, I hope."

2

All Heaven with its power

Meg sat propped up on pillows in the old brass bed in the
attic and tried to read, because thinking hurt too much,
was not even thinking but projection into a fearful future. And Calvin was not beside her, to share, to
strengthen . . . She let the book drop; it was one of her
old volumes of fairy tales. She looked around the room,
seeking comfort in familiar things. Her hair was down for
the night and fell softly about her shoulders. She glanced
at herself in the old, ripply mirror over the chest of
drawers and despite her anxiety was pleased at the reflection. She looked like a child again, but a far lovelier
child than she actually had been.

Her ears pricked up as she heard a soft, velvety tread, and a stripy kitten minced across the wide floorboards, sprang up onto the bed, and began grooming itself while purring loudly. There was always at least one kitten around, it seemed. She missed the old black dog. What would Fortinbras have made of the events of the evening? She would have been happier if the old dog had been in his usual forbidden place at the foot of the bed, because he had an unusual degree of sensitivity, even for a dog, to anything which could help or harm his human family.

Meg felt cold and pulled her battered quilt about her shoulders. She remembered Mrs. O'Keefe calling on all Heaven with its power, and thought shudderingly that she would settle for one large, loving dog. Heaven had shown considerable power that evening, and it was too wild and beyond control for comfort.

And Charles Wallace. She wanted her brother. Mrs. O'Keefe had called on Charles to stop Branzillo: he'd need all the powers Heaven could give him.

He had said good night to Meg in a brusque and preoccupied way, and then given her one quick blue glance which had made her keep the light on and the book open. Sleep, in any event, was far away, lost somewhere in that time which had been shattered by the President's phone call.

The kitten rose high on its legs, made three complete turns, and dropped, heavily for such a little creature, into the curve of her body. The purr slowly faded out and it slept. Meg wondered if she would ever again sleep in that secure way, relinquishing consciousness without fear of what might happen during the night. Her eyes felt dry with fatigue but she did not want to close them and shut out the reassurance of the student lamp with its double yellow globes, the sagging bookshelves she had made with boards and bricks, the blue print curtains at the window; the hem of the curtains had been sagging for longer than she cared to remember and she had been meaning to sew it up since well before her marriage. —Tomorrow, she thought, —if there is a tomorrow.

When she heard footsteps on the attic stairs she stiffened, then relaxed. They had all got in the habit of automatically skipping the seventh step, which not only creaked when stepped on, but often made a sound like a shot. She and Charles Wallace had learned to put one foot on the extreme left of the step so that it let out only a long, slow sigh; when either one of them did this, it was a signal for a conference.

She listened to his progress across the attic, heard the rocking of the old wooden horse as he gave it his usual affectionate slap on the rump, followed by the whing of a dart going into the cork board: all the little signals they had built up over the years.

He pushed through the long strands of patterned rice which curtained the doorway, stood at the foot of the bed, and rested his chin on the high brass rail of the footboard. He looked at her without smiling, then climbed over the footboard as he used to do when he was a little boy, and sat cross-legged on the foot of the bed. "She really does expect me to do something."

Meg nodded.

"For once I'm feeling more in sympathy with the twins than with Mother and Father. The twins think the whole thing is unreasonable and impossible."

"Well—remember, Mother always said there's more to her than meets the eye."

"What about the rune?"

Meg sighed. "She gave it to you."

"What am I supposed to do with it?"

"Stop Branzillo. And I guess I'm feeling like the twins, too. It just doesn't make sense."

"Have you ever really talked with her? Do you know her at all?"

"No. I don't think anyone does. Calvin thinks she stopped herself from being hurt long, long ago by not letting herself love anybody or anything."

"What's her maiden name?" Charles Wallace asked abruptly.

Meg frowned. "I don't remember. Why?"

"I'm not sure. I feel completely in the dark. But she said her grandmother gave her the rune . . . Do you know her first name?"

Meg closed her eyes, thinking. "Branwen. That's it. And she gave me a pair of linen sheets for a wedding present. They were filthy. I had to wash them half a dozen times, and then they turned out to be beautiful. They must have been from her hope chest, and they had embroidered initials, bMz."

"Z and M for what?"

"I don't remember . . ."

"Think, Meg. Let me try to kythe it."

Again she closed her eyes and tried to relax. It was as though too much conscious intensity of thinking made her brain rigid and closed, and if she breathed slowly and deeply it opened up, and memories and thoughts were freed to come to her consciousness where she could share them with Charles Wallace.

"The M—" she said slowly. "I think it's Maddox."

"Maddox. It's trying to tell me something, Maddox, but I'm not sure what. Meg, I want you to tell me everything about her you possibly can."

"I don't know much."

"Meg—" The pupils of his eyes enlarged so that the iris was only a pale blue ring. "Somehow or other she's got something to do with Branzillo."

"That's—that's—"

"—absurd. That's what the twins would say. And it is. But she came tonight of all nights, when she's never been willing to come before. And you heard her say that she didn't want to come but she felt impelled to. And then she began to remember a rune she hadn't thought of since she was a child, and she told me to use it to stop Branzillo."

"And she said we thought she was crackers."

"But she isn't. Mother and Father know that. And nobody can accuse them of being dimwitted daydreamers. What does the Z stand for?"

Again Meg shook her head. "I don't know. I don't even remember if I asked, though I think I must have."

"Branwen Maddox. Branwen Z. Maddox." He rubbed

his fingers over his forehead. "Maddox. There's a clue there."

The kitten yawned and went *brrtt* as though they were disturbing it. Meg reached out and gently knuckled its hard little head and then scratched the soft fur under the chin until it started to purr again and slowly closed its eyes.

"Maddox—it's in a song, or a ballad, about two brothers fighting, like *Childe Harold* maybe. Or maybe a narrative poem—" He buried his head in his hands. "Why can't I remember!" he demanded in frustration.

"Is it that important?"

"Yes! I don't know why, but it is. Maddox—fighting his brother and angering the gods . . ."

"But, Charles—what does some old story have to do with anything?"

"It's a clue. But I can't get enough . . . Is it very cold out?"

Meg looked surprised. "I don't think so. Why?"

Charles Wallace gazed out the window. "The snow hasn't melted, but there isn't much wind. And I need to listen."

"The best listening place is the star-watching rock."

He nodded thoughtfully. The large, flattish glacial rock left over from the time when oceans of ice had pushed across the land, and which the family called the star-watching rock because it gave them a complete and unobstructed view of the sky, was indeed a good place to listen. When they lay on it to watch the stars they looked straight across the valleys to the hills. Behind the

rock was a small woods. There was no sight of civilization, and little sound. Occasionally they heard the roar
of a truck far away on the highway, or a plane tracking
across the sky. But mostly it was quiet enough so that
all they heard was the natural music of the seasons.
Sometimes in the spring Meg thought she could hear the
grass grow. In the autumn the tree toads sang back and
forth as though they couldn't bear to let the joys of
summer pass. In the winter when the temperature
dropped swiftly she was sometimes startled by the sound
of ice freezing with a sharp cracking noise like a rifle
retort. This Thanksgiving night—if nothing more unusual
or horrible happened—would be quiet. It was too late
in the year for tree toads and locusts and crickets. They
might hear a few tired leaves sighing wearily from their
branches, or the swoosh of the tall grasses parting as a
small nocturnal animal made its way through the night.

Charles Wallace said, "Good idea. I'll go."

"I'll go with you."

"No. Stay here."

"But—"

"You know Dr. Louise was afraid you were going to
get pneumonia last week when you had that bad chest
cold. You mustn't risk getting cold again, for the baby's
sake."

"All right, Charles, but, oh—"

"Meg," he said gently. "Something's blocking me, and
I need to get unblocked. I have to be alone. But I'll need
you to kythe with me."

She looked troubled. "I'm out of practice—" Kything

was being able to be with someone else, no matter how far away they might be, was talking in a language that was deeper than words. Charles Wallace was born with this gift; slowly she became able to read the thoughts he sent her, to know what he wanted her to know. Kything went far beyond ordinary ESP, and while it came to Charles Wallace as naturally as breathing, for Meg it took intense concentration. Charles Wallace and Calvin were the only two people with whom she was able to give and receive this language that went far beyond words.

Charles Wallace assured her. "It's like swimming, or riding a bike. Once you learn, you never forget."

"I know—but I want to go with you." She tried to hold back the thought, —To protect you.

"Meg." His voice was urgent. "I'm going to need you, but I'm going to need you *here,* to kythe with me, all the way."

"All the way where?"

His face was white and strained. "I don't know yet. I have a feeling it will be a long way, and yet what has to be done has to be done quickly."

"Why you?"

"It may not be me. We're not certain. But it has to be somebody."

—If it's not somebody, Meg thought, —then the world, at least the world as we know it, is likely to come to an end.

She reached out and gave her little brother a hug and a kiss. "Peace go with you."

She turned out the light and lay down to wait until she heard him in her mind. The kitten stretched and yawned and slept, and its very indifference was a comfort. Then the sharp sound of a dog barking made her sit up.

The barking continued, sharp and demanding, very much like Fortinbras when he was asking for attention. She turned on the light. The barking stopped. Silence. Why had it stopped?

She got out of bed and hurriedly slipped into a robe and slippers and went downstairs, forgetting the seventh step, which groaned loudly. In the kitchen she saw her parents and Charles Wallace all stroking a large, nondescript dog.

Mrs. Murry looked with no surprise at Meg. "I think our dog has found us."

Mr. Murry pulled gently at the dog's upright ear; the other drooped. "She's a 'yaller dog' in looks, but she appears to be gentle and intelligent."

"No collar or anything," Charles Wallace said. "She's hungry, but not overly thin."

"Will you fix her some food, Meg?" Mrs. Murry asked. "There's still some in the pantry left over from Fortinbras."

As Meg stirred up a bowl of food she thought, —We're all acting as though this dog is going to be with us for a long time.

It wasn't the coming of the dog that was strange, or their casual acceptance of it. Fortinbras had come to them in the same way, simply appearing at the door, an overgrown puppy. It was the very ordinariness of it which made tears prickle briefly against her lashes.

"What are we going to call her?" Mrs. Murry asked.

Charles Wallace spoke calmly. "Her name is Ananda."

Meg looked at him, but he only smiled slightly. She put the food down and the dog ate hungrily, but tidily.

"Ananda," Mrs. Murry said thoughtfully. "That rings some kind of bell."

"It's Sanskrit," Charles Wallace said.

Meg asked, "Does it mean anything?"

"That joy in existence without which the universe will fall apart and collapse."

"That's a mighty big name for one dog to carry," Mrs. Murry said.

"She's a large dog, and it's her name," Charles Wallace responded.

When Ananda had finished eating, licking Fortinbras's old bowl till it was clean, she went over to Meg, tail wagging, and held up one paw. Meg took it; the pads felt roughly leathery and cool. "You're beautiful, Ananda."

"She's hardly that," Mr. Murry said, smiling, "but she certainly knows how to make herself at home."

The kettle began to sing. "I'm making tea against the cold." Mrs. Murry turned off the burner and filled the waiting pot. "Then we'd better go to bed. It's very late."

"Mother," Meg asked, "do you know what Mrs. O'Keefe's first name is? Is it Branwen?"

"I think so, though I doubt if I'll ever feel free to call her that." She placed a steaming cup in front of Meg.

"You remember the sheets she gave us?"

"Yes, superb old linen sheets."

"With initials. A large M in the middle, with a smaller b and z on either side. Do you know what the Z stands for?"

"Zoe or Zillah or something unusual like that. Why?"

Meg answered with another question. "Does the name Branwen mean anything? It's sort of odd."

"It's a common enough Irish name. I think the first Branwen was a queen in Ireland, though she came from England. Perhaps she was a Pict, I'm not sure."

"When?" Charles Wallace asked.

"I don't know exactly. Long ago."

"More than two thousand years?"

"Maybe three thousand. Why?"

Charles Wallace poured milk into his tea and studied the cloudy liquid. "It just might be important. After all, it's Mom O'Keefe's name."

"She was born right here in the village, wasn't she?" Meg asked.

Her father replied, "There've been Maddoxes here as far back as anybody remembers. She's the last of the name, but they were an important family in the eighteenth and nineteenth centuries. They've known hard times since then."

"What happened?" Charles Wallace pursued.

Mr. Murry shook his head. "I keep thinking that one of these years your mother or I'll have time to do research into the early years of the village. Our roots are here, too, buried somewhere in the past. I inherited this

house from a great-aunt I hardly knew, just at the time
we were making up our minds to leave the pressures of
the city and continue our research in peace and quiet—
and getting the house swung the balance."

"As for time for other interests"—Mrs. Murry sounded
rueful—"we don't have any more time than we did in the
city. But at least here the pressure to work is our own,
and not imposed on us."

"This Branwen—" Charles Wallace persisted, "was
she an important queen?"

Mrs. Murry raised her fine brows. "Why this sudden
and intense interest?"

"Branwen Maddox O'Keefe was extraordinarily interesting this evening."

Mrs. Murry sipped her tea. "I haven't thought about
the mythologies of the British Isles since you all grew too
old for reading aloud at bedtime. I suspect Branwen
must have been important or I wouldn't remember her
at all. Sorry not to be able to tell you more. I've been
thinking more about cellular biology than mythology
these last few years."

Charles Wallace finished his tea and put the cup in the
sink. "All right if I go for a walk?"

"I'd rather not," his father said. "It's late."

"Please, Father, I need to listen." He sounded and
looked very young.

"Can't you listen here?"

"Too many distractions, too many people's thoughts
in the way . . ."

"Can't it wait?"

Charles Wallace looked at his father without answering.

Mr. Murry sighed. "None of us takes Mrs. O'Keefe and all that happened this evening lightly, but you've always tended to take too much on yourself."

The boy's voice strained. "This time I'm not taking it on myself. Mrs. O'Keefe put it on me."

His father looked at him gravely, then nodded. "Where are you going?"

"Not far. Just to the star-watching rock."

Mr. Murry rinsed his teacup, rinsed it, and rinsed it again. "You're still a child."

"I'm fifteen. And there's nothing to hurt me between home and the star-watching rock."

"All right. Don't stay long."

"No longer than necessary."

"Take Ananda with you."

"I need to be alone. Please, Father."

Mr. Murry took off his glasses, looked at his son through them at a distance, put them on again. "All right, Charles."

Meg looked at her mother and guessed that she was holding back from telling her youngest child not to forget to put on boots and a warm jacket.

Charles Wallace smiled toward their mother. "I'll wear the blue anorak Calvin brought me from Norway." He turned the last of his smile to his sister, then went into the pantry, shutting the kitchen door firmly behind him.

"Time for the rest of us to go to bed," Mrs. Murry said. "You particularly, Meg. You don't want to catch more cold."

"I'll take Ananda with me."

Her father objected. "We don't even know if she's housebroken."

"She ate like a well-trained dog."

"It's up to you, then."

Meg did not know why she felt such relief at the coming of the big yellow dog. After all, Ananda could not be her dog. When Calvin returned from London they would go back to their rented apartment, where pets were not allowed, and Ananda would remain with the Murrys. But that was all right; Ananda, she felt, was needed.

The dog followed Meg upstairs as though she'd been with the Murrys all her life, trotted through the cluttered attic and into Meg's room. The kitten was asleep on the bed, and the big dog sniffed the small puff of fur, tail wagging in an ecstasy of friendliness. Her tail was large and long, with a smattering of golden feathers, which might possibly indicate some kind of setter or Labrador blood in her genetic pattern, the kind of tail which could create as much havoc in a china shop as a bull. The kitten opened its eyes, gave a small, disinterested hiss, and went back to sleep. With one leap, Ananda landed on the bed, thumping heavily and happily with her mighty tail. The kitten rose and stalked to the pillow.

As she had so often said to Fortinbras, Meg announced, "Sleeping on the bed isn't allowed." Ananda's amber eyes looked at her imploringly and she whined softly. "Well—only up here. Never downstairs. If you want to be part of this household you'll have to understand that."

Ananda thumped; light from the student lamp glinted against her eyes, turning them to gold. Her coat shone with a healthy glow.

"Make way for me." Meg climbed back into bed. "Now, Ananda"—she was taking comfort in reverting to her child's habit of talking out loud to the family animals —"what we're going to do is listen, very intently, for Charles Wallace. You have to help me kythe, or you'll have to get off the bed." She rubbed her hand over Ananda's coat, which smelled of ferns and moss and autumn berries, and felt a warm and gentle tingling, which vibrated through her hand and up her arm. Into her mind's eye came a clear image of Charles Wallace walking across what had once been the twins' vegetable garden, but which was now a small grove of young Christmas trees, a project they could care for during vacations. Their magnificent vegetable garden had been plowed under when they went to college. Meg missed it, but she knew that both her parents were much too busy to tend to more than a small patch of lettuce and tomatoes.

Charles Wallace continued to walk along the familiar route.

Hand resting on Ananda, the tingling warmth flowing back and forth between them, Meg followed her brother's steps. When he reached the open space where the star-watching rock was, Ananda's breathing quickened; Meg could feel the rise and fall of the big dog's rib cage under her hand.

There was no moon, but starlight touched the winter grasses with silver. The woods behind the rock were a dark shadow. Charles Wallace looked across the valley, across the dark ridge of pines, to the shadows of the hills beyond. Then he threw back his head and called,

> *"In this fateful hour*
> *I call on all Heaven with its power!"*

The brilliance of the stars increased. Charles Wallace continued to gaze upward. He focused on one star which throbbed with peculiar intensity. A beam of light as strong as a ladder but clear as water flowed between the star and Charles Wallace, and it was impossible to tell whether the light came from the piercing silver-blue of the star or the light blue eyes of the boy. The beam became stronger and firmer and then all the light resolved itself in a flash of radiance beside the boy. Slowly the radiance took on form, until it had enfleshed itself into the body of a great white beast with flowing mane and tail. From its forehead sprang a silver horn which contained the residue of the light. It was a creature of utter and absolute perfection.

The boy put his hand against the great white flanks, which heaved as though the creature had been racing. He could feel the warm blood coursing through the veins as the light had coursed between star and boy. "Are you real?" he asked in a wondering voice.

The creature gave a silver neigh which translated itself into the boy's mind as "I am not real. And yet in a sense I am that which is the only reality."

"Why have you come?" The boy's own breath was rapid, not so much with apprehension as with excitement and anticipation.

"You called on me."

"The rune—" Charles Wallace whispered. He looked with loving appreciation at the glorious creature standing beside him on the star-watching rock. One silver-shod hoof pawed lightly, and the rock rang with clarion sound. "A unicorn. A real unicorn."

"That is what you call me. Yes."

"What are you, really?"

"What are *you*, really?" the unicorn countered. "You called me, and because there is great need, I am here."

"You know the need?"

"I have seen it in your mind."

"How is it that you speak my language?"

The unicorn neighed again, the sound translucent as silver bubbles. "I do not. I speak the ancient harmony."

"Then how is it that I understand?"

"You are very young, but you belong to the Old Music."

"Do you know my name?"

"Here, in this When and Where, you are called Charles Wallace. It is a brave name. It will do."

Charles Wallace stretched up on tiptoe to reach his arms about the beautiful beast's neck. "What am I to call you?"

"You may call me Gaudior." The words dropped on the rock like small bells.

Charles Wallace looked thoughtfully at the radiance of the horn. "Gaudior. That's Latin for *more joyful*."

The unicorn neighed in acquiescence.

"That joy in existence without which . . ."

Gaudior struck his hoof lightly on the rock, with the sound of a silver trumpet. "Do not push your understanding too far."

"But I'm not wrong about Gaudior?"

"In a sense, yes; in a sense, no."

"You're real and you're not real; I'm wrong and I'm right."

"What is real?" Gaudior's voice was as crystal as the horn.

"What am I supposed to do, now that I've called on all Heaven with its power and you've come?"

Gaudior neighed. "Heaven may have sent me, but my powers are closely defined and narrowly limited. And I've never been sent to your planet before. It's considered a hardship assignment." He looked down in apology.

Charles Wallace studied the snow-dusted rock at his feet. "We haven't done all that well by our planet, have we?"

"There are many who would like to let you wipe your-selves out, except it would affect us all; who knows what might happen? And as long as there are even a few who belong to the Old Music, you are still our brothers and sisters."

Charles Wallace stroked Gaudior's long, aristocratic nose. "What should I do, then?"

"We're in it together." Gaudior knelt delicately and indicated that Charles Wallace was to climb up onto his back. Even with the unicorn kneeling, it was with difficulty that the boy clambered up and sat astride, up toward the great neck, so that he could hold on to the silver mane. He pressed his feet in their rubber boots as tightly as he could against the unicorn's flanks.

Gaudior asked, "Have you ridden the wind before?"

"No."

"We have to be careful of Echthroi," Gaudior warned. "They try to ride the wind and throw us off course."

"Echthroi—" Charles Wallace's eyes clouded. "That means *the enemy.*"

"Echthroi," Gaudior repeated. "The ancient enemy. He who distorted the harmony, and who has gathered an army of destroyers. They are everywhere in the universe."

Charles Wallace felt a ripple of cold move along his spine.

"Hold my mane," the unicorn advised. "There's always the possibility of encountering an Echthros, and if we do, it'll try to unseat you."

Charles Wallace's knuckles whitened as he clutched the heavy mane. The unicorn began to run, skimming over the tops of the grasses, up, over the hills, flinging himself onto the wind and riding with it, up, up, over the stars . . .

3

The sun with its brightness

In her attic bedroom Meg regarded Ananda, who thumped her massive tail in a friendly manner. "What's this about?" Meg demanded.

Ananda merely thudded again, waking the kitten, who gave a halfhearted *brrtt* and stalked across the pillow.

Meg looked at her battered alarm clock, which stood in its familiar place on the bookcase. The hands did not seem to have moved. "Whatever's going on, I don't understand."

Ananda whined softly, an ordinary whine coming from an ordinary dog of questionable antecedents, a mongrel like many in the village.

"Gaudior," Meg murmured. "More joyful. That's a good name for a unicorn. *Gaudior, Ananda:* that joy without which the universe will fall apart and collapse. Has the world lost its joy? Is that why we're in such a mess?" She stroked Ananda thoughtfully, then held up the hand which had been pressing against the dog's flank. It glowed with radiant warmth. "I told Charles Wallace I'm out of practice in kything. Maybe I've been settling for the grownup world. How did you know we needed you, Ananda? And when I touch you I can kythe even more deeply than I've ever done before." She put her hand back on the comfortable flank and closed her eyes, shivering with the strain of concentration.

She saw neither Charles Wallace nor the unicorn. She saw neither the familiar earth with the star-watching rock, the woods, the hills, nor the night sky with its countless galaxies. She saw nothing. Nothing. There was no wind to ride or be blown by.

Nothing was. She was not. There was no dark. There was no light. No sight nor sound nor touch nor smell nor taste. No sleeping nor waking. No dreaming, no knowing.

Nothing.

And then a surge of joy.

All senses alive and awake and filled with joy.

Darkness was, and darkness was good. As was light.

Light and darkness dancing together, born together, born of each other, neither preceding, neither following, both fully being, in joyful rhythm.

The morning stars sang together and the ancient harmonies were new and it was good. It was very good.

And then a dazzling star turned its back on the dark, and it swallowed the dark, and in swallowing the dark it became the dark, and there was something wrong with the dark, as there was something wrong with the light. And it was not good. The glory of the harmony was broken by screeching, by hissing, by laughter which held no merriment but was hideous, horrendous cacophony.

With a strange certainty Meg knew that she was experiencing what Charles Wallace was experiencing. She saw neither Charles Wallace nor the unicorn, but she knew through Charles Wallace's knowing.

The breaking of the harmony was pain, was brutal anguish, but the harmony kept rising above the pain, and the joy would pulse with light, and light and dark once more knew each other, and were part of the joy.

Stars and galaxies rushed by, came closer, closer, until many galaxies were one galaxy, one galaxy was one solar system, one solar system was one planet. There was no telling which planet, for it was still being formed. Steam boiled upward from its molten surface. Nothing could live in this primordial caldron.

Then came the riders of the wind when all the riders sang the ancient harmonies and the melody was still new, and the gentle breezes cooled the burning. And the boiling, hissing, flaming, steaming, turned to rain, aeons of rain, clouds emptying themselves in continuing torrents of rain which covered the planet with healing darkness, until the clouds were nearly emptied and a dim light came through their veils and touched the water of the ocean so that it gleamed palely, like a great pearl.

Land emerged from the seas, and on the land green began to spread. Small green shoots rose to become great trees, ferns taller than the tallest oaks. The air was fresh and smelled of rain and sun, of green of tree and plant, blue of sky.

The air grew heavy with moisture. The sun burned like brass behind a thick gauze of cloud. Heat shimmered on the horizon. A towering fern was pushed aside by a small greenish head on a long, thick neck, emerging from a massive body. The neck swayed sinuously while the little eyes peered about.

Clouds covered the sun. The tropical breeze heightened, became a cold wind. The ferns drooped and withered. The dinosaurs struggled to move away from the cold, dying as their lungs collapsed from the radical change in temperature. Ice moved inexorably across the land. A great white bear padded along, snuffling, looking for food.

Ice and snow and then rain again and at last sunlight breaking through the clouds, and green again, green of grass and trees, blue of sky by day, sparkle of stars by night.

Unicorn and boy were in a gentle, green glade, surrounded by trees.

"Where are we?" Charles Wallace asked.

"We're here," the unicorn replied impatiently.

"Here?"

Gaudior snorted. "Don't you recognize it?"

Charles Wallace looked around at the unfamiliar landscape. Tree ferns spread their fronds skyward as though drinking blue. Other trees appeared to be lifting their branches to catch the breeze. The boy turned to Gaudior. "I've never been here before."

Gaudior shook his head in puzzlement. "But it's your own Where, even if it's not your own When."

"My own what?"

"Your own Where. Where you stood and called on all Heaven with its power and I was sent to you."

Again Charles Wallace scanned the unfamiliar landscape and shook his head.

"It's a very different When," Gaudior conceded. "You're not accustomed to moving through time?"

"I've moved through fifteen years' worth of time."

"But only in one direction."

"Oh—" Understanding came to the boy. "This isn't my time, is it? Do you mean that Where we are now is the same place as the star-watching rock and the woods and the house, but it's a different time?"

"For unicorns it is easier to move about in time than in space. Until we learn more what we are meant to do, I am more comfortable if we stay in the same Where."

"You know Where we are, then? I mean—When we are? Is it time gone, or time to be?"

"It is, I think, what you would call Once Upon a Time and Long Ago."

"So we're not in the present."

"Of course we are. Whenever we are is present."

"We're not in *my* present. We're not When we were when you came to me."

"When I was called to you," Gaudior corrected. "And When is not what matters. It's what happens in the When that matters. Are you ready to go?"

"But—didn't you say we're right here? Where the star-watching rock was—I mean, will be?"

"That's what I said." Gaudior's hoof pawed the lush green of the young grass. "If you are to accomplish what you have been asked to accomplish, you will have to travel in and out."

"In and out of time?"

"Time, yes. And people."

Charles Wallace looked at him in startlement. "What?"

"You have been called to find a Might-Have-Been, and in order to do this, you will have to be sent Within."

"Within—Within someone else? . . . But I don't know if I can."

"Why not?" Gaudior demanded.

"But—if I go Within someone else—what happens to my own body?"

"It will be taken care of."

"Will I get it back?"

"If all goes well."

"And if all does not go well?"

"Let us hold firmly to all going well."

Charles Wallace wrapped his arms about himself as though for warmth. "And you wonder that I'm frightened?"

"Of course you're frightened. I'm frightened, too."

"Gaudior, it's a very scary thing just to be told casually that you're going to be inside someone else's body. What happens to *me?*"

"I'm not entirely sure. But you don't get lost. You stay you. If all goes well."

"But I'm someone else, too?"

"If you're open enough."

"If I'm in another body, do I have to be strong enough for both of us?"

"Perhaps," Gaudior pointed out, "your host will be the stronger of the two. Are you willing?"

"I don't know . . ." He seemed to hear Meg warning him that it was always disastrous when he decided that he was capable of taking on, singlehanded, more than anyone should take on.

"It would appear," Gaudior said, "that you have been called. And the calling is never random, it is always according to the purpose."

"What purpose?"

Gaudior ignored him. "It appears that you are gifted in going Within."

"But I've never—"

"Are you not able to go Within your sister?"

"When we kythe, then, yes, a little. But I don't literally go Within Meg, or become Meg. I stay me."

"Do you?"

Charles Wallace pondered this. "When I'm kything with Meg, I'm wholly aware of her. And when she kythes with me, then she's more aware of me than she is of her-

self. I guess kything is something like your going Within
—that makes it sound a little less scary."

Gaudior twitched his beard. "Now you have been
called to go Within in the deepest way of all. And I have
been called to help you." The light in his horn pulsed
and dimmed. "You saw the beginning."

"Yes."

"And you saw how a destroyer, almost since the beginning, has tried to break the ancient harmonies?"

"Where did the destroyer come from?"

"From the good, of course. The Echthros wanted all
the glory for itself, and when that happens the good becomes not good; and others have followed that first
Echthros. Wherever the Echthroi go, the shadows follow, and try to ride the wind. There are places where
no one has ever heard the ancient harmonies. But there
is always a moment when there is a Might-Have-Been.
What we must do is find the Might-Have-Beens which
have led to this particular evil. I have seen many Might-
Have-Beens. If such and such had been chosen, then
this would not have followed. If so and so had been
done, then the light would partner the dark instead of
being snuffed out. It is possible that you can move into
the moment of a Might-Have-Been and change it."

Charles Wallace's fingers tightened in the silver mane.
"I know I can't avert disaster just because Mrs. O'Keefe
told me to. I may be arrogant, but not that arrogant. But
my sister is having a baby, and I can be strong enough
to attempt to avert disaster for her sake. And Mrs.
O'Keefe gave me the rune . . ." He looked around him

at the fresh green world. Although he was still wearing boots and the warm Norwegian anorak, he was not uncomfortable. Suddenly song surrounded him, and a flock of golden birds settled in the trees. "When are we, then? How long ago?"

"Long. I took us all the way back before this planet's Might-Have-Beens, before people came and quarreled and learned to kill."

"How did we get to here—to long ago?"

"On the wind. The wind blows where it will."

"Will it take us Where—When—you want us to go?"

The light of the unicorn's horn pulsed, and the light in the horn, holding the blue of the sky, was reflected in Charles Wallace's eyes. "Before the harmonies were broken, unicorns and winds danced together with joy and no fear. Now there are Echthroi who are greedy for the wind, as for all else, so there are times when they ride the wind and turn it into a tornado, and you had better be grateful we didn't ride one of those—it's always a risk. But we did come to When I wanted, to give us a little time to catch our breaths."

The golden birds fluttered about them, and then the sky was filled with a cloud of butterflies which joined the birds in patterned flight. In the grass little jeweled lizards darted.

"Here the wind has not been troubled," Gaudior said. "Come. This glimpse is all I can give you of this golden time."

"Must we leave so soon?"

"The need is urgent."

Yes, the need was indeed urgent. Charles Wallace looked up at the unicorn. "Where do we go now?"

Gaudior pawed the lush green impatiently. "Not Where; can you not get that through your human skull? When. Until we know more than we know now, we will stay right here in your own Where. There is something to be learned here, and we have to find out what."

"You don't know?"

"I am a mere unicorn." Gaudior dropped his silver lashes modestly. "All I know is that there is something important to the future right here in this place where you watch stars. But whatever it was did not happen until the ancient music of the spheres was distorted. So now we go to a When of people."

"Do you know when that When is?"

The light in Gaudior's horn dimmed and flickered, which Charles Wallace was beginning to recognize as a sign that the unicorn was troubled or uncertain. "A far When. We can ride this wind without fear, for here the ancient harmonies are still unbroken. But it may roughen if the When we enter is a dissonant one. Hold on tight. I will be taking you Within."

"Within—who am I going Within?" Charles Wallace twined the mane through his fingers.

"I will ask the wind."

"You don't know?"

"Questions, questions." Gaudior stomped one silver hoof. "I am not some kind of computer. Only machines have glib answers for everything." The light in the horn pulsed with brilliance; sparks flew from Gaudior's hoofs,

and they were off and up. The smooth flanks became
fluid, and slowly great wings lifted and moved with the
wind.

The boy felt the wind swoop under and about them.
Riding the unicorn, riding the wind, he felt wholly in
freedom and joy; wind, unicorn, boy, merged into a
single swiftness.

Stars, galaxies, circled in cosmic pattern, and the joy
of unity was greater than any disorder within.

And then, almost without transition, they were in a
place of rocks and trees and high grasses and a large
lake. What would, many centuries later, become the star-
watching rock was a small mountain of stone. The woods
behind the rock was a forest of towering fern trees and
giant umbrageous trees he did not recognize. In front of
the rock, instead of the valley of Charles Wallace's When,
there was a lake stretching all the way to the hills, sparkling in the sunlight. Between the rock and the lake were
strange huts of stone and hide, half house, half tent, form-
ing a crescent at the lake's edge.

In front of and around the dwellings was activity and
laughter, men and women weaving, making clay from
the lake into bowls and dishes, painting the pottery with
vivid colors and intricate geometrical designs. Children
played at the water's edge, splashing and skipping peb-
bles.

A boy sat on an outcropping of rock, whittling a spear
with a sharp stone. He was tanned and lean, with shin-

ing hair the color of a blackbird's wing, and dark eyes which sparkled like the water of the lake. His cheekbones were high, and his mouth warm and full. He gave the making of the spear his full concentration. He looked across the glinting waters of the lake and sniffed the scent of fish. Then he turned back to his spear, but his sensitive nostrils quivered almost imperceptibly as he smelled in turn the green of grass, the blue of sky, the red blood of an animal in the forest. He did not appear to notice the unicorn standing behind him on the hill of stone, or if he did, he took the beautiful creature completely for granted. Gaudior's wings were folded back into the flanks now, so that they were invisible; the light in the horn was steady.

Meg pressed her hand intently against Ananda. The big dog turned her head and licked her hand reassuringly with her warm, red tongue.

Meg felt her senses assailed with an awareness she had never experienced with such intensity before, even in childhood. The blue of sky was so brilliant it dazzled her inner eye. Although it was cold in the attic, she could feel the radiant warmth of the day; her skin drank the loveliness of sun. She had never before smelled rock, nor the richness of the dark earth, nor the wine of the breeze, as she smelled them now.

Why? How? She could see the unicorn, but she could not see Charles Wallace. Where was he?

Then she understood.

Charles Wallace was Within the boy on the rock. In

some strange way, Charles Wallace *was* the boy on the
rock, seeing through his eyes, hearing through his ears
(never had bird song trilled with such sparkling clarity),
smelling through his nose, and kything all that his awak-
ened senses received.

Gaudior neighed softly. "You must be careful," he
warned. "You are not Charles Wallace Murry. You must
lose yourself as you do when you kythe with your sister.
You must become your host."

"My host—"

"Harcels, of the People of the Wind. You must not
know more than he knows. When you think thoughts
outside his thoughts, you must keep them from him. It is
best if you do not even think them."

Charles Wallace stirred timidly within Harcels. How
would he, himself, accept such an intrusion by another?
Had he ever been so intruded?

"No," Gaudior replied, speaking only to that part of
Charles Wallace which was held back from complete
unity with Harcels. "We do not send anyone Within unless the danger is so great that—"

"That—"

The light in the horn flickered. "You know some of the
possibilities if your planet is blown up."

"A few," Charles Wallace said starkly. "It just might
throw off the balance of things, so that the sun would
burst into a supernova."

"That is one of the possibilities, yes. Everything that
happens within the created Order, no matter how small,

has its effect. If you are angry, that anger is added to all the hate with which the Echthroi would distort the melody and destroy the ancient harmonies. When you are loving, that lovingness joins the music of the spheres."

Charles Wallace felt a ripple of unease wash over him. "Gaudior—what am I supposed to do—Within Harcels?"

"You might start by enjoying being Within him," Gaudior suggested. "In this When, the world still knows the Old Music."

"Does he see you, as I do?"

"Yes."

"He is not surprised."

"To joy, nothing is surprising. Relax, Charles. Kythe with Harcels. *Be* Harcels. Let yourself go." He struck one hoof against rock, drawing sparks, leapt from the rock in a great arc, and galloped into the woods.

Harcels rose, stretched languorously. He, too, leapt from the rock with the gravity-defying ease of a ballet dancer, landed on the springy grass, rolled over in merriment, sprang to his feet, and ran to the water's edge, calling to the children, the weavers, the potters.

At the edge of the lake he stood very still, isolating himself from the activity around him. He pursed his lips and whistled, a long sweet summons, and then called softly, "Finna, Finna, Finna!"

Halfway across the lake there was a disturbance in the water and a large creature came swimming, leaping, flying, toward Harcels, who in turn flung himself into the water and swam swiftly to meet it.

Finna was akin to a dolphin, though not as large, and

her skin was an iridescent blue-green. She had the gracious smile of a dolphin, and the same familiarity with sea and air. As she met Harcels she sent a small fountain of water through her blowhole, drenching the boy, who shouted with laughter.

For a few moments they wrestled together, and then Harcels was riding Finna, leaping through the air, holding tight as Finna dove down, down deep below the surface, gasping as she flashed again up into the sunlight, sending spray in every direction.

It was sheer joy.

What Charles Wallace had known in occasional flashes of beauty was Harcels's way of life.

In the attic bedroom Meg kept her hand on Ananda. A shudder moved like a wave over them both. "Oh, Ananda," Meg said, "why couldn't it have stayed that way? What happened?"

—When? Charles Wallace wondered. —When are we?

For Harcels, all Whens were Now. There was yesterday, which was gone, which was only a dream. There was tomorrow, which was a vision not unlike today. When was always Now, for there was little looking either backward or forward in this young world. If Now was good, yesterday, though a pleasurable dream, was not necessary. If Now was good, tomorrow would likely continue to be so.

The People of the Wind were gentle and harmonious. On the rare occasions when there was a difference of opinion, it was mediated by the Harmonizer, and his judgment was always accepted. Fish were caught, flesh shot with bow and arrow, never more than needed. Each person in the tribe knew what he was born to do, and no gift was considered greater or less than another. The Harmonizer held a position no more lofty than the youngest cook just learning to build a fire or clean a fish.

One day a wild boar of monstrous size chased a small party of hunters, and the smallest and slowest among them was gored in the side. Harcels helped carry him home, and knelt all through the night with the Healer, bringing fresh cool moss to lay against the fevered wound, singing the prayers of healing as each star moved in its own ordained dance across the sky.

In the morning there was great rejoicing, for not only was the fiery wound cooling but it was recognized that Harcels had found his gift and would be apprenticed to the Healer, and when the Healer went to dwell with those who move among the stars, Harcels would take his place.

The melody was clear and pure. The harmony was undistorted. Time was still young and the sun was bright by day and moved without fear to rest in the realm of distant stars by night.

Harcels had many friends among his people, but his heart's companions were beasts: Finna, and Eyrn, a great bird something between an eagle and a giant gull, and large enough for Harcels to ride. Eyrn's feathers were white, tipped with rose, shading to purple. She was crowned with a tuft of rosy feathers, and her eyes were ruby. With Harcels firmly astride she would fly high, high, higher, until the air was thin and the boy gasped for breath. She flew far and high, so that he could see the dwellings of distant tribes, could see the ocean that stretched, it seemed, across all the rest of the world.

Harcels asked the Teller of Tales about the other tribes.

"Leave them be," the Teller of Tales said in the sharpest voice he had ever been heard to use.

"But it might be fun to know them. They might have things to teach us."

"Harcels," the Teller of Tales said, "I, too, have ridden a creature like your Eyrn, and I have had my steed descend in a hidden place, that I might watch unseen. I saw a man kill a man."

"But why? Why ever would one man kill another?"

The Teller of Tales looked long into the clear eyes of the boy. "Let us hope you will never have to know."

It was easy for Charles Wallace to live Within Harcels, in the brightness of the young sun, where darkness was the friend of light. One day when Harcels was astride Eyrn, they flew over a cluster of dwellings and the boy started to ask Eyrn to descend, but Charles Wallace gently drew his thoughts to the pleasure of flight as Eyrn threw himself upon a stream of wind and glided with the merest motion of wings. Charles Wallace was not certain that this small interference was permissible; he knew only that if Harcels learned the ways of the tribes who knew how to kill, his joy would vanish with his innocence.

—It was the right thing to do, Meg kythed to him fiercely. —It has to be the right thing.

She looked again at the clock. The hands had barely moved. While the seasons were following each other in swift succession in that Other Time where Charles Wallace lived Within Harcels, time was arrested in her own present moment. Time was moving only in that When in which the land so familiar and dear to her was different, where the flat star-watching rock was a hill of stone, the green valley a lake, and the little woods a dark forest.

She sighed achingly for a time so full of joy that it was difficult to realize it had once been real.

Ananda whined and looked at Meg with great anxious eyes.

"What is it?" Meg asked in alarm. She heard Gaudior's neigh, and saw a pulsing of silver light, the diamond-brilliant light which lit the unicorn's horn.

Charles Wallace was astride Gaudior's great neck, looking from within his own eyes at Harcels, Within whom he had known such spontaneity and joy that his own awareness would evermore share in it. He rubbed his cheek gently against the unicorn's silver neck. "Thank you," he whispered.

"Don't thank me," Gaudior snorted. "I'm not the one to decide whom you go Within."

"Who does, then?"

"The wind."

"Does the wind tell you?"

"Not until you are Within. And don't expect it to be this way every time. I suspect that you were sent Within Harcels to help get you accustomed to Within-ing in the easiest way possible. And you must let yourself go even more deeply into your hosts if you are to recognize the right Might-Have-Beens."

"If I let myself go, how can I recognize?"

"That you will have to discover for yourself. I can only tell you that this is how it works."

"Am I to be sent Within again now?"

"Yes."

"I'm not as afraid as I was, but, Gaudior, I'm still afraid."

"That's all right," Gaudior said.

"And if I let more of myself go, how can I kythe properly with Meg?"

"If you're meant to, you will."

"I'm going to need her . . ."

"Why?"

"I don't know. I just know that I am."

Gaudior blew three iridescent bubbles. "Hold tight, tight, tight. We're off on the wind, and there may be Echthroi this time who will try to take you from my back and throw you off the rim of the world."

4

The snow with its whiteness

The great unicorn flung himself into the wind and they were soaring among the stars, part of the dance, part of the harmony. As each flaming sun turned on its axis, a singing came from the friction in the way a finger moved around the rim of a crystal goblet will make a singing, and the song varies in pitch and tone from glass to glass.

But this song was exquisite as no song from crystal or wood or brass can be. The blending of melody and harmony was so perfect that it almost made Charles Wallace relax his hold on the unicorn's mane.

"No!" Meg cried aloud. "Hold on, Charles! Don't let go!"

A blast of icy cold cut across the beauty of the flight, a cold which carried a stench of death and decay.

Retching, Charles Wallace buried his face in Gaudior's mane, his fingers clenching the silver strands as the Echthroid wind tried to drag him from the unicorn's back. The stench was so abominable that it would have made him loosen his grasp had not the pungent scent of Gaudior's living flesh saved him as he pressed his face against the silver hide, breathing the strangeness of unicorn sweat. Gaudior's bright wings beat painfully against invisible wings of darkness beating at them. The unicorn neighed in anguish, his clear tones lost in the howling of the tempest.

Suddenly his hoofs struck against something solid. He whinnied with anxiety. "Hold on tightly, don't let go," he warned. "We've been blown into a Projection."

Charles Wallace could hardly be clutching the mane with more intensity. "A what?"

"We've been blown into a Projection, a possible future, a future the Echthroi want to make real." His breath came in gasping gulps; his flanks heaved wildly under Charles Wallace's legs.

The boy shivered as he remembered those darkly flailing wings and the nauseous odor. Whatever the Echthroi wanted to make real would be something fearful.

They were on a flat plain of what appeared to be solidified lava, although it had a faint luminosity alien to lava. The sky was covered with flickering pink cloud. The air was acrid, making them cough. The heat was intense and he was perspiring profusely under the light anorak, which held in the heat like a furnace.

"Where are we?" he asked, wanting Gaudior to tell him that they were not in his own Where, that this could not possibly be the place of the star-watching rock, of the woods, only a few minutes' walk from the house.

Gaudior's words trembled with concern. "We're still here, in your own Where, although it is not yet a real When."

"Will it be?"

"It is one of the Projections we have been sent to try to prevent. The Echthroi will do everything in their power to make it real."

A shudder shook the boy's slight frame as he looked around the devastated landscape. "Gaudior—what do we do now?"

"Nothing. You mustn't loosen your hold on my mane. They want us to do something, and anything we do might be what they need to make this Projection real."

"Can't we get away?"

The unicorn's ears flicked nervously. "It's very difficult to find a wind to ride when one has been blown into a Projection."

"But what do we do?"

"There is nothing to do but wait."

"Is anybody left alive?"

"I don't know."

Around them a sulfurous wind began to rise. Both boy

and unicorn were convulsed with paroxysms of coughing, but Charles Wallace did not loosen his grasp. When the seizure was over, he dried his streaming eyes on the silver mane.

When he looked up again, his heart lurched with horror. Waddling toward them over the petrified earth was a monstrous creature with a great blotched body, short stumps for legs, and long arms, with the hands brushing the ground. What was left of the face was scabrous and suppurating. It looked at the unicorn with its one eye, turned its head as though calling behind it to someone or something, and hurried toward them as fast as its stumps would take it.

"Oh, Heavenly Powers, save us!" Gaudior's neigh streaked silver.

The anguished cry called Charles Wallace back to himself. He cried,

> "With Gaudior in this fateful hour
> I call on all Heaven with its power
> And the sun with its brightness,
> And the snow with its whiteness . . ."

He took a deep breath and hot air seared his lungs and again he was assailed by an unquellable fit of coughing. He buried his face in the unicorn's mane and tried to control the spasm which shook him. It was not until the racking had nearly passed that he became aware of something cool brushing his burning face.

He raised his eyes and with awed gratitude he saw

snow, pure white snow drifting down from the tortured sky, covering the ruined earth. The monster had stopped its ponderous approach and was staring up at the sky, mouth open to catch the falling flakes.

With the snow came a light wind, a cool wind. "Hold!" Gaudior cried, and raised his wings to catch the wind. His four hoofs left the ground and he launched himself into the wind with a surge of power.

Charles Wallace braced, trying to tighten the grip of his legs about the unicorn's broad neck. He could feel the wild beating of Gaudior's heart as with mighty strokes he thrust along the wind through the darkness of outer space, until suddenly they burst into a fountain of stars, and the stench and the horror were gone.

The unicorn's breath came in great gulps of star-lit air; the wings beat less frantically, and they were safely riding the wind again and the song of the stars was clear and full.

"Now," said Gaudior, "we go."

"Where?" Charles Wallace asked.

"Not Where," Gaudior said. "When."

Up, up, through the stars, up to the far reaches of the universe where the galaxies swirled in their starry dance, weaving time.

Exhausted, Charles Wallace felt his eyelids drooping.

"Do not go to sleep," Gaudior warned.

Charles Wallace leaned over the unicorn's neck. "I'm not sure I can help it," he murmured.

"Sing, then," Gaudior commanded. "Sing to keep yourself awake." The unicorn opened his powerful jaws and music streamed out in full and magnificent harmony. Charles Wallace's voice was barely changing from a pure treble to a warm tenor. Now it was the treble, sweet as a flute, which joined Gaudior's mighty organ tones. He was singing a melody he did not know, and yet the notes poured from his throat with all the assurance of long familiarity.

They moved through the time-spinning reaches of a far galaxy, and he realized that the galaxy itself was part of a mighty orchestra, and each star and planet within the galaxy added its own instrument to the music of the spheres. As long as the ancient harmonies were sung, the universe would not entirely lose its joy.

He was hardly aware when Gaudior's hoofs struck ground and the melody dimmed until it was only a pervasive beauty of background. With a deep sigh Gaudior stopped his mighty song and folded his wings into his flanks.

Meg sighed as the beauty of the melody faded and all she heard was the soft movement of the wind in the bare trees. She realized that the room was cold, despite the electric heater which augmented the warm air coming up the attic stairs from the radiators below. She reached over Ananda to the foot of the bed and pulled up her old eiderdown and wrapped it around them both. A gust of wind beat at the window, which always rattled unless secured by a folded piece of cardboard or a sliver of wood stuck between window and frame.

"Ananda, Ananda," she said softly, "the music—it was more—more real than any music I've ever heard. Will we hear it again?"

The wind dropped as suddenly as it had risen, and once again she could feel the warmth coming from the little heater. "Ananda, he's really a very small boy . . . Where is Gaudior going to take him now? Whom is he going to go Within?" She closed her eyes, pressing the palm of her hand firmly against the dog.

It was the same Where as the Where of Harcels, but there were subtle differences, though it was still what Gaudior had called Once Upon a Time and Long Ago, so perhaps men still lived in peace and Charles Wallace would be in no danger. But no: time, though still young, was not as young as that, she felt.

The lake lapped close to the great rock and stretched across the valley to the horizon, a larger lake than the lake of Harcels's time. The rock itself had been flattened by wind and rain and erosion, so that it looked like an enormous, slightly tilted tabletop. The forest was dark and deep, but the trees were familiar, pine and hemlock and oak and elm.

Dawn.

The air was pure and blue and filled with the fragrance of spring. The grass around the rock looked as though it had been covered with a fall of fresh snow, but the snow was a narcissus-like flower with a spicy scent.

On the tabletop stood a young man.

She did not see Charles Wallace. She did not see the unicorn. Only the young man.

A young man older than Charles Wallace. Harcels had been younger. This young man was older, perhaps not as old as Sandy and Dennys, but more than fifteen. She saw no hint of Charles Wallace within the man, but she knew that somehow he was there. As Charles Wallace had been himself and yet had been Harcels, so Charles Wallace was Within the young man.

He had been there all night, sometimes lying on his back to watch the stars swing slowly across the sky; sometimes with his eyes closed, as he listened to the lapping of the small waves on the pale sand, the clunkings of frogs and the hoot of a night bird, the sound of an occasional fish slipping through the water. Sometimes he neither heard nor saw; he did not sleep, but abandoned his senses and lay on the rock patiently opening himself to the wind.

Perhaps it was his gift of kything practiced with Meg that helped Charles Wallace slip more and more deeply into the being of another.

Madoc, son of Owain, king of Gwynedd.

Madoc, on the dawning of his wedding day.

Meg's eyes slowly lowered; her body relaxed under the warmth of the eiderdown; but her hand remained on Ananda as she slid into sleep.

Madoc!

It was for Charles Wallace as though a shuttered window had suddenly been opened. It was not a ballad or a song he was trying to remember, it was a novel about a Welsh prince named Madoc.

He heard Gaudior's warning neigh. "You are Within Madoc. Do not disturb him with outside thoughts."

"But, Gaudior, Madoc was the key figure in the book— oh, *why* can't I remember more!"

Again Gaudior cut him off. "Stop trying to think. Your job now is to let yourself go into Madoc. Let go."

Let go.

It was almost like slipping down, deeper and deeper, into the waters of a pool, deeper and deeper.

Let go.

Fall into Madoc.

Let go.

Madoc rose from the rock and looked to the east, awaiting the sunrise with exalted anticipation. His fair skin was tanned, with a reddishness which showed that he was alien to so fierce a sun. He looked toward the indigo line of horizon between lake and sky, with eyes so blue that the sky paled in comparison. His hair, thick and gold as a lion's mane, was nearly covered with an elaborate crown of early spring flowers. A lavish chain of flowers was flung over his neck and one shoulder. He wore a kilt of ferns.

The sky lightened, and the sun sent its fiery rays over

the edge of the lake, reaching up into the sky, pulling itself, dripping, from the waters of the night. As the sun seemed to make a great leap out of the dark, Madoc began to sing in a strong, joyful baritone.

> *"Lords of fire and earth and water,*
> *Lords of rain and wind and snow,*
> *When will come the Old Man's daughter?*
> *Time to come, or long ago?*
> *Born of friend or borne by foe?*
>
> *Lords of water, earth, and fire,*
> *Lords of wind and snow and rain,*
> *Where is found the heart's desire?*
> *Has she come? will come again?*
> *Born, as all life's born, with pain?"*

When he finished, still looking out over the water, his song was taken up as though by an echo, a strange, thin, cracked echo, and then an old man, dressed with the same abundance of flowers as Madoc, came out of the forest.

Madoc bent down and helped the old man up onto the rock. For all the Old One's age, his stringy-looking muscles were strong, and though his hair was white, his dark skin had a glow of health.

> *"Lords of snow and rain and wind,*
> *Lords of water, fire, and earth,*
> *Do you know the one you send?*
> *Does it call for tears or mirth?*
> *Shall we sing for death or birth?"*

When the strange duet was ended, the old man held up his hand in a gesture of blessing. "It is the day, my far-sent son."

"It is the day, my to-be-father. Madoc, son of Owain, king of Gwynedd, will be Madoc, son of Reschal, Old One of the Wind People."

"A year ago today, you sang the song in your delirium," Reschal said, "and it was the child of my old age who found you in the forest."

"And it is mirth that is called for," the young man affirmed, "and we shall sing today for birth, for the birth of the new One which Zyll and I will become when you join us together."

"On the night that Zyll was born," the Old One said, "I dreamed of a stranger from a distant land, across a lake far greater than ours—"

"From across the ocean"—the young man put his hand lightly on the Old One's shoulder—"from the sea which beats upon the shores of Cymru, the sea which we thought went on and on until a ship would fall off at the end of the world."

"The end of the world—" the old man started, but broke off, listening.

The young man listened, too, but heard nothing. "Is it the wind?"

"It is not the wind." Reschal looked at the young man and put a gnarled hand on the richly muscled arm. "Madoc, son of Owain, king of Gwynedd—how strange those syllables sounded to us. We did not know what is a king, nor truly do we yet."

"You have no need of a king, Old One of the People of the Wind. Owain, my father, is long buried: I am a lifetime away from Gwynedd in Cymru. When the soothsayer looked into the scrying glass and foretold my father's death, he saw also that I would live my days far from Gwynedd."

The old man again lifted his head to listen.

"Is it the wind?" Still, Madoc could hear nothing beyond the sounds of early morning, the lapping of the lake against the shore, the stirring of the wind in the hemlocks which made a distant roaring which always reminded him of the sea he had left behind him.

"It is not the wind." There was no emotion in the old man's face, only a continuing, controlled listening.

The young man could not hide the impatience in his voice. "When is Zyll coming?"

The dark Old One smiled at him with affection. "You have waited how many years?"

"I am seventeen."

"Then you can wait a while longer, while Zyll's maidens make her ready. And there are still questions I must ask you. Are you certain in your heart that you will never want to leave Zyll and this small, inland people and go back to the big water and your ship with wings?"

"My ship was broken by wind and wave when we attempted to land on the rocky shores of this land. The sails are torn beyond mending."

"Another ship could be built."

"Old One, even had I the tools to fell the trees for lumber for a new ship, even had my brother and my companions not perished, I would never wish to leave Zyll and my new brethren."

"And your brother and your companions?"

"They are dead," Madoc said bleakly.

"Yet you hold them back so that they cannot continue their journey."

"We were far from home." Madoc spoke softly. "It is a long journey for their spirits."

"Are the gods of Gwynedd so weak they cannot care for their own?"

Madoc's blue eyes were dark with grief. "When we left Gwynedd in Cymru because of the quarreling of my brethren over our father's throne, it seemed to us the gods had already abandoned us. For brothers to wish to kill each other for the sake of power is to anger the gods."

"Perhaps," the old man said, "you must let the gods of Gwynedd go, as you must free your companions from your holding."

"I brought them to their death. When my father died, and my brothers became drunk with lust for power, as no wine can make a man drunk, I felt the gods depart. In a dream I saw them turn their backs on our quarreling, saw them as clearly as anything the soothsayers see in their scrying glass. When I awoke, I took Gwydyr aside and said that I would not stay to watch brother against brother, but that I would go find the land the Wise Ones said was at the farther end of the sea. Gwydyr demurred at first."

"He thought he might become king?"

"Yes, but Gwydyr and I were the youngest. The throne

was not likely to be ours while the other five remained alive."

"Yet you, Madoc, the seventh son, were the favored of the people."

"Had I let them proclaim me king, there would have been no way to avoid bloodshed. I left Gwynedd to prevent the horror of brother against brother."

"Have you"—the old man regarded Madoc keenly—"in fact left it?"

"I have left it. Gwynedd in Cymru is behind me. It will be ruled by whomever the gods choose. I do not wish to know. For now I am Madoc, son-to-be of Reschal, soon to be husband of Zyll of the People of the Wind."

"And Gwydyr? Have you let him go?"

Madoc gazed across the lake. "In many ways it seemed that I was older than he, though there were seven years between us. When we came to the tribe on the Far Side of the Lake he was afraid of their dark skins and hair and their strange singing that was full of hoots and howls, and he ran from them. They kept me as guest, yet I was a prisoner, for they would not let me go into the forest to look for my brother. They sent a party of warriors to search for him, and when they returned they carried only the belt with the jeweled buckle which marked him as the son of a king. They told me he had been killed by a snake; Gwydyr did not know what a snake is, for we have none in Gwynedd. They told me that he had called my name before he died, and that he had left me the Song of the King's Sons. And they buried him out in the forest. Without me, they buried my brother, and I do not even know the place where he is laid."

"That is the way of the People on the Far Side of the Lake," the old man said. "They fear the dead and try to escape the ancient terror."

"The ancient terror?"

Reschal looked at the tender sky of early morning. "That which went wrong. Once there were no evil spirits to blight the crops, to bring drought or flood. Once there was nothing to fear, not even death."

"And what happened to bring fear?"

"Who knows? It was so long ago. But is it not in Gwynedd, too?"

"It is in Gwynedd," Madoc replied soberly, "or brother would not have turned against brother. Yes, we too know what you call the ancient terror. Death, it is thought, or at least the fear of death, came with it. Reschal, I would that I knew where those across the lake had laid my brother, that I may say the prayers that will free his soul."

"It is their way to put the dead far from them and then to lose the place. They hide the dead, even from themselves, that their spirits may not come to the lake and keep the fish away."

"And your people?"

The old man pulled himself up proudly. "We do not fear the spirits of our dead. When there has been love during life, why should that change after death? When one of us departs we have a feast of honor, and then we send the spirit to its journey among the stars. On clear nights we feel the singing of their love. Did you not feel it last night?"

"I watched the stars—and I felt that they accepted me."

"And your brother? Did you feel his light?"

Madoc shook his head. "Perhaps if I could have found the place where they buried him . . ."

"You must let him go. For the sake of Zyll you must let him go."

"When will come the Old Man's daughter?" Madoc asked. "I left the People on the Far Side of the Lake to try to find my brother's grave, and in the forest I was quickly lost. For days I wandered, trying to make my way back, straying farther and farther from them. I was nearly dead when Zyll came hunting the healing herbs which are found only in the deepest part of the forest. *When will come the Old Man's daughter? Where is found the heart's desire?* Here, Reschal."

"You will let Gwydyr go to his place among the stars?"

"Does it call for tears or mirth? Shall we sing for death or birth?" Madoc sang softly. "I have shed my tears for the past. Today is for mirth. Why have you dragged me through tears again?"

"So that you may leave them behind you," Reschal said, and raised his withered arms to the sun. The lake, the shore, the rock, the forest behind, were bathed in golden light, and as though in response to Reschal's gesture there came a sound of singing, a strange wild song of spring and flowers and sunlight and growing grass and the beating of the heart of all of those young and in love. And Madoc's tears were dried, and thoughts of his lost companions and brother receded as the singing filled him with expectancy and joy.

The children of the tribe came first, wearing chains of flowers which flapped against their brown bellies as they danced along. Madoc, shining with delight, turned from the children to the Old One. But Reschal's eyes were focused on the unseen distance across the lake and he was listening, not to the children, but to that sound for which he had been straining before. And now Madoc thought that he, too, heard a throbbing like a distant heartbeat. "Old One, I hear it now. What is it?"

Reschal gazed across the water. "It is the People Across the Lake. It is their drums."

Madoc listened. "We have heard their drums before, when the wind blows from the south. But today the wind blows from the north."

The old man's voice was troubled. "We have always lived in peace, the People of the Wind and those Across the Lake."

"Perhaps," Madoc suggested, "they come to my wedding celebration?"

"Perhaps."

The children had gathered around the rock and were looking expectantly at Madoc and Reschal. The Old One raised his arm again, and singing drowned out the steady beating of the drums, and the men and women of the tribe, ranging from coltish girls and boys to men and women with white hair and wrinkled skin, came dancing toward the great rock. In their midst, circled by a group of young women, was Zyll. She wore a crown on her head to match Madoc's, and a short skirt made entirely of spring flowers. Her copper skin glowed as though lit by the sun from within, and her eyes met Madoc's with a sparkle of love.

Nowhere, Madoc thought, could wedding garments be more beautiful, no matter how much gold was woven into the cloth, nor with how many jewels the velvets and satins were decorated.

The flower-bedecked crowd parted to let Zyll come to the rock. Madoc stooped for her upraised hands, and gently lifted her so that she stood between him and Reschal. She bowed to her father, and then began to move in the ritual wedding dance. Madoc, during the year he had spent with the Wind People, had seen Zyll dance many times before: at the birth of each moon; at the feast of the newborn sun in winter; at the spring and autumn equinox, dance for the Lords of the lake, the sky, the rain and rainbow, the snow and the wind.

But for the Wind Dancers, as well as for all the other Wind People with their various gifts, there was only one Wedding Dance.

Madoc stood transfixed with joy as Zyll's body moved with the effortless lightness of the spring breeze. Her body leapt upward and it seemed that gravity had no power to pull her down to earth. She drifted gently from sky to rock as the petals fall from flowering trees.

Then she held out her hands to Madoc, and he joined

in the dance, marveling as he felt some of Zyll's effortless-
ness of movement enter his own limbs.

At first, when Zyll had found Madoc half dead in the
forest, and had brought him to the Wind People, they
had been afraid of him. His blue eyes, his pale skin,
reddened by exposure, his tawny hair, were unlike anything they had ever seen. They approached him shyly,
as though he were a strange beast who might turn on
them. As they became accustomed to his presence, some
of the Wind People proclaimed him a god. But then his
anger flashed like lightning, and though there were some
who said that his very fieriness announced him the Lord
of the storm, he would have none of their attempts to set
him apart.

"Stay with your own wind gods," he commanded. "You
have served them well, and you live in the light of their
favor. I, too, will serve the Lords of this place, for it is
their pleasure that I am still alive."

Gradually the Wind People began to accept him as one
of themselves, to forget his outer differences. The Old
One said, "It is not an easy thing to refuse to be worshipped."

"When people are worshipped, then there is anger and
jealousy in the wake. I will not be worshipped, nor will
I be a king. People are meant to worship the gods, not
themselves."

"You are wise beyond your years, my son," Reschal
said.

"My father did not want to be worshipped. But some
of his sons did. That is why I am here."

Across the lake the drums were silent.

The Old One watched Madoc and Zyll as their bodies slowly ceased the motions of the dance. Then he lifted Madoc's hand and placed it over Zyll's, and then put a hand on each of their heads. And as he did so, the sound of drums came again. Loud and close. Threatening.

A ripple went through the Wind People as they saw three dugout canoes approaching swiftly, each paddled by many men. Standing in the bow of the middle and largest dugout was a tall, fair-skinned, blue-eyed man.

With a glad shout Madoc leapt from the rock and ran to the water's edge. "Gwydyr!"

5

The fire with all the strength
it hath

In the attic Meg lay quietly in bed, her eyes closed. Her hand continued to rub rhythmically against Ananda, receiving the tingling warmth. Behind her lids her eyes moved as though she were dreaming. The kitten stood up, stretched its small back into a high arch, yawned, and curled up at her feet, purring.

Charles Wallace-within-Madoc felt the young man's surge of joy at seeing his brother alive, the brother he had thought dead and buried in a forgotten part of the forest.

The man in the dugout jumped overboard and ran splashing to shore.

"Gwydyr! You are alive!" Madoc held out his arms to his brother.

Gwydyr did not move into the embrace. His blue eyes were cold, and set close together. It was then that Madoc noticed the circlet around his brother's head, not of flowers, but of gold.

"Gwydyr, my elder brother." The joy slowly faded from the sunny blue of Madoc's eyes. "I thought you dead."

Gwydyr's voice was as cold as his eyes. "It was my wish that you should think so."

"But why should you wish such a thing!"

At the pain in Madoc's voice, Zyll dropped lightly from the rock and came to stand close by him.

"Did you not learn in Gwynedd that there is room for one king only?"

Madoc's eyes kept returning to Gwydyr's golden crown. "We left Gwynedd for that reason, to find a place of peace."

Gwydyr gestured behind him, and the drummers began to beat slowly on the taut skins. The paddles were rested and the men splashed into the shallow water, and pulled the dugouts onto the shore.

Gwydyr raised the corners of his lips into what was more a grimace than a smile. "I have come to claim the Old Man's daughter."

The sound of the drums was an aching pain in Madoc's

ears. "My brother, I wept for your death. I thought to rejoice to see you alive."

Gwydyr spoke with grim patience as though to a dim-witted child. "There is room for no more than one king in this place, little brother, and I, who am the elder, am that king. In Gwynedd I had no hope against six brothers. But here I am king and god and I have come to let the Wind People know that I reign over the lake and all the lands around. The Old Man's daughter is mine."

Zyll pressed against Madoc, her fingers tight on his arm.

Reschal spoke in his cracked voice. "The People of the Wind are people of peace. Always we have lived in amity with those Across the Lake."

Again Gwydyr's lips distorted into a smile. "Peace will continue as long as you give us half of your fish and half of all you hunt and if I take with me across the water the princess who stands beside my brother."

Zyll did not move from Madoc's side. "You come too late, Elder Brother. Madoc of Reschal and I have been made One."

"Madoc of Reschal. Ha! My laws are stronger than your laws." Gwydyr gestured imperiously. The men with the paddles pulled the blades off the shafts, and stood holding dangerously pointed spears.

A united cry of disbelief, then anger, came from the Wind People.

"No!" Madoc cried, outrage giving his voice such volume that it drowned out the beating of the drums, the shouting of the warriors with the spears, the anger of the Wind People. "There will be no bloodshed here because of the sons of Owain." He stepped away from Zyll and Reschal and confronted Gwydyr. "Brother, this is between you and me." And now he smiled. "Unless, of course, you are afraid of Madoc and need your savages with spears to protect you."

Gwydyr made an enraged gesture. "And what of your peaceable Wind People?"

Then Madoc saw that the festive garlands were gone from the young men, flung in a heap in front of the great rock. Instead of flowers they carried spears, bows and arrows.

Reschal looked at him gravely. "I have been hearing the war drums since last sundown. I thought it better to be prepared."

Madoc flung his arms wide. There was grim command in his voice. "Put down your arms, my brothers. I came to you in peace. I will not be the cause of war."

The young men looked first at Madoc, then at the People Across the Lake, their spears threatening.

"Brother," Madoc said to Gwydyr, "have your men put down their spears. Or do you fear to fight me in fair combat?"

Gwydyr snarled an order, and the men on the shore behind him placed their spears carefully on the sand in easy reach.

Then the Old One nodded at the young men, and they, too, put down their weapons.

Gwydyr shouted, "If we are to fight for the Old Man's daughter, little brother, I choose the weapon."

"That is fair," Madoc replied.

Zyll made a soft moan of anxiety and placed her hand on his arm.

"I choose fire," Gwydyr announced.

Madoc sang:

> *"Lords of water, earth, and fire,*
> *Where is found the heart's desire?"*

"Fire it shall be, then. But in what form?"

"You must *make* fire, little brother," Gwydyr said. "If your fire cannot overcome mine, then I will be king of the Wind People as well as those Across the Lake, and I will claim the Old Man's daughter for my own." His close-set eyes flickered greedily.

Reschal walked slowly toward him. "Gwydyr, sixth son of Owain, pride has turned the light behind your eyes to ice, so that you can no longer see clearly. You will never take my daughter."

Gwydyr gave the old man a mighty shove, so that he fell sprawling on the beach, face down. Zyll screamed, and her scream was arrested in mid-air, to hang there.

Madoc sprang to help the old man, and bent down on one knee to raise Reschal from the sand. But his eyes followed the Old One's to a small pool of water in a declivity in the sand, and his movements, like Zyll's scream, were suspended. Only the reflection in the small pool of water moved. Gwydyr's face was quivering in the

wind-stirred puddle, his face so like and so unlike
Madoc's. The eyes were the same blue, but there was no
gold behind them, and they turned slightly in to a nose
pinched with cruelty and lust. This was not, Madoc
thought, the brother who had come with him to the
New World. Or was it? and he had never truly seen his
brother before, only Gwydyr as he hoped him to be.

Ripples moved over the shallow oval and the reflection
shimmered like the reflections in the soothsayers' scrying
glass in Gwynedd.

Madoc had always feared the scrying glass; so he feared
the small oval of water which reflected Gwydyr's face,
growing larger and larger, and darker and darker, quivering until it was no longer the face of a man but of a screaming baby. The face receded until Madoc saw a black-
haired woman holding and rocking the baby. 'You shall be
great, little Madog,' she said, 'and call the world your own,
to keep or destroy as you will. It is an evil world, little
Madog.' The baby looked at her, and his eyes were set
close together, like Gwydyr's, and turned inward, just
so, and his mouth pouted with discontent. Again the face
grew larger and larger in the dark oval and was no longer
the face of a baby, but a man with an arrogant and
angry mien. 'We will destroy, then, Mother,' the man
said, and the face rippled until it was a small, slightly
pear-shaped sphere, and on the sphere were blotches of
green and brown for land, and blue and grey for seas,
and a soft darkness for clouds, and from the clouds came
strange dark objects which fell upon the land and fell
upon the sea, and where they fell, great clouds arose,

umbrellaing over the earth and the sea; and beneath the bulbous clouds was fire, raging redly and driven wild by wind.

Gwydyr's voice rippled across the scrying oval of water. "I choose fire, little brother. Where is your fire?"

The flames vanished and the oval was only a shallow pool reflecting nothing more than the cloud that moved across the sun.

Time resumed, and Zyll's scream continued as though it had never been broken. Madoc raised Reschal from the beach, stepping into the oval as he did so, splashing the shallow water onto the sand. "Stand back, Old One," he said. "I will break the scry." And he stamped once more on the water left in the puddle, until there was not enough to hold the least reflection.

From the central dugout came one of the warriors, carrying a smoking brazier. Gwydyr took one of the spears and held the sharp end over the coals. "You must make your own fire, Madoc!" He laughed derisively.

Madoc turned to the rock where the young men had laid their chains of flowers. He gathered the flowers in his arms and placed them in a heap over the oval where the water had been. Then he took the crown of flowers from his head and added it to the garlands. As though responding to a signal, Zyll cast hers on the fragrant pile. One by one all the men, women, children of the Wind People threw their headpieces onto the heap of flowers, Reschal last of all.

"What do you think you're doing?" Gwydyr screamed,

dancing about on the sand, thrusting his flaming spear at his brother.

Madoc leapt aside. "Wait, Gwydyr. You chose fire. You must let me fight fire with fire."

"You, you alone must make the fire. These are my rules."

Madoc replied quietly, "You were always one for making your own rules, Brother Gwydyr."

"I am the king, do you hear me, I am the king!" Gwydyr's voice rose hysterically.

Madoc, moving as though in a dream, pushed his brother's words aside, and focused the blue fire of his eyes on the great pyre of flowers. The scent of crushed blossoms rose like smoke. Madoc thrust his arms shoulder-deep into the garlands and pushed them aside so that once more he could see the oval. A thin film of water had bubbled up from the sand.

"No more of Gwydyr's nightmares," he commanded, staring fixedly at the water, which sparkled from the sun. The water rippled and shimmered and resolved itself once again into a mother holding a baby, but a different baby, eyes wide apart, with sunlight gleaming through the blue, a laughing, merry baby. "You will do good for your people, El Zarco, little Blue Eyes," the mother crooned. "Your eyes are an omen, a token for peace. The prayer has been answered in you, blue for birth, blue for mirth."

Then the oval broke into shimmering, and all that was reflected was the cloudy sky. Madoc looked heavenward then, and cried in a loud voice,

> *"I, Madoc, in this fateful hour*
> *Place all Heaven with its power*
> *And the sun with its brightness,*
> *And the snow with its whiteness,*
> *And the fire with all the strength it hath . . ."*

The sun burst from behind the clouds and shafted directly onto the garlands. The scent of roses mingled with the thin wisp of smoke which rose from the crushed petals. When the smoke was joined by a small tongue of flame, Madoc leapt toward his brother. "There is my fire, Gwydyr." He wrenched the spear from his brother and threw it with all his might into the lake. "Now we will fight in fair combat." And he clasped Gwydyr to him as though in love.

For time out of time the two brothers wrestled by the lake, both panting with exertion, but neither seeming to tire beyond the other. Their bodies swayed back and forth in a strange dance, and the People of the Wind and those Across the Lake watched in silence.

The sun completed its journey across the sky and dropped into the forest for the night's rest, and still the brothers held each other in an anguished grip and their breathing was louder than the wind in the trees.

The fire slowly consumed the garlands, and when there was nothing left but a handful of ashes, Madoc forced Gwydyr into the lake, and held him down under the water until rising bubbles told him that his brother was screaming for mercy. Then he raised him from the lake and water spewed from Gwydyr's mouth as dark as blood, and he hung limply in Madoc's arms.

Madoc gestured to the People Across the Lake. "Bring out your boats and take your king back to your own land." His voice held scorn and it held pain and his blue eyes were softened by tears.

The three boats pushed into the water. The spear-oars were returned to their blades. Madoc dumped Gwydyr like a sack of grain into the center dugout. "Go. Never let us hear the sound of the war drums again." He reached into the canoe and took the golden circlet from Gwydyr's head and tossed it far out into the lake.

Then he turned his back on his brother and splashed ashore.

Zyll was waiting for him.

Madoc looked at her and sang,

> *"Lords of water, earth, and fire*
> *Lords of rain and snow and water,*
> *Nothing more do I aspire,*
> *For I have the Old Man's daughter,*
> *For I have my heart's desire."*

And to him Zyll sang,

> *"Now we leave our tears for mirth.*
> *Now we sing, not death, but birth."*

Madoc held her close in his arms. "Tomorrow I will mourn for my brother, for this death is far worse than the other. But tonight we rejoice."

The children lifted their voices and began to sing, and then all the People of the Wind were singing, and Reschal said softly to Madoc, "That which your brother

wanted us to believe from the scry is part of his nightmare. Perhaps our dreams will be stronger than his."

"Yes, Old One," Madoc said, but he thought of the
things he had seen falling from the sky, and the strange
mushrooming clouds and the fire, and shuddered. He
looked at the water that had seeped into the oval. But
all that he saw was the smiling face of the moon.

The moon slipped behind the trees to join, briefly, her
brother, sun. The stars danced their intricate ritual across
the sky. The People Across the Lake looked at Gwydyr,
and his golden crown was gone, and so was his power.

Madoc's arms encircled Zyll and he cried out in his
sleep and tears slid through his closed eyelids and wet
his lashes, and while he still slept, Zyll held him and
kissed the tears away.

"Come," Gaudior said.

Charles Wallace stood by the unicorn, blinking. "Was
it a dream?" He looked at the dark lake lapping the
shore, at the tilted rock; it was empty.

Gaudior blew silver bubbles that bounced off his
beard. "You were Within Madoc, deep Within this time."

"Madoc, son of Owain, king of Gwynedd. The Madoc
of the book. And hasn't there been a recurring theory
that Welsh sailors came here before Leif Ericson? . . .
Something about Indians with blue or grey eyes . . ."

"You should know," Gaudior chided. "You were
Within Madoc."

"It can't all have been real."

"Reality was different in those days," Gaudior said. "It was real for Madoc."

"Even the fire among the garlands?"

"Roses often burn. Theirs is the most purifying flame of all."

"And the scry—what Madoc saw in the water—was that a kind of Projection?"

The light in Gaudior's horn flickered. "Gwydyr was on the side of evil, and so he was open to the Projections of the Echthroi."

"So the terrible baby was a Projection the Echthroi want to have happen?"

"I'm never entirely sure about Projections," Gaudior admitted.

"And there was the other baby . . ." Charles Wallace closed his eyes to try to visualize the scry. "The blue-eyed baby, the answer to prayer, who was going to bring peace. So he's equally possible, isn't he?"

"It's all very confusing"—Gaudior shook his mane—"because we move in different dimensions, you and I."

Charles Wallace rubbed his fingers over his forehead as he had done in Meg's room. "It's all in the book somewhere. Why am I being blocked on that book?" The unicorn did not reply. "A book against war, a book about the legend of Madoc and Gwydyr, who came from Wales to this land . . . and what else? I can't get it . . ."

"Leave it alone," Gaudior advised.

Charles Wallace leaned against the unicorn, pressing his forehead against the silver hide, thinking out loud.

"All we know is that a Welsh prince named Madoc did come to the New World with his brother Gwydyr and that Madoc married Zyll of the People of the Wind. Gaudior, if, unknowing, while I was Within Madoc I gave him the rune, would that have been changing a Might-Have-Been?"

The unicorn replied unhelpfully, "It's all very complicated."

"Or—did Madoc have the rune himself? How could he, if it came from Ireland and St. Patrick?"

Gaudior raised his head and pulled back the dark silver of his lips in a ferocious grimace, baring his dangerous teeth. But all he did was open his mouth and drink wind as though quenching a terrible thirst.

Charles Wallace looked about, and as he looked, the scene rippled like the waters in the scrying oval on the beach, and the lake receded until he was looking across a wintry valley, and the rock was no longer a slightly tilted table but the flat star-watching rock, thinly crusted with snow.

Gaudior lowered his head and licked wind from his lips. "Gwydyr did not stay with the People Across the Lake."

"I wouldn't think he would, but how do you know?"

Gaudior raised tufted brows. "I have just been talking with the wind. Gwydyr left the lake in disgrace, and moved southward, ending up in South America."

Charles Wallace clapped his hand to his forehead. "That's it! It's in the book, too. Gwydyr going to Patagonia. And Vespugia is part of Patagonia. And there was a connection that was lost and had to be found, but what *was* it? I keep almost remembering, and then it's as if someone slams a door on my memory."

Gaudior sniffed. "Echthroi, probably. They'll try to block anything that might be a clue to the Might-Have-Been they don't want you to discover."

Charles Wallace nodded. "Mad Dog Branzillo was born in Vespugia. But right here, where we stand, Madoc came and married Zyll and made the roses burn for peace. What happened to the Wind People? Where are they now?"

"They were lovers of peace," Gaudior replied shortly. "Your planet does not deal gently with lovers of peace."

Charles Wallace sat on the rock, the thin rim of snow crackling beneath him. He put his head down on his knees. "I think I have to find out what the connection is between Wales and Vespugia, between Madoc and Gwydyr and Mad Dog Branzillo."

Meg stirred and opened her eyes. Her hand lay lightly on Ananda. "Such dreams, Fortinbras," she murmured, "such strange dreams." Her sleepy gaze drifted toward the clock and suddenly she was wide awake. "Ananda! For a moment I thought you were Fort. And it wasn't dreaming, was it? It was kything, but not clear and sharp, the way it was when Charles Wallace was Within Harcels. He was deeper Within Madoc, and so I have to dig deeper to find the kythe. And Charles wants me to find something out for him . . . but what?" She pushed her fingers through her hair, closed her eyes tightly, and concentrated, her hand pressing against Ananda. "Something about a lake . . . about burning roses . . . and two brothers fighting . . . yes . . . and Mad Dog Branzillo and Wales. That's it. He wants me to find a connection between Mad Dog Branzillo and Wales. And that hardly seems possible, much less likely." She listened to the sounds within the silence of the night, the sounds which were so familiar that they were part of the silence. The old house creaked comfortably. The wind brushed softly against the window. —Nobody's likely to be asleep, not tonight. And Sandy's a history buff. I'll go ask him.

She got out of bed, pushed her feet into furry slippers, and went downstairs. There was light shining under the door of the twins' room, so she knocked.

"What are you doing up, Sis?" Dennys asked. "You need your sleep."

"So do you, doc. I'm up for the same reason you are."

"I often study late," Dennys said. "What can we do for you?"

"What do you know about Vespugia?"

Dennys said, "With your hair down like that, you look about fifteen."

"I'm an old married woman. What about Vespugia?"

Sandy replied, "I was just reading about it in the encyclopedia. It's part of what used to be called Patagonia. Sort of between Argentina and Chile."

"Branzillo was born there?"

"Yes."

"Who colonized Vespugia?"

"Oh, the usual mishmash. Spaniards, a few English, and a group from Wales while it was still part of Patagonia."

Madoc was from Wales. She asked carefully, "Wales—when was that?"

"There's a legend that some Welshmen came to North America even before Leif Ericson, and that one of them went south, looking for a warm climate, and eventually settled in Vespugia—or where Vespugia is now. But that's only legend. However, it's fact that in 1865 a party left Wales for Patagonia and settled in the open wastelands near the Chubut River."

"So maybe Mad Dog Branzillo has some Welsh blood in him?"

"It's perfectly possible, although Branzillo hardly sounds Welsh."

"What year did you say the group left Wales?"

"1865."

"Are those the only times Wales is mentioned in connection with Vespugia?"

"In this encyclopedia."

She thought for a minute. "All right. What happened in 1865 that I ought to know about?"

Dennys said, "Meg, sit down if you're going to get Sandy to give you a history lesson. Is this something to do with being pregnant, like a passion for strawberries?"

"Raspberries. And I don't think it has much to do with being pregnant."

"Let me get *The Time Tables of History*." Sandy reached for the bookcase and pulled out a large and battered volume, and began turning the pages. "Aha. 1865. Appomatox was on April 9, and Lincoln was assassinated on the fourteenth. The Civil War ended on May 26."

"Quite a year."

"Yup. In England, Lord Palmerston died, and was succeeded as Prime Minister by Lord John Russell."

"I don't know much about him."

"And back to the once-more-United States, the Thirteenth Amendment abolished slavery."

"Would there have been slavery in Vespugia?"

"Not sure. Bolivar died in 1830, and his influence would likely have filtered through to Vespugia. So I doubt if there'd have been slaves."

"Well, good."

"Okay, and also in 1865 the Atlantic cable was finally completed. Oh, and here's something for you, Den: Lister caused a scandal by insisting on antiseptic surgery and using carbolic acid on a compound wound."

Dennys applauded. "You're almost as veritable an encyclopedia as Charles Wallace."

"Charles has it in his head and I have to look it up in a reference book. My sphere of knowledge is considerably more limited. Mendel came out with his law of heredity that year"—he peered down at the book again—"and the Ku Klux Klan was founded, and Edward Whymper climbed the Matterhorn. And Lewis Carroll wrote *Alice's Adventures in Wonderland.*"

"Indeed, 1865 was quite a year," Dennys said. "What have you learned, Meg?"

"I think maybe a lot. Thanks, both of you."

"Get back into bed," Dennys chided. "You don't want to get chilled wandering around this drafty old barn in the middle of the night."

"I'm warm." She indicated her heavy robe and slippers. "I'm taking care. But thanks."

"If we made you some hot chocolate, would you drink it?"

"I'm off hot chocolate."

"Some consommé or bouillon?"

"No, thanks, really, I don't want anything. I'll get back into bed."

Sandy called after her, "And also in 1865 Rudyard Kipling was born, and Verlaine wrote *Poèmes saturniens,* and John Stuart Mill wrote *Auguste Comte and Positivism,* and Purdue, Cornell, and the universities of Maine were founded."

She waved back at him, then paused as he continued, "And Matthew Maddox's first novel, *Once More United,* was published."

She turned back, asking in a carefully controlled voice, "Maddox? I don't think I've ever heard of that author."

"You stuck to math in school."

"Yeah, Calvin always helped me with my English papers. Did this Matthew Maddox write anything else?"

Sandy flipped through the pages. "Let's see. Nothing in 1866, 1867. 1868, here we are, *The Horn of Joy.*"

"Oh, that," Dennys said. "I remember him now. I had to take a lit course my sophomore year in college, and

I took nineteenth-century American literature. We read that, Matthew Maddox's second and last book, *The Horn of Joy*. My prof said if he hadn't died he'd have been right up there with Hawthorne and James. It was a strange book, passionately anti-war, I remember, and it went way back into the past, and there was some weird theory of the future influencing the past—not my kind of book at all."

"But you remember it," Meg remarked.

"Yeah, I remember it, for some reason. There was a Welsh prince whose brothers were fighting for the throne. And he left Wales with one of his brothers, and was shipwrecked and landed somewhere on the New England coast. There was more, but I can't think of it right now."

"Thanks," Meg said. "Thanks a lot."

Ananda greeted her joyfully at the head of the stairs. Meg fondled the dog's floppy ear. "I really would have liked something hot to drink, but I didn't want Sandy and Dennys coming up to the attic and staying to talk when we have to concentrate on kything with Charles Wallace." She got back into bed and Ananda jumped up beside her and settled down. The clock's hands had moved ahead fifteen minutes, the length of time she had spent with Sandy and Dennys. And time was of the essence. But she felt that the trip downstairs had been worth it. She had found the author and the title of the book for Charles Wallace. And she had found a connection between Wales and Vespugia in 1865. But what did the connection mean? Madoc was Welsh, but he didn't go to Vespugia, he came here, and married here.

She shook her head. Maybe Charles Wallace and Gaudior could make something out of it.

And how any of this could connect with Mrs. O'Keefe was a mystery.

6

The lightning with
its rapid wrath

"Thanks, Meg," Charles Wallace whispered. "Oh, Gaudior, she really did help us, she and the twins." He leaned forward to rest his cheek against the unicorn's neck. "The book was by Matthew Maddox. I don't think I ever read it, but I remember Dennys talking about it. And Mrs. O'Keefe was a Maddox, so she's *got* to be descended from Matthew."

"Descended," Gaudior snorted. "You make it sound like a fall."

"If you look at Mrs. O'Keefe, that's what it's like," Charles Wallace admitted. "1865. Can we go there?"

"Then," the unicorn corrected. "When. We can try, if

you think it's important. We'll hope for a favorable
wind."

Charles Wallace looked alarmed. "You mean we might
get blown into another Projection?"

"It's always a risk. We know the Echthroi are after us,
to stop us. So you must hold on."

"I'll hold on for dear life. The last thing I want is to
get blown into another Projection."

Gaudior blew softly through his teeth. "I find our most
recent information not very helpful."

"But it could be important, a group of Welshmen going
to South America in 1865. I think we should try to go to
Vespugia."

"That's a long way, and unicorns do not travel well to
different Wheres. And to try to move in *both* space and
time—I don't like it." He flicked his tail.

"Then how about trying to move to 1865, right here,
the year Matthew Maddox published his first novel?
Then we could try to move from 1865 here to 1865 in
Vespugia. And maybe we could learn something from
Matthew Maddox."

"Very well. It's less dangerous to go elsewhen first than
to try to go elsewhen and elsewhere simultaneously." He
began to gallop, and as he flung himself onto a gust of
wind, the wings lifted and they soared upward.

The attack, just as they went through a shower of stars,
was completely unexpected. A freezing gust blasted the
wind on which they were riding, taking away Charles
Wallace's breath. His knuckles whitened as he clenched

the mane, which seemed to strengthen into steel wire to help him hold his grasp. He had a horrible sense of Gaudior battling with a darkness which was like an anti-unicorn, a flailing of negative wings and iron hoofs. The silver mane was torn from his hands as he was assailed by the horrible stench which accompanied Echthroi. Dark wings beat him from the unicorn's back and he felt the burning cold of outer space. This was more horrible than any Projection. His lungs cracked for lack of air. He would become a burnt-out body, a satellite circling forever the nearest sun . . .

A powerful wrench, and air rushed into his battered lungs. He felt a sharp tug at the nape of his neck, and the blue anorak tightened against his throat. The agonizing stench was gone and he was surrounded by the scent of unicorn breath, smelling of stars and frost. Gaudior was carrying him in his mouth, great ivory teeth clamped on the strong stuff of the anorak.

Gaudior's iridescent wings beat against the dark. Charles Wallace held his breath. If Gaudior dropped him, the Echthroi would be waiting. His armpits were cut from the pulling of the anorak, but he knew that he must not struggle. Gaudior's breath gusted painfully from between clenched teeth.

Then the silver hoofs touched stone, and they were safely at the star-watching rock. Gaudior opened his teeth and dropped the boy. For the first moments Charles Wallace was so weak that he collapsed onto the rock. Then he struggled to his feet, still trembling from the near disaster. He stretched his arms to ease his sore armpits and shoulders. Gaudior was breathing in great, panting gusts, his flanks heaving.

The soft breeze around them filled and healed their seared lungs.

Gaudior rolled his lips, and took a deep draught of clear air. Then he bent down and nuzzled Charles Wallace in the first gesture of affection he had shown. "I wasn't sure we were going to get away. The Echthroi are enraged that the wind managed to send you Within Madoc, and they're trying to stop you from going Within anyone else."

Charles Wallace stroked the unicorn's muzzle. "You saved me. I'd be tumbling in outer space forever if you hadn't grabbed my anorak."

"It was one chance in a million," Gaudior admitted. "And the wind helped me."

Charles Wallace reached up to put his arms around Gaudior's curving neck. "Even with help, it wasn't easy. Thank you."

Gaudior made a unicorn shrug; his curly beard quivered. "Unicorns find it embarrassing to be thanked. Please desist."

It was a hot, midsummer's day, with thunderheads massed on the horizon. The lake was gone, and the familiar valley stretched to the hills. The woods was a forest of mighty elms and towering oaks and hemlock. In the far distance was what looked like a cluster of log cabins.

"I don't think this looks like 1865," he told Gaudior.

"You'd know more about that than I would. I didn't have much opportunity to learn earth's history. I never expected this assignment."

"But, Gaudior, we have to know When we are."

"Why?"

Charles Wallace tried to quell his impatience, which was all the sharper after the terror of the attack. "If there's a Might-Have-Been we're supposed to discover, we have to know When it is, don't we?"

Gaudior's own impatience was manifested by prancing. "Why? We don't have to know everything. We have a charge laid on us, and we have to follow where it leads. You've been so busy trying to do the leading that we almost got taken by the Echthroi."

Charles Wallace said nothing.

"Perhaps," Gaudior granted grudgingly, "it wasn't entirely your fault. But I think we should not try to control the Whens and the Wheres, but should go Where we're sent. And what with all that contretemps with the Echthroi, you're still in your own body, and you're supposed to be Within."

"Oh. What should I do?"

Gaudior blew mightily through flared nostrils. "I will have to ask the wind." And he raised his head and opened his jaws. Charles Wallace waited anxiously until the unicorn lowered his head and raised one wing, stretching it to its full span. "Step close to me," he ordered.

Charles Wallace moved under the wing and leaned against Gaudior's flank. "Did the wind say When we are?"

"You make too many demands," Gaudior chided, and folded his wing until Charles Wallace felt smothered. Gasping for breath, he tried to push his way out into the air, but the wing held him firmly, and at last his struggling ceased.

When he opened his eyes the day had vanished, and trees and rock were bathed in moonlight.

He was Within. Lying on the rock, looking up at the moon-bathed sky. Only the most brilliant stars could compete with the silver light. Around him the sounds of summer sang sweetly. A mourning dove complained from her place deep in the darkest shadows. A grandfather frog boomed his bull-call. A pure trilling of bird song made him sit up and call out in greeting, "Zylle!"

A young woman stepped out from the shadows of the forest. She was tall and slender, except for her belly, which was heavy with child. "Thanks for meeting me, Brandon."

Charles Wallace-within-Brandon Llawcae gave her a swift hug. "Anything I do with you is fun, Zylle."

Again, as when he was Within Harcels, he was younger than fifteen, perhaps eleven or twelve, still very much a child, an eager, intelligent, loving child.

In the moonlight she smiled at him. "The herbs I need to ease the birthing of my babe are found only when the moon is full, and only here. Ritchie fears it would offend Goody Adams, did she know."

Goody, short for Goodwife. That's what the Pilgrims said, instead of Mrs. This was definitely not 1865, then.

More than a century earlier, perhaps even two centuries. Brandon Llawcae must be the son of early settlers . . .

"Let yourself go," Gaudior knelled. "Let yourself be Brandon."

"But why are we here?" Charles Wallace demurred. "What can we learn here?"

"Stop asking questions."

"But I don't want to waste time . . ." Charles Wallace said anxiously.

Gaudior whickered irritably. "You are here, and you are in Brandon. Let go."

Let go.

Be Brandon.

Be.

"So," Zylle continued, "it is best that Ritchie not know, either. I can always trust you, Brandon. You don't open your mouth and spill everything out when to do so would bring no good."

Brandon ducked his head shyly, then looked swiftly up at Zylle's eyes, which were a startling blue in her brown face. "I have learned from the People of the Wind that 'tis no harm to hold a secret in the heart."

Zylle sighed. "No, it is no harm. But it grieves me that you and I may not share our gifts with those we love."

"My pictures." Brandon nodded. "My parents want me to try not to see my pictures."

"Among my people," Zylle said, "you would be known as a Seer, and you would be having the training in prayer and trusting that would keep your gift very close to the

gods, from whom the gift comes. My father had hoped
that Maddok might have the gift, because it is rare to
have two with blue eyes in one generation. But my little
brother's gift is to know about weather, when to plant
and when to harvest, and that is a good gift, and a
needed one."

"I miss Maddok." Bran scowled down at the rock. "He
never comes to the settlement any more."

Zylle placed her hand lightly on his shoulder. "It's different in the settlement now that there are more families.
Maddok no longer feels welcome."

"I welcome him!"

"He knows that. And he misses you, too. But it isn't
only that the settlement is larger. Maddok is older, and
has to do more work at home. But he will always be your
friend."

"And I'll always be his. Always."

"Your pictures—" Zylle looked at him intently. "Are
you able to stop seeing them?"

"Not always. When I look at something that holds a
reflection, sometimes the pictures come, whether I will
or no. But I try not to ask them to come."

"When you see your pictures, it is all right to tell me
what you see, the way you used to tell Maddok."

"Ritchie is afraid of them."

She pressed his shoulder gently. "Life has been nothing
but hard work for Ritchie, with no time for seeing pictures or dreaming dreams. Your mother tells me that in
Wales there are people who are gifted with the second

sight, and that these people may be feared for their gift but they are not frowned on."

"Ritchie says I would be frowned on. It is different here than in Wales. Especially since Pastor Mortmain came and built the church and scowled whenever Maddok visited the settlement or I went to the Indian compound."

"Pastor Mortmain would try to separate the white people from the Indians."

"But *why?*" Brandon demanded. "We were friends."

"And still are," Zylle assured him. "When did you last see a picture?"

"Tonight," he told her. "I saw the reflection of a candle on the side of the copper kettle Mother had just polished, and I saw a picture of here, this very place, but the rock was much higher, and there"—he pointed to the valley—"it was all a lake, with the sun sparkling on the water."

She looked at him wonderingly. "My father, Zillo, says that the valley was once a lake bed."

"And I saw Maddok—at least, it wasn't Maddok, because he was older, and his skin was fair, but he looked so like Maddok, at first I thought it was."

"The legend," she murmured. "Oh, Brandon, I feel we are very close, you and I. Perhaps it is having to keep our gifts hidden that brings us added closeness." While they were talking she had been gathering a small plant that grew between the grasses. She held the blossoms out to the moonlight. "I know where to find the healing herbs, herbs that will keep babies from choking to death in the winter, or from dying of the summer sickness when the weather is hot and heavy as it is now. But your mother warns me that I must not offer these gifts; they would not be well received. But for myself, and the birthing of Ritchie's and my baby, I will not be without the herbs which will help give me a good birthing and a fine child." She began to spread the delicate blossoms on the rock. As the moonlight touched them, petals and leaf alike appeared to glow with inner silver. Zylle looked up at the moon and sang,

> *"Lords of fire and earth and water,*
> *Lords of moon and wind and sky,*
> *Come now to the Old Man's daughter,*
> *Come from fathers long gone by.*
> *Bring blue from a distant eye.*
>
> *Lords of water, earth, and fire,*
> *Lords of wind and snow and rain,*
> *Give to me my heart's desire.*
> *Life as all life comes with pain,*
> *But blue will come to us again."*

Then she knelt and breathed in the fragrance of the blossoms, took them up in her hands, and pressed them against her forehead, her lips, her breasts, against the roundness of her belly.

Brandon asked, "Do we take the flowers home with us?"

"I would not want Goody Adams to see them."

"When Ritchie and I were born, there wasn't a mid-wife in the settlement."

"Goody Adams is a fine midwife," Zylle assured him. "Had she been here, your mother might not have lost those little ones between you and Ritchie. But she would not approve of what I have just done. We will leave the birthing flowers here for the birds and moon and the wind. They have already given me their help."

"When—oh, Zylle, do you know when the baby will come?"

"Tomorrow." She stood. "It's time we went home. I would not want Ritchie to wake and find me not beside him."

Brandon reached for her long, cool fingers. "It was the best day in the world when Ritchie married you."

She smiled swiftly, concealing a shadow of worry in her eyes. "The people of the settlement look with suspicion on an Indian in their midst, and a blue-eyed Indian at that."

"If they'd only listen to our story that comes from Wales, and to your story—"

She pressed his fingers. "Ritchie warns me not to talk about our legend of the white man who came to us in the days when there were only Indians on this continent."

"Long ago?"

"Long, long ago. He came from across the sea, from a land at the other end of the world, and he was a brave man, and true, who lusted neither after power nor after land. My little brother is named after him."

"And the song?" Brandon asked.

"It's old, very old, the prayer for a blue-eyed baby to keep the strength of the prince from over the sea within the Wind People, and the words may have changed over the years. And I have changed, for I have made my life with the white people, as the Golden Prince made his with the Wind People. For love he stayed with the princess of a strange land, and made her ways his ways. For love I leave my people and stay with Ritchie, and my love is deep, deep, for me to be able to leave my home. I sing the prayer because it is in my blood, and must be sung; and yet I wonder if my child will be allowed to know the Indian half of himself?"

"He?"

"It will be a boy."

"How do you know?"

"The trees have told me in the turning of their leaves under the moonlight. I would like a girl baby, but Ritchie will be pleased to have a son."

The footpath through the grasses led them to a brook, which caught the light of the moon and glimmered in the shifting shadows of the leaves. The brook was spanned by a natural stone bridge, and here Zylle paused, looking down at the water.

Brandon, too, looked at their reflections shifting and shimmering as the wind stirred the leaves. While he looked at Zylle's reflection, the water stirring her mouth into a tender smile, he saw, too, a baby held close in her arms, a black-haired, blue-eyed baby with gold behind its eyes.

Then, while he gazed, the eyes changed in the child and turned sullen, and the face was no longer the face of a baby but the face of a man, and he could not see

Zylle anywhere. The man wore a strange-looking uniform with many medals, and his jowls were dark, jutting pridefully. He was thinking to himself, and he was thinking cruel thoughts, vindictive thoughts, and then Brandon saw fire, raging fire.

His body gave a mighty shudder and he gasped and turned toward Zylle, then glanced fearfully at the brook. The fire was gone, and only their two faces were reflected.

She asked, "What did you see?"

Eyes lowered, gazing on the dark stone of the bridge, he told her, trying not to let the images reappear in his mind's eye.

She shook her head somberly. "I make nothing out of it. Certainly nothing good."

Still looking down, Brandon said, "Before I was made to feel afraid of my pictures, they were never frightening, only beautiful."

Zylle squeezed his hand reassuringly. "I'd like to tell my father about this one, for he is trained in the interpretation of visions."

Brandon hesitated, then: "All right, if you want to."

"I want him to give me comfort," she said in a low voice.

They turned from the brook and walked on home in silence, to the dusty clearing with its cluster of log cabins.

The Llawcaes' cabin was the first, a sizable building with a central room for sitting and eating, and a bedroom at either end. Brandon's room was a shed added to his parents' room, and was barely large enough to hold a small bed, a chest, and a chair. But it was all his, and Ritchie had promised that after the baby was born he would cut a fine window in the wall, as people were beginning to do now that the settlement was established.

Brandon's cubbyhole was dark, but he was used to his own room's night and moved in it as securely as though he had lit a candle. Without undressing, he lay down on the bed. In the distance the thunder growled, and with the thunder came an echo, a low, rhythmic rumbling which Brandon recognized as the drums of the Wind People as they sang their prayers for rain.

In the morning when he wakened, he heard bustling in the central room, and went in to find his mother boiling water in the big black kettle suspended from a large hook in the fireplace. Goody Adams, the midwife, was bustling about, exuding importance.

"This is a first birth," she said. "We'll need many kettles of water for the Indian girl."

"Zylle is our daughter," Brandon's mother reminded the midwife.

"Once an Indian, always an Indian, Goody Llawcae. Not forgetting that we're all grateful that her presence among us causes us to live in peace with the savage heathen."

"They're not—" Brandon started fiercely.

But his mother said, "The chores are waiting, Brandon."

Biting his lip, he went out.

The morning was clear, with a small mist drifting across the ground and hazing the outline of the hills. When the sun was full, the mist would go. The settlers were grateful for the mist and the heavy dews, which were all that kept the crops from drying up and withering completely, for there had been no rain for more than a moon.

Brandon went to the small barn behind the cabin to let their cow out into the daylight. She would graze with the other cattle all day, and at dusk Brandon would ride out on his pony to bring her home for milking. He gave the pony some oats, then fed the horse. In the distance he could hear hammering. Goodman Llawcae and his son Ritchie were the finest carpenters for many miles around, and were always busy with orders.

—I'm glad Ritchie didn't hear Goody Adams call Zylle's people savage heathens, he thought. —It's a good thing he was in with Zylle. Then he started back to the house. The picture he had seen in the brook the night before troubled him. He was afraid of the dark man with cruel thoughts, and he was afraid of the fire. Since he had tried to repress the pictures, they had become more and more frightening.

When he reached the cabin and went in through the door, which was propped open to allow all the fresh air possible to enter, his mother came out of the bedroom and spoke to Ritchie, who was pacing up and down in front of the fireplace.

"Your father needs you, Ritchie. Zylle is resting now, between pains. I will call you at once should she need you."

Goody Adams muttered, "The Indian girl does not cry. It is an omen."

Ritchie flung back his head. "It is the mark of the Indian, Goody. Zylle will shed no tears in front of you."

"Heathen—" Goody Adams started.

But Goody Llawcae cut her short. "Ritchie. Brandon. Go to your father."

Ritchie flung out the door, not deigning to look at the midwife. Brandon followed him, calling, "Ritchie—"

Ritchie paused, but did not turn around.

"I hate Goody Adams!" Brandon exploded.

Now Ritchie looked at his young brother. "Hate never did any good. Everyone in the settlement feels the lash of Goody Adams's tongue. But her hands bring out living babies, and there's been no childbed fever since she's been here."

"I liked it better when I was little and there was only us Llawcaes, and the Higginses, and Davey and I used to play with Maddok."

"It was simpler then," Ritchie agreed, "but change is the way of the world."

"Is change always good?"

Ritchie shook his head. "There was more joy when there were just the two families of us, and no Pastor Mortmain to put his dead hand on our songs and stories. I cannot find it in me to believe that God enjoys long

faces and scowls at merriment. Get along with you now,
Bran. I have work to do, and so do you."

When Brandon finished his chores and hurried back to
the cabin, walking silently, one foot directly in front of
the other, as Maddok had taught him, Ritchie, too, had
returned, and was standing in the doorway. The sun was
high in the sky and beat fiercely on the cabins and the
dusty compound. The grass was turning brown, and the
green leaves had lost their sheen.

Ritchie shook his head. "Not yet. It's fiercely hot. Look
at those thunderheads."

"They've been there every day." Brandon looked at the
heavy clouds massed on the horizon. "And not a drop of
rain."

A low, nearly inaudible moan came from the cabin,
and Ritchie hurried indoors. From the bedroom came a
sharp cry, and Brandon's skin prickled with gooseflesh,
despite the heat. "Oh God, God, make Zylle be all right."
He focused on one small cloud in the dry blue, and there
he saw a picture of Zylle and the black-haired, blue-eyed
baby. And as he watched, both mother and child
changed, and the mother was still black-haired, but
creamy of skin, and the baby was bronze-skinned and
blue-eyed, and the joy in the face of the mother was
the same as in the picture of Zylle. But the fair-skinned
mother was not in the familiar landscape but in a wild,
hot country, and her clothes were not like the homespun
or leather he was accustomed to, but different, finer than
clothes he had seen before.

The baby began to cry, but the cry came not from the baby in the picture but from the cabin, a real cry, the healthy squall of an infant.

Goody Llawcae came to the door, her face alight. "It's a nephew you have, Brandon, a bonny boy, and Zylle beaming like the sun. Though sorrow endure for a night, joy cometh in the morning."

"It's afternoon."

"Don't be so literal, lad. Run to let your father know. Now!"

"But when may I see Zylle and the baby?"

"After his grandfather has had the privilege. Run!"

When Goody Adams had at last taken herself off, the Llawcaes gathered about the mother and child. Zylle lay on the big carved bed which Richard Llawcae had made for her and Ritchie as a wedding present. Light from the door to the kitchen–living room fell across her as she held the newborn child in her arms. Its eyes were tightly closed, and it waved tiny fists in searching gestures, and its little mouth opened and closed as though it were sipping its strange new element, air.

"Oh, taste and see," Zylle murmured, and touched her lips softly to the dark fuzz on the baby's head. His copper skin was still moist from the effort of birth and the humidity of the day. In the distance, thunder growled.

"His eyes?" Brandon whispered.

"Blue. Goody Adams says the color of the eyes often changes, but Bran's won't. No baby could ask for a better uncle. May we name him after you?"

Brandon nodded, blushing with pleasure, and reached out with one finger to touch the baby's cheek.

Richard Llawcae opened the big, much-used Bible, and read aloud, "I love the Lord, because he hath heard my voice and my supplications. The sorrows of death compassed me, and the pains of hell gat hold upon me: I found trouble and sorrow. Then called I upon the name of the Lord. Gracious is the Lord, and righteous. I was brought low, and he helped me. Return unto thy rest, O my soul; for the Lord hath dealt bountifully with thee."

"Amen," Zylle said.

Richard Llawcae closed the Book. "You are my beloved daughter, Zylle. When Ritchie chose you for his betrothed, his mother and I were uncertain at first, as were your own people. But it seemed to your father, Zillo, and to me that two legends were coming together in this union. And time has taught us that it was a blessed inevitability."

"Thank you, Father." She reached out to his leathery hand. "Goody Adams did not like it that I shed no tears."

Goody Llawcae ran her hand gently over Zylle's shining black hair. "She knows that it is the way of your people."

—Savages, heathen savages, Brandon thought. —That's what Goody Adams thinks of Zylle's people.

When Bran went to do his evening chores a shadow materialized from behind the great trunk of a pine tree. Maddok.

Brandon greeted him with joy. "I'm glad, glad to see you! Father was going to send me to the Indian compound after chores, but now I can tell you: the baby's come! A boy, and all is well."

The shadow of a smile moved across Maddok's face, in which the blue eyes were as startling as they were in Zylle. "My father will be glad. Your family will allow us to come tonight, to see the baby?"

"Of course."

Maddok's eyes clouded. "It's not 'of course.' Not any more."

"It is with us Llawcaes. Maddok—how did you know to come, just now?"

"I saw Zylle yesterday. She told me it would be today."

"I didn't see you."

"You weren't alone. Davey Higgins was with you."

"But you and Davey and I always played together. It was the three of us."

"Not any more. Davey has been forbidden to leave the settlement and come to the compound. Your medicine man's gods do not respect our gods."

Brandon let his breath out in a sigh that was nearly a groan. "Pastor Mortmain. It's not our gods that don't respect your gods. It's Pastor Mortmain."

Maddok nodded. "And his son is courting Davey's sister."

Brandon giggled. "I'd love to see Pastor Mortmain's face if he heard himself referred to as a medicine man."

"He is not a good medicine man," Maddok said. "He will cause trouble."

"He already has. It's his fault Davey can't see you."

Maddok looked intently into Brandon's eyes. "My father also sent me to warn you."

"Warn? Of what?"

"We have had runners out. In the town there is much talk of witchcraft."

Witchcraft. It was an ugly word. "But not here," Brandon said.

"Not yet. But there is talk among your people."

"What kind of talk?" Brandon asked sharply.

"My sister shed no tears during the birth."

"They know that it is the way of the Indian."

"It is also the mark of a witch. They say that a cat ran screaming through the street at the time of the birth, and that Zylle put her pain into the cat."

"That is nonsense." But Brandon's eyes were troubled.

"My father says there are evil spirits abroad, hardening men's hearts. He says there is lust to see evil in innocence. Brandon, my friend and brother, take care of Zylle and the baby."

"Zylle and I picked herbs for the birthing," Brandon said in a low voice.

"Zylle was taught all the ways of a good delivery, and she has the healing gifts. But that, too, would be looked upon as magic. Black magic."

"But it's not magic—"

"No. It is understanding the healing qualities of certain plants and roots. People are afraid of knowledge that is not yet theirs. My father is concerned for Zylle, and for you."

Brandon protested. "But we are known as God-loving people. Surely they couldn't think—"

"Because you are known as such, they will wish to think," Maddok said. "My father says you should go more with the other children of the settlement, where you can see and hear. It's better to be prepared. I, too, will keep my ears open." Without saying goodbye, he disappeared into the forest.

Late in the evening, when most of the settlement was sleeping, Zylle's people came through the woods, silently, in single file, approaching the cabin from behind, as Maddok had done in the afternoon.

They clustered around Zylle and the baby, were served Goody Llawcae's special cold herb tea, and freshly baked bread, fragrant with golden cheese and sweet butter.

Zillo took his grandson into his arms, and a shadow of tenderness moved across his impassive face. "Brandon, son of Zylle of the Wind People and son of Ritchie of Llawcae, son of a prince from the distant land of Wales; Brandon, bearer of the blue," he murmured over the sleeping baby, rocking him gently in his arms.

Out of the corner of his eye, Brandon saw one of the Indian women go to his mother, talking to her softly. His mother put her hand to her head in a worried gesture.

And before the Indians left, he saw Zillo take his father aside.

Despite his joy in his namesake, there was heaviness in his heart when he went to bed, and it was that, as much as the heat, which kept him from sleeping. He could hear his parents talking with Ritchie in the next room, and he shifted position so that he could hear better.

Goody Llawcae was saying, "People do not like other people to be different. It is hard enough for Zylle, being an Indian, without being part of a family marked as different, too."

"Different?" Ritchie asked sharply. "We were the first settlers here."

"We come from Wales. And Brandon's gift is feared."

Richard asked his wife, "Did one of the Indians give you a warning?"

"One of the women. I had hoped this disease of witch-hunting would not touch our settlement."

"We must try not to let it start with us," Goodman Llawcae said. "At least the Higginses will stand by us."

"Will they?" Ritchie asked. "Goodman Higgins seems much taken with Pastor Mortmain. And Davey Higgins hasn't come to do chores with Brandon in a long time."

Richard said, "Zillo warned me of Brandon, too."

"Brandon—" Goody Llawcae drew in her breath.

"He saw one of his pictures last night."

On hearing this, Brandon hurried into the big room. "Zylle told you!"

"She did not, Brandon," his father said, "and eaves-droppers seldom hear anything pleasant. You did give Zylle permission to speak to her father, and it was he who told me. Are you ashamed to tell us?"

"Ashamed? No, Father, not ashamed. I try not to ask for the pictures, because you don't want me to see them, and I know it disturbs you when they come to me anyhow. That is why I don't tell you. I thought you would prefer me not to."

His father lowered his head. "It is understandable that you should feel this way. Perhaps we have been wrong to ask you not to see your pictures if they are God's gift to you."

Brandon looked surprised. "Who else would send them?"

"In Wales it is believed that such gifts come from God. There is not as much fear of devils there as here."

"Zylle and Maddok say my pictures come from the gods."

"And Zillo warned me," his father said, "that you must not talk about your pictures in front of anybody, especially Pastor Mortmain."

"What about Davey?"

"Not anybody."

"But Davey knows about my pictures. When we were little, I used to describe them to Davey and Maddok."

The parents looked at each other. "That was long ago. Let's hope Davey has forgotten."

Ritchie banged his fist against the hard wood of the bedstead. Richard held up a warning hand. "Hush. You will wake your wife and son. Once the heat breaks, people's temperaments will be easier. Brandon, go back to bed."

Back in his room, Brandon tossed hotly on his straw pallet. Even after the rest of the household was quiet, he could not sleep. In the distance he heard the drums. But no rain came.

The next evening when he was bringing the cow home
from the day's grazing, Davey Higgins came up to him.
"Bran, Pastor Mortmain says I am not to speak to you."

"You're speaking."

"We've known each other all our lives. I will speak as
long as I can. But people are saying that Zylle is prevent-
ing the rain. The crops are withering. We do not want
to offend the Indians, but Pastor Mortmain says that
Zylle's blue eyes prove her to be not a true Indian, and
that the Indians were afraid of her and wished her onto
us."

"You know that's not true!" Brandon said hotly. "The
Indians are proud of the blue eyes."

"I know it," Davey said, "and you know it, but we are
still children, and people do not listen to children. Pastor
Mortmain has forbidden us to go to the Indian compound, and Maddok is no longer welcome here. My father believes everything Pastor Mortmain says, and my
sister is being courted by his son, that pasty-faced Duthbert. Bran, what do your pictures tell you of all this?"
Davey gave Brandon a sidewise glance.

Brandon looked at him directly. "I'm twelve years old
now, Davey. I'm no longer a child with a child's pictures." He left Davey and took the cow to the shed, feeling that denying the pictures had been an act of be-
trayal.

Maddok came around the corner of the shed. "My father has sent me to you, in case there is danger. I am to

follow you, but not be seen. But you know Indian ways, and you will see me. So I wanted you to know, so that you won't be afraid."

"I am afraid," Brandon said flatly.

"If only it would rain," Maddok said.

"You know about weather. Will it rain?"

Maddok shook his head. "The air smells of thunder, but there will be no rain this moon. There is lightning in the air, and it turns people's minds. How is Zylle? and the baby?"

Now Brandon smiled. "Beautiful."

At family prayers that evening the Llawcae faces were sober. Richard asked for wisdom, for prudence, for rain. He asked for faithfulness in friendship, and for courage. And again for rain.

The thunder continued to grumble. The heavy night was sullen with heat lightning. And no drop fell.

The children would not talk with Brandon. Even Davey shamefacedly turned away. Mr. Mortmain, confronting Brandon, said, "There is evil under your roof. You had better see to it that it is removed."

When Brandon reported this, Ritchie exploded. "The evil is in Mr. Mortmain's own heart."

The evil was as pervasive as the brassy heat.

Pastor Mortmain came in the evening to the Llawcaes' cabin, bringing with him his son, Duthbert, and Goodman Higgins. "We would speak with the Indian woman."

"My wife—" Ritchie started, but his father silenced him.

"It is late for this visit, Pastor Mortmain," Richard said. "My daughter-in-law and the baby have retired."

"Then they must be wakened. It is our intention to discover if the Indian woman is a Christian, or—"

Zylle walked into the room, carrying her child. "Or what, Pastor Mortmain?"

Duthbert looked at her, and his eyes were greedy.

Goodman Higgins questioned her gently. "We believe you to be a Christian, Zylle. That is true, is it not?"

"Yes, Goodman Higgins. When I married Ritchie I accepted his beliefs."

"Even though they were contrary to the beliefs of your people?" Pastor Mortmain asked.

"But they are not contrary."

"The Indians are pagans," Duthbert said.

Zylle looked at the pasty young man over the baby's head. "I do not know what pagan means. I only know that Jesus of Nazareth sings the true song. He knows the ancient harmonies."

Pastor Mortmain drew in his breath in horror. "You say that our Lord and Saviour sings! What more do we need to hear?"

"But why should he not sing?" Zylle asked. "The very stars sing as they turn in their heavenly dance, sing praise of the One who created them. In the meeting house do we not sing hymns?"

Pastor Mortmain scowled at Zylle, at the Llawcaes, at

his son, who could not keep his eyes off Zylle's loveliness, at Goodman Higgins. "That is different. You are a heathen and you do not understand."

Zylle raised her head proudly. "Scripture says that God loves every man. That is in the Psalms. He loves my people as he loves you, or he is not God."

Higgins warned, "You must not blaspheme, child."

"Why," demanded Pastor Mortmain, "are you holding back the rain?"

"Why ever should I wish to hold back the rain? Our corn suffers as does yours. We pray for rain, twice daily, at morning and at evening prayer."

"The cat," Duthbert said. "What about the cat?"

"The cat is to keep rodents away from house and barn, like all the cats in the settlement."

Pastor Mortmain said, "Goody Adams tells us the cat is to help you fly through the air."

Duthbert's mouth dropped slightly, and Ritchie shouted with outrage. But Zylle silenced him with a gesture, asking, "Does your cat help you to fly through the air, Pastor Mortmain? No more does mine. The gift of flying through the air is given to only the most holy of people, and I am only a woman like other women."

"Stop, child," Goodman Higgins ordered, "before you condemn yourself."

"Are you a true Indian?" Pastor Mortmain demanded.

She nodded. "I am of the People of the Wind."

"Indians do not have blue eyes."

"You have heard our legend."

"Legend?"

"Yes. Though we believe it to be true. My father has the blue eyes, too, as does my little brother."

"Lies!" Pastor Mortmain cried. "Storytelling is of the devil."

Richard Llawcae took a step toward the small, dark figure of the minister. "How strange that you should say that, Pastor Mortmain. Scripture says that Jesus taught by telling stories. *And he spake many things unto them in parables . . . and without a parable spake he not unto them.* That is in the thirteenth chapter of the Gospel according to Matthew."

Pastor Mortmain's face was hard. "I believe this Indian woman to be a witch. And if she is, she must die like a witch. That, too, is in Scripture." He gestured to Goodman Higgins and Duthbert. "We will meet in church and make our decision."

"Who will make the decision?" Ritchie demanded, not heeding his father's warning hand. "All the men of the settlement, in fair discussion, or you, Pastor Mortmain?"

"Be careful," Goodman Higgins urged. "Ritchie, take care."

"David Higgins," Richard Llawcae said, "our two cabins were the first in this settlement. You have known us longer than anyone else here. Do you believe that my son would marry a witch?"

"Not knowingly, Richard."

"You were here with us during the evenings when the Indians came to listen to our stories, and we heard their own legend that matched ours. You saw how the Indian legend and the Welsh one insured peace between us and the People of the Wind, did you not, now, David?"

"Yes, that is so."

Pastor Mortmain intervened. "Goodman Higgins has told me of the storytelling which preceded the sop of reading from Scripture."

"Scripture was never a sop for us, Pastor. Those early years were hard. Goody Higgins died birthing Davey, and after her death in one week three of David's children died of diphtheria, and another only a year later coughed his life away. My wife lost four little ones between Richard and Brandon, one at birth, the other three as children. We were sustained and strengthened by Scripture then, as we are still. As for the stories, the winter evenings were long, and it was a pleasant way to while away the time as we worked with our hands."

Goodman Higgins shuffled his feet. "There was no harm in the stories, Pastor Mortmain. I have assured you of that."

"Perhaps not for you," Pastor Mortmain said. "Come."

Goodman Higgins did not look up as he followed Pastor Mortmain and Duthbert out of the cabin.

Nightmare. Brandon wanted to scream, to make himself wake up, but he was not asleep, and the nightmare was happening. When he did his chores he was aware that Maddok was invisibly there, watching over him. Sometimes he heard him rustling up in the branches of a tree. Sometimes Maddok let Brandon have a glimpse of him behind a tree trunk, behind the corner of a barn or cabin. But wherever he went, Maddok was there, and that meant that the Indians knew all that was happening.

A baby in the settlement died of the summer sickness, which had always been the chief cause of infant mortality during the hot months, but it was all that was needed to convict Zylle.

Pastor Mortmain sent to the town for a man who was said to be an expert in the detection of witches. He had sent many people to the gallows.

"And that's supposed to make him an expert?" Ritchie demanded.

The settlement crackled with excitement. It seemed to Brandon that people were enjoying it. The Higgins daughter walked along the dusty street with Duthbert, and did not raise her eyes, but Pastor Mortmain's son smiled, and it was not a pleasant smile. People lingered in their doorways, staring at Pastor Mortmain and the expert on witches as they stood in front of the church. Davey Higgins stayed in his cabin and did not come out, though the other children were as eager as their parents to join in the witch hunt.

It was part of the nightmare when the man from the city who had hanged many people gave Pastor Mortmain and the elders of the village his verdict: there was no doubt in his mind that Zylle was a witch.

A sigh of excitement, of horror, of pleasure, went along the street.

That evening when Brandon went to the common pasture to bring the cow home, one of the other boys spat on the ground and turned away. Davey Higgins, tying the halter on the Higgins cow, said, "It is the Lord's will that the witch should die."

"Zylle is not a witch."

"She's a heathen."

"She's a Christian. A better one than you are."

"She's a condemned witch, and tomorrow they take her to the jail in town, though she'll be brought back here to be hanged—"

"So we can all see." One of the boys licked his lips in anticipation.

"No!" Brandon cried. "No!"

Davey interrupted him. "You'd better hold your tongue, or I could tell things about you to make Pastor Mortmain condemn you as a witch, too."

Brandon looked levelly at Davey while the others teased him to tell.

Davey flushed. "No. I didn't mean anything. Brandon is my friend. It's not his fault his brother married a witch."

"How could you let them take Zylle and the baby away?" Brandon demanded of Ritchie and his parents. "How could you!"

"Son," Richard Llawcae said, "Zylle is not safe here, not now with feelings running high. There are those who would hang her immediately. Your brother and I are going to town tomorrow to speak to people we know there. We think they will help us."

But the witch-hunting fever was too high. There was

no help. There was no reason. There was only nightmare.

Goody Llawcae stayed in the town to tend Zylle and the baby; that much was allowed, but it was not through kindness; there were those who feared that Zylle might try to take her own life, or that something might happen to prevent them seeing a public hanging.

Richard and Ritchie refused to erect the gallows.

Avoiding their eyes, Goodman Higgins pleaded, "You must not refuse to do this, or you, too, will be accused. In the town they have convicted entire families."

Richard said, "There was another carpenter, once, and he would have refused to do this thing. Him I will follow."

There were others more than willing to erect a crude gallows. A gallows is more easily built than a house, or a bed, or a table.

The date for the hanging was set.

On the eve, Brandon went late to bring the cow in from the pasture, in order to avoid the others. When he got to the barn, Maddok was waiting there in the shadows.

"My father wants to see you."

"When?" Bran asked.

"Tonight. After the others are asleep, can you slip away without being seen?"

Bran nodded. "You have taught me how to do that. I will come. It has meant much to me to know that you have been with me."

"We are friends," Maddok said without a smile.

"Is it going to rain soon?" Brandon asked.

"No. Not unless prayer changes things."

"You pray every night. So do we."

"Yes. We pray," Maddok said, and slipped silently into the woods.

In the small hours of the morning, before dawn, when he was sure everybody in the settlement would be asleep, Brandon left the cabin and ran swiftly as a young deer into the protecting shadows of the woods.

Maddok was standing at the edge of the forest, waiting. "Come. I know the way in the dark more easily than you."

"Zillo knows everything? You've told him?"

"Yes. But he wants to meet with you."

"Why? I'm still only a child."

"You have the gift of seeing."

Brandon shivered.

"Come," Maddok urged. "My father is waiting."

They traveled swiftly, Brandon following Maddok as he led the way, over the brook, through the dark shadows of the forest.

At the edge of the Indian clearing, Zillo stood. Maddok nodded at his father, then vanished into the shadows.

"You won't let it happen?" Brandon begged. "If Zylle is harmed, Ritchie will kill."

"We will not let it happen."

"The men of the settlement expect the Indians to come. They have guns. They are out of their right minds, and they will not hesitate to shoot."

"They must be prevented. Have you seen anything in a vision lately?"

"I have tried not to. I am afraid."

"No one knows you are here?"

"Only Maddok."

Zillo pulled a polished metal sphere from a small pouch and held it out to catch the light of the late moon. "What do you see?"

Brandon hesitantly looked into it. "This is right for me to do, when my father . . . ?"

Zillo's eyes were expressionless. "I have held this action in prayer all day. It is not your father's wish to deny a gift of the gods, and at this time we have no one in the tribe with the gift of seeing."

As Brandon looked, the light in the metal sphere shifted, and he saw clouds moving swiftly across the sky, clouds reflected in water. Not taking his eyes from the scrying metal he said, "I see a lake where the valley should be, a lake I have seen before in a picture. It is beautiful."

Zillo nodded. "It is said there was a lake here in long gone days. In the valley people have found stones with the bones of fish in them."

"The sky is clouding up," Brandon reported. "Rain is starting to fall, spattering into the water of the lake."

"You see no fire?"

"Before, I saw fire, and I was afraid. Now there is only rain."

The severity of Zillo's face lifted barely perceptibly.

"That is good, that picture. Now I will teach you some words. You must learn them very carefully, and you must make sure that you do not use them too soon. Only the blue-eyed children of the Wind People are taught these words, and never before have they been given to one not of the tribe. But I give them to you for Zylle's saving."

On the morning of the execution Zylle was returned to the settlement. Infant Brandon was taken from her and given to Goody Llawcae.

"He is too young to be weaned," Goody Llawcae objected. "He will die of the summer sickness."

"The witch will not harm her own child," Pastor Mortmain said.

It took six of the strongest men in the settlement to restrain Ritchie and Richard.

"Tie the witch's hands," the man from the city ordered.

"I will do it," Goodman Higgins said. "Hold out your hands, child."

"Show her no gentleness, Higgins," Pastor Mortmain warned, "unless you would have us think you tainted, too. After all, you have listened to their tales."

Goody Llawcae, holding the crying baby, said, "Babies have died of the summer sickness for years, long before Zylle came to dwell among us, and no one thought of witchcraft."

Angry murmurs came from the gathered people. "The witch made another baby die. Let her brat die as well."

Ritchie, struggling compulsively, nearly broke away.

Pastor Mortmain said, "When the witch is dead, you

will come back to your senses. We are saving you from the evil."

The people of the settlement crowded about the gallows in ugly anticipation of what was to come. Davey Higgins stayed in the doorway of his cabin.

Goodman Higgins and Pastor Mortmain led Zylle across the dusty compound and up the steps to the gallows.

Brandon thought his heart would beat its way out of his body. He felt a presence beside him, and there was Maddok, and he knew that the rest of the tribe was close by.

"Now," Maddok whispered.

And then Brandon cried aloud the words which Zillo had taught him.

> *"With Zylle in this fateful hour*
> *I call on all Heaven with its power*
> *And the sun with its brightness,*
> *And the snow with its whiteness,*
> *And the fire with all the strength it hath,*
> *And the lightning with its rapid wrath—"*

Thunderstorms seldom came till late afternoon. But suddenly the sky was cleft by a fiery bolt, and the church bore the power of its might. The crash of thunder was almost simultaneous. The sky darkened from a humid blue to a sulfurous dimness. Flame flickered about the doorway of the church.

The Indians stepped forward until the entire settlement was aware of their presence, silent and menacing. Several men raised guns. As Duthbert fired, lightning flashed again and sent Duthbert sprawling, a long burn down his arm, his bullet going harmlessly into the air. Flames wreathed the belfry of the church.

Zillo sprang across the compound and up the steps to the gallows. "No guns," he commanded, "or the lightning will strike again. And this time it will kill."

Duthbert was moaning with pain. "Put down the guns —don't shoot—"

Pastor Mortmain's face was distorted. "You are witches, all of you, witches! The Llawcae boy has the Indian girl's devil with him that he can call lightning! He must die!"

The Indians drew in closer. Maddok remained by Brandon. And then Davey Higgins came from the door of his cabin and stood on Brandon's other side.

Ritchie broke away from the men who were holding him, and sprang up onto the gallows. "People of the settlement!" he cried. "Do you think all power is of the devil? What we have just seen is the wrath of God!" He turned his back on the crowd and began to untie Zylle.

The mood of the people was changing. Richard was let loose and he crossed the dusty compound to Pastor Mortmain. "Your church is burning because you tried to kill an innocent woman. Our friends and neighbors would never have consented to this madness had you not terrified them with your fire and brimstone."

Goodman Higgins moved away from Pastor Mortmain. "That is right. The Llawcaes have always been God-fearing people."

The Indians drew closer.

Ritchie had one arm about Zylle. He called out again:

"The Indians have always been our friends. Is this how we return their friendship?"

"Stop them—" Pastor Mortmain choked out. "Stop the Indians! They will massacre us—stop them—"

Ritchie shouted, "Why should we? Do you want us to show you more compassion than you have shown us?"

"Ritchie!" Zylle faced him. "You are not like Pastor Mortmain. You have a heart in you. Show them your compassion!"

Zillo raised a commanding hand. "This evil has been stopped. As long as nothing like this ever happens again, you need not fear us. But it must never happen again."

Murmurs of "Never, never, we are sorry, never, never," came from the crowd.

Pastor Mortmain moaned, "The fire, the fire, my God, the church, the church is burning."

Ritchie led Zylle down the steps and to his mother, who put the baby into her daughter-in-law's waiting arms. Brandon, standing between Maddok and Davey, watched as his mother and Zylle, his father and brother, turned their backs on the burning church and walked across the compound, past their chastened neighbors, past the watchful Indians, and went into their cabin. He stayed, his feet rooted to the ground as though he could not move, while the people of the settlement brought ineffectual buckets of water to try to control the flames and keep the fire from spreading to the cabins around the church. He watched the belfry collapse, a belfry erected more to the glory of Pastor Mortmain than to the glory of God.

And then he felt the rain, a gentle rain which would fall all day and sink into the thirsty ground, a rain which would continue until the deepest roots of plant and tree had their chance to drink. A rain which put out the fire before it spread to any of the dwellings.

Behind the three boys the People of the Wind stood silently, watching, as the people went slowly into their cabins. When there was no one left by the empty gallows except the three children, Zillo barked a sharp command and the Indians quickly dismantled the ill-built platform and gallows, threw the wood on the smoking remains of the church, and left, silently.

The horror was over, but nothing would ever be the same again.

When Brandon and Maddok went into the Llawcae cabin, Zillo was there, holding the baby. The kettle was simmering, and Goody Llawcae was serving herb tea, "to quieten us."

"I am angry." Ritchie looked past Brandon to his mother. "Your herbs will not stop my anger."

"You have cause to be angry," his father said. "Anger is not bitterness. Bitterness can go on eating at a man's heart and mind forever. Anger spends itself in its own time. Small Brandon will help to ease the anger."

Zillo handed the baby to Ritchie, who took his son and held him against his strong shoulder. Ritchie looked, then, at his brother. "Where did you get those words you called out just before the storm?"

"From Zillo."

"When?"

"Last night. He sent for me."

Zillo looked at Richard and Ritchie, his eyes fathomless. "He is a good lad, your young one."

Richard Llawcae returned Zillo's gaze, and put his arm lightly around Brandon's shoulders. "The ways of the Lord are mysterious, and we do not need to understand them. His ways are not our ways—though we would like them to be. We do not need to understand Brandon's gifts, only to know that they are given to him by God." He turned to the Bible and leafed through the pages until he had found the passage he wanted. "The Lord is faithful, who shall establish you, and keep you from evil. And the Lord direct your hearts into the love of God. Now the Lord of peace himself give you peace always by all means . . ."

Brandon, worn out by lack of sleep, by terror and tension, put his head down on his arms and slid into sleep, only half hearing as Ritchie said that he could not continue to live in the settlement. He would take Zylle and the baby and return to Wales, where they could start a new life . . .

The world was bleak for Brandon when Ritchie and Zylle and the baby left.

One day as he was doing his chores, Maddok appeared, helped him silently, and then together they went through the woods toward the Indian compound.

Under the great shadowing branches of an oak, Maddok paused. He looked long at Brandon. "It is right that Zylle should have gone with Ritchie."

Brandon looked at Maddok, then at the ground.

"And it is right that you and I should become brothers. My father will perform the ceremony tonight, and you will be made one of the People of the Wind."

A spark of the old light appeared in Brandon's face. "Then no one can keep us apart."

"No one. And perhaps you will marry one of the People of the Wind. And perhaps our children will marry, so that our families will be united until eternity."

Brandon reached for Maddok's hands. "Until eternity," he said.

7

The winds with their swiftness

And Charles Wallace was on Gaudior's back.

"I've read about the Salem trials, of course," he mused aloud. "Is there—oh, Gaudior, do other planets have the same kind of horror as ours?"

"There are horrors wherever the Echthroi go."

"Brandon: he's younger than I. And yet—am I like Brandon? Or is he like me?"

"I do not think you would be accepted by a host who is alien to what you are—Gwydyr, for instance."

"I hate to think I caused Brandon so much pain—"

"Do not take too much on yourself," Gaudior warned.

"We don't know what would have happened had you not been Within Brandon."

"What did we learn Within? It's a strange triangle: Wales and here; Wales and Vespugia; Vespugia and here. It's all interconnected, and we have to find the connections—oh!" He stepped back from Gaudior with a startled flash of comprehension.

"What now?" Gaudior asked.

Charles Wallace's voice rose with excitement. "When Madoc is spelled the Welsh way, it's Madog! Get it?"

Gaudior blew a small bubble.

"Madog. Mad Dog. It's a play on words. Mad Dog Branzillo may really be Madog. El Rabioso. Mad Dog. It's a ghastly sort of pun. Madoc: Madog: Mad Dog."

The unicorn looked down his long nose. "You may have something there."

"So there's another connection! Gaudior, we have to go to Patagonia, to Vespugia. I understand that it isn't easy for unicorns to move in both time and space, but you've got to try."

Gaudior raised his wings and stretched them up toward the sky. "The last time we gave explicit directions to the wind, look what happened."

"We didn't get to 1865. But we did learn important things about Madoc's descendants."

"Is that all you remember?" The unicorn folded his wings.

"It's in the book, Matthew Maddox's—"

"Somehow or other," Gaudior said, "we are blundering closer and closer to the Might-Have-Been which the Echthroi don't want us to get to, and the closer we get, the more they will try to prevent us. Already you have changed small things, and they are angry."

"What have I changed?"

"Don't you know?"

Charles Wallace bowed his head. "I tried to stop Harcels from seeing the ways of other men."

"And . . ."

"Zylle—I tried to stop them from hanging her. Would she have been hanged—without the rune?"

"There are many things unicorns do not feel they need to know."

"And there are some things we do need to know if we're to succeed in doing what Mrs. O'Keefe asked me to do." For a moment he looked startled, remembering Calvin's mother. "How strange that it should have come from Mrs. O'Keefe—the charge. And the rune."

"That should teach you something."

"It does. It teaches me that we have to go to Vespugia to find the connection between Mom O'Keefe and Mad Dog Branzillo."

The light in Gaudior's horn flickered rapidly.

"I know—" Charles Wallace stroked the unicorn's neck. "The Echthroi nearly got us when we were aiming for 1865 in our own Where. Perhaps we have to leave the star-watching rock and aim for 1865 in Patagonia, when the Welsh group arrived there. Perhaps they met Gwydyr's descendants. I think we have no choice now except to go to Patagonia."

"They may attack us again." Gaudior's anxious neigh

broke into silver shards. "It might be a good idea for you
to tie yourself to me. If the Echthroi tear you from my
back again, it isn't likely that I'd be able to catch you a
second time."

Charles Wallace looked all around him, carefully, and
saw nothing but the woods, the rock, the valley, the
mountains beyond. Then: "I know!" He slid off Gaudior's
back to the rock. "I forgot to bring in the hammock this
autumn. Meg usually does it. It's just a few yards along
the path, between two old apple trees. It's a woven rope
one, and it's hung on good stout laundry rope, from
Mortmain's General Store—Mortmain! Gaudior, do you
suppose—"

"We don't have time for suppositions," Gaudior warned.
"Bind yourself to me."

Charles Wallace hurried along the path, with the unicorn following, prancing delicately as bare blackberry
canes reached across the path and tore at his silver hide.

"Here we are. Mother likes the hammock to be far
away from the house so that she can't possibly hear the
telephone." He started untying one end of the hammock.
The branches of the apple trees were bare of leaves, but
a few withered apples still clung palely to the topmost
branches. The earth around the trees and under the hammock smelled of cider vinegar and mulching leaves.

"Make haste slowly," Gaudior advised, as Charles Wallace's trembling fingers fumbled with the knots. The air
was cold, and the unicorn bent his neck so that he could
breathe on Charles Wallace's fingers to warm them.

"Think only about untying the knots. The Echthroi are near."

Warmed by the unicorn's breath, the boy's fingers began to lose their stiffness, and he managed to untie the first knot. Two more knots, and one end of the hammock dropped to the leafy ground, and Charles Wallace moved to the second tree, where the hammock seemed even more firmly secured to the gnarled trunk. He worked in silence until the hammock was freed. "Kneel," he told the unicorn.

Charles Wallace dragged one end of the hammock under the unicorn, so that the heavy webbing was under Gaudior's great abdomen. With difficulty he managed to fling the rope up over Gaudior's flanks. He clambered up and bound the rope securely around his waist. "It's a good thing Mother always uses enough rope for five hammocks."

Gaudior whickered. "Are you tied on securely?"

"I think so. The twins taught me to make knots."

"Hold on to my mane, too."

"I am."

"I don't like this," Gaudior objected. "Are you sure you think we ought to try to go to Patagonia?"

"I think it's what we have to do."

"I'm worried." But Gaudior began to run, until he had gathered enough speed to launch himself.

The attack came almost immediately, Echthroi surrounding boy and unicorn. Charles Wallace's hands were torn from Gaudior's mane, but the rope held firm. The breath was buffeted out of him, and his eyelids were sealed tight against his eyes by the blasting wind, but the Echthroi did not succeed in pulling him off Gaudior's back. The rope strained and groaned, but the knots held.

Gaudior's breath came in silver streamers. He had folded his wings into his flanks to prevent the Echthroid wind from breaking them. Boy and unicorn were flung through endless time and space.

A cold, stenching wind picked them up and they were flung downward with a violence over which the unicorn had no control. Helplessly they descended toward a vast darkness.

They crashed.

They hit with such impact that Charles Wallace thought fleetingly, just before he lost consciousness, that the Echthroi had flung them onto rock and this was the end.

But the descent continued. Down down into blackness and cold. No breath. A feeling of strangling, a wild ringing in the ears. Then he seemed to be rising, up, up, and light hit his closed eyes with the force of a blow, and clear cold air rushed into his lungs. He opened his eyes.

It was water and not rock they had been thrown against.

"Gaudior!" he cried, but the unicorn floated limply on the surface of the darkness, half on his side, so that one of Charles Wallace's legs was still in the water. The boy bent over the great neck. No breath came from the silver nostrils. There was no rise and fall of chest, no beat of heart. "Gaudior!" he cried in anguish. "Don't be dead! Gaudior!"

Still, the unicorn floated limply, and small waves plashed over his face.

"Gaudior!" With all his strength Charles Wallace beat against the motionless body. —The rune, he thought wildly, —the rune . . .

But no words came, except the unicorn's name. "Gaudior! Gaudior!"

A trembling stirred the silver body, and then Gaudior's breath came roaring out of him like an organ with all the stops pulled out. Charles Wallace sobbed with relief. The unicorn opened eyes which at first were glazed, then cleared and shone like diamonds. He began to tread water. "Where are we?"

Charles Wallace bent over the beautiful body, stroking neck and mane in an ecstasy of relief. "In the middle of an ocean."

"Which ocean?" Gaudior asked testily.

"I don't know."

"It's your planet. You're supposed to know."

"Is it my planet?" Charles Wallace asked. "The Echthroi had us. Are you sure we aren't in a Projection?"

Unicorn and boy looked around. The water stretched to the horizon on all sides. Above them the sky was clear, with a few small clouds.

"It's not a Projection." Gaudior whickered. "But we could be anywhere in Creation, on any planet in any galaxy which has air with oxygen and plenty of water. Does this seem to you like an ordinary earth ocean?" He shook his head, and water sprayed out from his mane. "I am not thinking clearly yet . . ." He gulped air, then regurgitated a large quantity of salt water. "I have drunk half this ocean."

"It looks like a regular ocean," Charles Wallace said tentatively, "and it feels like winter." His drenched anorak clung to his body in wet folds. His boots were full of water, which sloshed icily against his feet. "Look!" He pointed ahead of them to a large crag of ice protruding from the water. "An iceberg."

"Which direction is land?"

"Gaudior, if we don't even know what galaxy or planet we're on, how do you expect me to know where land is?"

With difficulty Gaudior stretched his wings to their fullest extent, so that they shed water in great falls that splashed noisily against the waves. His legs churned with a mighty effort to keep afloat.

"Can you fly?" Charles Wallace asked.

"My wings are waterlogged."

"Can't you ask the wind where we are?"

A shudder rippled along the unicorn's flanks. "I'm still half winded—the wind—the wind—we hit water so hard it's a wonder all our bones aren't broken. The wind must have cushioned our fall. Are you still tied on?"

"Yes, or I wouldn't be here. Ask the wind, please."

"Winded—the wind—the wind—" Again Gaudior shook water from his wings. He opened his mouth in his characteristic gesture of drinking, gulped in the cold, clear breeze, his lips pulled back to reveal the dangerous-looking teeth. He closed his eyes and his long lashes were dark against his skin, which had paled to the color of moonlight. He opened his eyes and spat out a great fountain of water. "Thank the galaxies."

"Where are we?"

"Your own galaxy, your own solar system, your own planet. Your own Where."

"You mean this is the place of the star-watching rock? Only it's covered by an ocean?"

"Yes. And the wind says it's midsummer."

Charles Wallace looked at the iceberg. "It's a good thing it's summer, or we'd be dead from cold. And summer or no, we'll die of cold if we don't get out of water and onto land, and soon."

Gaudior sighed. "My wings are still heavy with water and my legs are tiring."

A wave dashed over them. Charles Wallace swallowed a mouthful of salty water and choked, coughing painfully. His lungs ached from the battering of the Echthroid wind and the cold of the sea. He was desperately sleepy. He thought of travelers lost in a blizzard, and how in the end all they wanted was to lie down in the snow and go to sleep, and if they gave in to sleep they would never wake up again. He struggled to keep his eyes open, but it hardly seemed worth the effort.

Gaudior's legs moved more and more slowly. When the next wave went over them, the unicorn did not kick back up to the surface.

As water and darkness joined to blot out Charles

Wallace's consciousness, he heard a ringing in his ears, and through the ringing a voice calling, "The rune, Chuck! Say it! Say the rune!"

But the weight of the icy water bore him down.

Ananda's frantic whining roused Meg.

"Say it, Charles!" she cried, sitting bolt-upright.

Ananda whined again, then gave a sharp bark.

"I'm not sure I remember the words—" Meg pressed both hands against the dog, and called out,

"With Ananda in this fateful hour
I place all Heaven with its power
And the sun with its brightness,
And the snow with its whiteness,
And the fire with all the strength it hath,
And the lightning with its rapid wrath,
And the winds with their swiftness along their path . . ."

The wind lifted and the whitecaps were churned into rolling breakers, and unicorn and boy were raised to the surface of the water and caught in a great curling comber and swept along with it across the icy sea until they were flung onto the white sands of dry land.

8

The sea with its deepness

Unicorn and boy vomited sea water and struggled to breathe, their lungs paining them as though they were being slashed by knives. They were sheltered from the wind by a cliff of ice onto which the sun was pouring, so that water was streaming down in little rivulets. The warmth of the sun which was melting the ice also melted the chill from their sodden bodies, and began to dry the unicorn's waterlogged wings. Gradually their blood began to flow normally and they breathed without choking on salt water.

Because he was smaller and lighter (and billions of years younger, Gaudior pointed out later), Charles Wallace recovered first. He managed to wriggle out of the still-soaking anorak and drop it down onto the wet sand. Then with difficulty he kicked off the boots. He looked at the ropes which still bound him to the unicorn; the knots were pulled so tight and the cord was by now so sodden that it was impossible to untie himself. Exhausted, he bent over Gaudior's neck and felt the healing sun send its rays deep into his body. Warmed and soothed, his nose pressed against wet unicorn mane, he fell into sleep, a deep, life-renewing sleep.

When he awoke, Gaudior was stretching his wings out to the sun. A few drops of water still clung to them, but the unicorn could flex them with ease.

"Gaudior," Charles Wallace started, and yawned.

"While you were sleeping," the unicorn reproved gently, "I have been consulting the wind. Praise the Music that we're in the When of the melting of the ice or we could not have survived." He, too, yawned.

"Do unicorns sleep?" Charles Wallace asked.

"I haven't needed to sleep in aeons."

"I feel all the better for a nap. Gaudior, I'm sorry."

"For what?"

"For making you try to get us to Patagonia. If I hadn't, we might not have been nearly killed by the Echthroi."

"Apology accepted," Gaudior said briskly. "Have you learned?"

"I've learned that every time I've tried to control things we've had trouble. I don't know what we ought to do now, or Where or When we ought to go from here. I just don't know . . ."

"I think"—Gaudior turned his great head to look at the boy—"that our next step is to get all these knots untied."

Charles Wallace ran his fingers along the rope. "The knots are all sort of welded together from wind and water and sun. I can't possibly untie them."

Gaudior wriggled against the pressure of the ropes. "They appear to have shrunk. I am very uncomfortable."

After a futile attempt at what looked like the most pliable of the knots, Charles Wallace gave up. "I've got to find something to cut the rope."

Gaudior trotted slowly up and down the beach. There were shells, but none sharp enough. They saw a few pieces of rotting driftwood, and some iridescent jellyfish and clumps of seaweed. There were no broken bottles or tin cans or other signs of mankind, and while Charles Wallace was usually horrified at human waste and abuse of nature, he would gladly have found a broken beer bottle.

Gaudior turned inland around the edge of the ice cliff, moving up on slipping sand runneled by melting ice. "This is absurd. After all we've been through, who would have thought I'd end up like a centaur with you permanently affixed to my back?" But he continued to struggle up until he was standing on the great shoulder of ice.

"Look!" Charles Wallace pointed to a cluster of silvery plants with long spikes which had jagged teeth along the sides. "Do you think you could bite one of those off, so I can saw the rope with it?"

Gaudior splashed through puddles of melted ice, lowered his head, and bit off one of the spikes as close to the root as his large teeth permitted. Holding it between his teeth he twisted his head around until Charles Wallace, straining until the rope nearly cut off his breath, managed to take it from him.

Gaudior wrinkled his lips in distaste. "It's repellent. Careful, now. Unicorn's hide is not as strong as it looks."

"Stop fidgeting."

"It itches." Gaudior flung his head about with uncontrollable and agonized laughter. "Hurry."

"If I hurry I'll cut you. It's coming now." He moved the plant-saw back and forth with careful concentration, and finally one of the ropes parted. "I'll have to cut one more, on the other side. The worst is over now."

But when a second rope was severed, Charles Wallace was still bound to the unicorn, and the plant was limp and useless. "Can you bite off another spike?"

Gaudior bit and grimaced. "Nothing really has to taste that disagreeable. But then, I am not accustomed to any food except starlight and moonlight."

At last the ropes were off boy and beast, and Charles Wallace slid to the surface of the ice cliff. Gaudior was attacked by a fit of sneezing, and the last of the sea water flooded from his nose and mouth. Charles Wallace looked at the unicorn and drew in his breath in horror. Where the lines of rope had crossed the flanks there were red welts, shocking against the silver hide. The entire abdominal area, where the webbed hammock had rubbed, was raw and oozing blood. The water which had flooded from Gaudior's nostrils was pinkish.

The unicorn in turn inspected the boy. "You're a mess," he stated flatly. "You can't possibly go Within in this condition. You'd only hurt your host."

"You're a mess, too," Charles Wallace replied. He looked at his hands, and the palms were as raw as Gaudior's belly. Where the anorak and his shirt had slipped, the rope had cut into his waist as it had cut Gaudior's flanks.

"And you have two black eyes," the unicorn informed him. "It's a wonder you can see at all."

Charles Wallace squinted, first with one eye, then the other. "Things are a little blurry," he confessed.

Gaudior shook a few last drops from his wings. "We can't stay here, and you can't go Within now, that's obvious."

Charles Wallace looked at the sun, which was moving toward the west. "It's going to be cold when the sun goes down. And there doesn't seem to be any sign of life. And nothing to eat."

Gaudior folded his wings across his eyes and appeared to contemplate. Then he returned the wings to the bleeding flanks. "I don't understand earth time."

"What's that got to do with it?"

"Time is of the essence, we both know that. And yet it will take weeks, if not months, for us to heal."

When the unicorn stared at him as though expecting a response, Charles Wallace looked down at a puddle in the ice. "I don't have any suggestions."

"We're both exhausted. The one place I can take you

without fear of Echthroi is my home. No mortal has ever been there, and I am not sure I should bring you, but it's the only way I see open to us." The unicorn flung back his mane so that it brushed against the boy's bruised face with a silver coolness. "I have become very fond of you, in spite of all your foolishness."

Charles Wallace hugged the unicorn. "I have become fond of you, too."

Joints creaking painfully, Gaudior knelt. The boy clambered up, wincing as he inevitably touched the red welts which marred the flanks. "I'm sorry. I don't want to hurt you."

Gaudior neighed softly. "I know you don't."

The boy was so exhausted that he was scarcely aware of their flight. Stars and time swirled about him, and his lids began to droop.

"Wake up!" Gaudior ordered, and he opened his eyes to a world of starlit loveliness. The blurring of his vision had cleared, and he looked in awe at a land of snow and ice; he felt no cold, only the tenderness of a soft breeze which touched his cuts and bruises with healing gentleness. In the violet sky hung a sickle moon, and a smaller, higher moon, nearly full. Mountains heaved snow-clad shoulders skyward. Between the ribs of one of the foothills he saw what appeared to be a pile of enormous eggs.

Gaudior followed his gaze. "The hatching grounds. It has been seen by no other human eyes."

"I didn't know unicorns came from eggs," the boy said wonderingly.

"Not all of us do," Gaudior replied casually. "Only the

time travelers." He took in great draughts of moonlight, then asked, "Aren't you thirsty?"

Charles Wallace's lips were cracked and sore. His mouth was parched. He looked longingly at the moonlight and tentatively opened his mouth to it. He felt a cool and healing touch on his lips, but when he tried to swallow he choked.

"I forgot," Gaudior said. "You're human. In my excitement at being home it slipped my mind." He cantered off to one of the foothills and returned with a long blue-green icicle held carefully in his teeth. "Suck it slowly. It may sting at first, but it has healing properties."

The cool drops trickled gently down the boy's parched throat, like rays of moonlight, and at the same time that they cooled the burning, they warmed his cold body. He gave his entire concentration to the moonsicle, and when he had finished the last healing drops he turned to thank Gaudior.

The unicorn was rolling in the snow, his legs up in the air, rolling and rolling, a humming of sheer pleasure coming from his throat. Then he stood up and shook himself, flinging splashes of snow in all directions. The red welts were gone; his hide was smooth and glistening perfection. He looked at the sore places on Charles Wallace's waist and hands. "Roll, the way I did," he ordered.

Charles Wallace threw himself into the snow, which was like no other snow he had ever felt; each flake was separate and tingly; it was cool but not chilling, and he felt healing move not only over the rope burns but deep within his sore muscles. He rolled over and over, laughing with delight. Then came a moment when he knew that he was completely healed, and he jumped up. "Gaudior, where is everybody? all the other unicorns?"

"Only the time travelers come to the hatching grounds, and during the passage of the small moon they can be about other business, for the small moon casts its warmth on the eggs. I brought you here, to this place, and at this moon, so we'd be alone."

"But why should we be alone?"

"If the others saw you they'd fear for their eggs."

Charles Wallace's head came barely halfway up the unicorn's haunches. "Creatures your size would be afraid of me?"

"Size is immaterial. There are tiny viruses which are deadly."

"Couldn't you tell them I'm not a virus and I'm not deadly?"

Gaudior blew out a gust of air. "Some of them think mankind *is* deadly."

Charles Wallace, too, sighed, and did not reply.

Gaudior nuzzled his shoulder. "Those of us who have been around the galaxies know that such thinking is foolish. It's always easy to blame others. And I have learned, being with you, that many of my preconceptions about mortals were wrong. Are you ready?"

Charles Wallace held out his hands to the unicorn. "Couldn't I see one of the eggs hatch?"

"They won't be ready until the rising of the third moon, unless . . ." Gaudior moved closer to the clutch, each egg almost as long as the boy was tall. "Wait—" The unicorn trotted to the great globular heap, which shone with inner luminosity, like giant moonstones. Gaudior bent his curved neck so that his mane brushed softly over the surface of the shells. With his upper teeth he tapped gently on one, listening, ears cocked, the short ear-hairs standing up and quivering like antennae. After a moment he moved on to another shell, and then another, with unhurried patience, until he tapped on one shell twice, thrice, then drew back and nodded at the boy.

This egg appeared to have rolled slightly apart from the others, and as Charles Wallace watched, it quivered, and rolled even farther away. From inside the shell came a sound of tapping, and the egg began to glow. The tapping accelerated and the shell grew so bright the boy could scarcely look at it. A sharp cracking, and a flash of brilliance as the horn thrust up and out into the pearly air, followed by a head with the silver mane clinging damply to neck and forehead. Dark silver-lashed eyes opened slowly, and the baby unicorn looked around, its eyes reflecting the light of the moons as it gazed on its fresh new environment. Then it wriggled and cracked the rest of the shell. As fragments of shell fell onto the snowy ground they broke into thousands of flakes, and the shell became one with the snow.

The baby unicorn stood on new and wobbly legs, neighing a soft moonbeam sound until it gained its balance. It stood barely as tall as Charles Wallace, testing one forehoof, then the other, and kicking out its hind legs. As Charles Wallace watched, lost in delight, the baby unicorn danced under the light of the two moons.

Then it saw Gaudior, and came prancing over to the big unicorn; by slightly lowering the horn it could have run right under the full-grown beast.

Gaudior nuzzled the little one's head just below the horn. Again the baby pranced with pleasure, and Gaudior began to dance with it, leading the fledgling in steps ever more and more intricate. When the baby began to tire, Gaudior slowed the steps of the dance and raised his head to the sickle moon, drew back his lips in an exaggerated gesture, and gulped moonlight.

As the baby had been following Gaudior in the steps of the dance, so it imitated him now, eagerly trying to drink moonlight, the rays dribbling from its young and inexperienced lips and breaking like crystal on the snow. Again it tried, looking at Gaudior, until it was thirstily and tidily swallowing the light as it was tipped out from the curve of the moon.

Gaudior turned to the nearly full moon, and again with exaggerated gestures taught the little one to drink. When its flanks were quivering with fullness, Gaudior turned to the nearest star, and showed it the pleasures of finishing a meal by quenching its thirst with starlight. The little one sipped contentedly, then closed its mouth with its tiny, diamond-like teeth, and, replete, leaned against Gaudior.

Only then did it notice Charles Wallace. With a leap of startlement, it landed on all four spindly legs, squealed in terror and galloped away, tail streaming silver behind it.

Charles Wallace watched the little creature disappear over the horizon. "I'm sorry I frightened it. Will it be all right?"

Gaudior nodded reassuringly. "It's gone in the direction of the Mothers. They'll tell it you're only a bad dream it had coming out of the shell, and it'll forget all about you." He knelt.

Reluctantly Charles Wallace mounted and sat astride the great neck. Holding on to a handful of mane, he looked about at the wild and peaceful landscape. "I don't want to leave."

"You human beings tend to want good things to last forever. They don't. Not while we're in time. Do you have any instructions for me?"

"I'm through with instructions. I don't even have any suggestions."

"We'll go Where and When the wind decides to take us, then?"

"What about Echthroi?" Charles Wallace asked fearfully.

"Because we're journeying from the home place the wind should be unmolested, as it was when we came here. After that we'll see. We've been in a very deep sea, and I never thought we'd get out of it. Try not to be afraid. The wind will give us all the help it can." The wings stretched to their full span and Gaudior flew up between the two moons, and away from the unicorn hatching grounds.

Meg sighed with delight.

"Oh, Ananda, Ananda, that was the most beautiful kythe! How I wish Charles Wallace could have stayed there longer, where he's safe . . ."

Ananda whined softly.

"I know. He has to leave. But the Echthroi are after him, and I feel so helpless . . ."

Ananda looked up at Meg, and the tufts of darker fur above the eyes lifted.

Meg scratched the dog between the ears. "We did send him the rune when he was in the Ice Age sea, and the wind came to help." Anxiously she placed her hand on Ananda, and closed her eyes, concentrating.

She saw the star-watching rock, and two children, a girl and a boy, perhaps thirteen and eleven, the girl the elder. The boy looked very much like a modern Brandon Llawcae, a Brandon in blue jeans and T-shirt—so it was definitely not 1865.

Charles Wallace was Within the boy, whose name was not Brandon.

Chuck.

Mrs. O'Keefe had called Charles Wallace *Chuck*.

Chuck was someone Mrs. O'Keefe knew. Someone Mrs. O'Keefe had said was not an idiot.

Now he was with a girl, yes, and someone else, an old woman. Chuck Maddox, and his sister, Beezie, and their grandmother. They were laughing, and blowing dandelion clocks, counting the breaths it took for the lacy white spores to leave the green stem.

Beezie Maddox had golden hair and bright blue eyes and a merry laugh. Chuck was more muted, his hair a soft brown, his eyes blue-grey. He smiled more often than laughed. He was so much like Brandon that Meg was sure he must be a direct descendant.

"Ananda, why am I so terribly frightened for him?" Meg asked.

"Let's blow dandelion clocks," Beezie had suggested.

"Not around the store you don't," their father had said. "I'll not have my patch of lawn seeded with more dandelion spore than blows here on its own."

So Chuck and Beezie and the grandmother came on a Sunday afternoon, across the brook, along to the flat rock. In the distance they could hear the sound of trucks on the highway, although they could not see them. Occasionally a plane tracked across the sky. Otherwise, there was nothing to remind them of civilization, and this was one of the things Chuck liked best about crossing the brook and walking through the woods to the rock.

Beezie handed him a dandelion. "Blow."

Chuck did not much like the smell of the spore; it was heavy and rank, and he wrinkled his nose with distaste.

"It doesn't smell all that bad to me," Beezie said. "When I squish the stem it smells green, that's all."

The grandmother held the snowy fronds to her nose. "When you're old, nothing smells the way it used to." She blew, and the white snowflakes of her dandelion flew in all directions, drifting on the wind.

Chuck and his sister had to blow several times before the clock told its time. The grandmother, who was quickly out of breath, and who had pressed her hand against her heart as she struggled up the fern-bordered path from the brook, blew lightly, and all the spores flew from the stem, danced in the sunny air, and slowly settled.

Chuck looked at Beezie, and Beezie looked at Chuck.

"Grandma, Beezie and I huff and puff and you blow no stronger than a whisper and it all blows away."

"Maybe you blow too hard. And when you ask the time, you mustn't fear the answer."

Chuck looked at the bare green stem in his grandmother's fingers. "I blew four times, and it isn't nearly four yet. What time does your dandelion tell, Grandma?"

The spring sun went briefly behind a small cloud, veiling the old woman's eyes. "It tells me of time past, when the valley was a lake, your pa says, and a different people roamed the land. Do you remember the arrowhead you found when we were digging to plant tulip bulbs?" Deftly she changed the subject.

"Beezie and I've found lots of arrowheads. I always carry one. It's better'n a knife." He pulled the flat chipped triangle from his jeans pocket.

Beezie wore jeans, too, thin where her sharp knees were starting to push through the cloth. Her blue-and-white-checked shirt was just beginning to stretch tightly across her chest. She dug into her pockets like her brother, pulling out an old Scout knife and a bent spoon. "Grandma, blowing the dandelion clocks—that's just superstition, isn't it?"

"And what else would it be? Better ways there are of telling the time, like the set of the sun in the sky and the shadows of the trees. I make it out to be nigh three in the afternoon, and near time to go home for a cup of tea."

Beezie lay back on the warm ledge of rock, the same kind of rock from which the arrowhead had been chipped. "And Ma and Pa'll have tea with us because it's Sunday, and the store's closed, and nobody in it but Pansy. Grandma, I think she's going to have kittens again."

"Are you after being surprised? What else has Pansy to do except frighten the field mice away."

Despite the mention of tea, Chuck too lay back, putting his head in his grandmother's lap so she could ruffle his hair. Around them the spring breeze was gentle; the leaves whispered together; and in the distance a phoebe called wistfully. The roaring of a truck on the distant highway was a jarring note.

The grandmother said, "When we leave the village and cross the brook it's almost as though we crossed out of time, too. And then there comes the sound of the present"—she gestured toward the invisible highway—"to remind us."

"What of, Grandma?" Beezie asked.

The old woman looked into an unseen distance. "The world of trucks isn't as real to me as the world on the other side of time."

"Which side?" Chuck asked.

"Either side, though at the present I know more about the past than the future."

Beezie's eyes lit up. "You mean like in the stories you tell us?"

The grandmother nodded, her eyes still distant.

"Tell us one of the stories, Grandma. Tell us how

Queen Branwen was taken from Britain by an Irish king."

The old woman's focus returned to the children. "I may have been born in Ireland, but we never forgot we came from Branwen of Britain."

"And I'm named after her."

"That you are, wee Beezie, and after me, for I'm Branwen, too."

"And Zillah? I'm Branwen Zillah Maddox." Beezie and Chuck knew the stories of their names backwards and forwards but never lost pleasure in hearing them.

Meg opened her eyes in amazement.
Branwen Zillah Maddox. B.Z. Beezie.
Mrs. O'Keefe.
That golden child was Mrs. O'Keefe.
And Chuck was her brother.

"Zillah comes from your Maddox forebears," the grandmother told the children, "and a proud name it is, too. She was an Indian princess, according to your pa, from the tribe which used to dwell right here where we be now, though the Indians are long gone."

"But you don't know as much about Zillah as you do about Branwen."

"Only that she was an Indian and beautiful. There are too many men on your father's side of the family, and stories come down, nowadays, through women. But in Branwen's day there were men who were bards."

"What's bards?" Chuck asked.

"Singers of songs and tellers of tales. Both my grandma

and my grandpa told me the story of Branwen, but mostly my grandma, over and over, and her grandma told her before that, and the telling goes back beyond memory. Britain and Ireland have long misunderstood each other, and this misunderstanding goes back beyond memory, too. And in the once upon a time and long ago when the Irish king wooed the English princess, 'twas thought there might at last be peace between the two green and pleasant lands. There was feasting for many moons at the time of the nuptials, and then the Irish king sailed for Ireland with his wife."

"Wouldn't Branwen have been homesick?" Beezie asked.

"And of course she'd have been homesick. But she was born a princess and now she was a queen, and queens know how to mind their manners—or did in those days."

"And the king? What was he like?"

"Oh, and handsome he was, as the Irish can be, as was my own sweet Pat, who bore well the name of the blessed saint, with black hair and blue eyes. Branwen knew not that he was using her to vent his spleen against her land and her brethren, knew it not until he trumped up some silly story of her sitting in the refectory and casting her eye on one of his men. So, to punish her—"

"For what?" Chuck asked.

"For what, indeed? For his own jealous fantasies. So, to punish her, he sent her to tend the swine and barred her from the palace. So she knew he had never loved her, and her heart burned within her with anguish. Then she thought to call on her brother in England, and she used

the rune, and whether she and hers gave the rune to
Patrick, or whether their guardian angels gave it to each
of them, she called on all Heaven with its power—"
The children chanted the rune with her.

> *"And the sun with its brightness,*
> *And the snow with its whiteness,*
> *And the fire with all the strength it hath,*
> *And the lightning with its rapid wrath,*
> *And the winds with their swiftness along their path,*
> *And the sea with its deepness,*
> *And the rocks with their steepness,*
> *And the earth with its starkness,*
> *All these I place*
> *By God's almighty help and grace*
> *Between myself and the powers of darkness!"*

The grandmother continued, "And the sun shone on
her fair hair and warmed her, and the gentle snow fell
and made all clean the sty in which the Irish king had set
her, and the fire burst from the fireplace of his wooden
palace and the lightning struck it and it burned with
mighty rage and all within fled the fury. And the wind
blew from Britain and the sails of her brother Bran's ship
billowed as it sped over the deep sea and landed where
the rocks were steep and the earth stark. And Bran's men
scaled the rock and rescued their beloved Branwen."

"Is it a true story, Grandma," Beezie asked, "really?"

"To those with the listening ear and the believing
heart."

"Chuck has the believing heart," Beezie said.

The grandmother patted his knee. "One day maybe

you will be the writer your father wanted to be. He was not cut out for a storekeeper."

"I love the store," Beezie said defensively. "It smells good, of cinnamon and fresh bread and apples."

"I'm hungry," Chuck said.

"And wasn't I after saying before we got into storytelling that we should get along home for tea? Pull me up, both of you."

Chuck and Beezie scrambled to their feet and heaved the old woman upright. "We'll pick a bouquet for Ma and Pa on the way," Beezie said.

The narrow path was rough with rocks and hummocks of grass, and walking was not easy. The grandmother leaned on a staff which Chuck had cut for her from a grove of young maples which needed thinning. He went ahead, slowing down when he saw Beezie and his grandmother lagging behind him. A bouquet of field flowers was growing in Beezie's hands, for she paused whenever she saw that the old woman was out of breath. "Look, Chuck! Look, Grandma! Three more jacks-in-the-pulpit!"

Chuck was hacking away with his arrowhead at a strand of bittersweet snaking around a young fir tree, strangling it with coils strong as a boa constrictor's. "Ma used to have us looking for bittersweet a year or so ago, and now it's taking over. It'll kill this tree unless I cut through it. You two go along and I'll catch up."

"Want my knife?" Beezie offered.

"No. My arrowhead's sharp."

For a moment he stared after his sister and grandmother as they wended their slow way. He sniffed the fragrance of the air. Although the apple trees were green, the pink and white blossoms were still on the ground. The scent of lilac mingled with the mock orange. He might be able to hear the trucks on the road and see the planes in the sky, but at least here he couldn't smell them.

Chuck liked neither the trucks nor the planes. They all left their fumes behind them, blunting the smell of sunlight, of rain, of green and growing things, and Chuck 'saw' with his nose almost more than with his eyes. Without looking he could easily tell his parents, his grandmother, his sister. And he judged people almost entirely by his reaction to their odor.

'I don't smell a thing,' his father had said after Chuck had wrinkled his nose at a departing customer.

Chuck had said calmly, 'He smells unreliable.'

His father gave a small, surprised laugh. 'He *is* unreliable. He owes me more than I can afford to be owed, for all his expensive clothes.'

When the strand of bittersweet was severed, Chuck stood leaning against the rough bark of the tree, breathing in its resiny smell. In the distance he could see his grandmother and Beezie. The old woman smelled to him of distance, of the sea, which was fifty or more miles away, but perhaps it was a farther sea which clung to her. 'And you smell green,' he had told her. 'Ah, and that's because I come from a far green country and the scent of it will be with me always.'

'What color do I smell?' Beezie had asked.

'Yellow, like buttercups and sunlight and butterfly wings.'

Green and gold. Good smells. Home smells. His mother was the blue of sky in early morning. His father was the rich mahogany of the highboy in the living room, with the firelight flickering over the polished wood. Comfortable, safe smells.

And suddenly the thought of the odor of cookies and freshly baked bread called to him, and he ran to catch up.

The family lived over the store in a long, rambling apartment. The front room, overlooking the street, was a storeroom, filled with cartons and barrels. Behind it were three bedrooms: his parents', his own little cubbyhole, and the bigger room Beezie shared with the grandmother. Beyond these were the kitchen and the large long room which served as living and dining room.

There was a fire crackling in the fireplace, for the spring evenings were apt to be chilly. The family was seated about a large round table set for tea, with cookies and bread still warm from the oven, a pitcher of milk, and a big pot of tea covered with the cozy the grandmother had brought with her from Ireland.

Chuck took his place, and his mother poured his tea. "Did you save another tree?"

"Yes. I really should take Pa's big clippers with me next time."

Beezie pushed the plate of bread and butter to him. "Take your share quickly or I'll eat it all up."

Chuck's sensitive nostrils twitched. There was a smell in the room which was completely unfamiliar to him, and of which he was afraid.

The father helped himself to a cookie. "This is one of the times I wish Sunday afternoons came more than once a week."

"You've been acting tired lately." His wife looked at him anxiously.

"Being tired is the natural state of a country store-keeper who doesn't have much business sense."

The grandmother moved creakily from her chair at the table to her rocker. "Hard work's not easy. You need more help."

"Can't afford it, Grandma. How about telling us a story?"

"You've heard them all as many times as there are stars in the sky."

"I never tire of them."

"I'm told out for today."

"Oh, come on, Grandma," Mr. Maddox cajoled. "You never tire of storytelling, and you know you make most of it up as you go along."

"Stories are like children. They grow in their own way." She closed her eyes. "I will just take a small snooze."

"You tell me about the Indian princess, then, Pa," Beezie ordered.

"I don't know much about her as far as provable facts are concerned. My illustrious forebear, Matthew Maddox, from whom I may have inherited an iota of talent, wrote about her in his second novel. It was a best-seller in its day. Sad he couldn't have known about its success, but it was published posthumously. It was a strange sort of fantasy, with qualities which make some critics call it the first American science-fiction novel, because it played with time, and he'd obviously heard of Mendel's theories of genetics. Anyhow, Beezie love, it's a fictional account of the two brothers from ancient Wales who came to this country after their father's death, the first Europeans to set foot on these uncharted shores. And, as the brothers had quarreled in Wales, so they quarreled in the New World, and the elder of the two made his way to South America. Madoc, the younger brother, stayed with the Indians in a place which is nameless but which Matthew Maddox implies is right around here, and he married the Indian princess Zyll, or Zillah, and in the novel it is his strain which is lost, and must be found again."

"Sounds interesting," Chuck said.

Beezie wrinkled her nose. "I don't much like science fiction. I like fairy tales better."

"*The Horn of Joy* has elements of both. The idea that the proud elder brother must be defeated by the inconsequential but honest younger brother is certainly a fairy-tale theme. There was also a unicorn in the story, who was a time traveler."

"Whyn't you tell us about it before?" Beezie asked.

"Thought you'd be too young to be interested. Anyhow, I sold my copy when I was offered an outrageously large sum for it when I . . . it was too large an amount to turn down. Matthew Maddox, for a nineteenth-century writer, had an uncanny intuition about the theories of space, time, and relativity that Einstein was to postulate generations later."

"But that's not possible," Beezie protested.

"Precisely. But it's all in Matthew's book, nevertheless. It's an evocative, haunting novel, and since Matthew Maddox assumed that he was descended from the younger Welshman, the one who stayed here, and the Indian princess, I've followed his fancy that the name Maddox comes from Madoc." A shadow moved across his face. "When my father had a stroke and I had to leave my poet's garret in the city and come help out with the store, I had to give up my dream of following in Matthew's footsteps."

"Oh, Pa—" Chuck said.

"I'm mainly sorry for you children. I never had a chance to prove whether or not I could be a writer, but I'm a failure as a merchant." He rose. "I'd better go down to the store for an hour or so and work on accounts."

When he left, holding on to the banister as he went down the steep stairs, the smell that made Chuck afraid went with him.

Chuck told no one, not even Beezie, about the smell which was in his father but was not of his father.

Twice that week, Chuck had nightmares. When he cried out in terror his mother came hurrying, but he told her only that he had had a bad dream.

Beezie wasn't put off so easily. "You're worried about something, Chuck."

"There's always something to worry about. Lots of people owe Pa money, and he's worried about bills. I heard a salesman say he couldn't give Pa any more credit."

Beezie said, "You're too young to worry about things like that. Anyhow, it isn't the kind of thing you worry about."

"I'm getting older."

"Not that old."

"Pa's giving me more to do. I know more about the business now."

"But that's not what you're worried about."

He tried another tack. "I don't like the way Paddy O'Keefe's always after you in school."

"Paddy O'Keefe's repeated sixth grade three times. He may be good at baseball, but I'm not one of the girls who thinks the sun rises and sets on him."

"Maybe that's why he's after you." He had succeeded in deflecting her attention.

"I don't let him near me. He never washes. What does he smell like, Chuck?"

"Like a dandruffy woodchuck."

One evening after supper Beezie said, "Let's go see if the fireflies are back." It was Friday, and no school in the morning, so they could go to bed when they chose.

Chuck felt an overwhelming desire to get out of the house, away from the smell, which nearly made him retch. "Let's go."

It was still twilight when they reached the flat rock.

They sat, and the stone still held the warmth of the day's sun. At first there were only occasional sparkles, but as it got darker Chuck was lost in a daze of delight as a galaxy of fireflies twinkled on and off, flinging upward in a blaze of light, dropping earthward like falling stars, moving in continuous effervescent dance.

"Oh, Beezie!" he cried. "I'm dazzled with gorgeousness."

Behind them the woods were dark with shadows. There was no moon, and a thin veil of clouds hid the stars. "If it were a clear night," Beezie remarked, "the fireflies wouldn't be as bright. I've never seen them this beautiful." She lay back on the rock, looking up at the shadowed sky, then closing her eyes. Chuck followed suit.

"Let's feel the twirling of the earth," Beezie said. "That's part of the dance the fireflies are dancing, too. Can you feel it?"

Chuck squeezed his eyelids tightly closed. He gave a little gasp. "Oh, Beezie! I felt as though the earth had tilted!" He sat up, clutching at the rock. "It made me dizzy."

She gave her bubbling little giggle. "It can be a bit scary, being part of earth and stars and fireflies and clouds and rocks. Lie down again. You won't fall off, I promise."

He leaned back, feeling the radiance soak into his body. "The rock's still warm."

"It's warm all summer, because the trees don't shade it. And there's a rock in the woods that's always cool, even on the hottest day, because the leaves are so close together that the sun's fingers never touch it."

Chuck felt a cold shadow move over him and shuddered.

"Someone walk over your grave?" Beezie asked lightly.

He jumped up. "Let's go home."

"Why? What's wrong? It's so beautiful."

"I know—but let's go home."

When they got back, everything was in confusion. Mr. Maddox had collapsed from pain, and been rushed to the hospital. The grandmother was waiting for the children.

The frightening smell had exploded over Chuck with the violence of a mighty wave as he entered.

The grandmother pulled the children to her and held them.

"But what is it? What's wrong with Pa?" Beezie asked.

"The ambulance attendant thought it was his appendix."

"But he will be all right?" she pleaded.

"Dear my love, we'll have to wait and pray."

Chuck pressed against her, quivering, not speaking. Slowly the smell was dissipating, leaving a strange emptiness in its wake.

Time seemed to stand still. Chuck would glance at the clock, thinking an hour had passed, only to find it barely a minute. After a long while Beezie fell asleep, her head in her grandmother's lap. Chuck was watchful, looking from the clock to the telephone to the door. But at length he, too, slept.

In his sleep he dreamed that he was lying on the flat rock, and feeling the swing of the earth around the sun, and suddenly the rock tilted steeply, and he was sliding off, and he scrabbled in terror to keep from falling off the precipice into a sea of darkness. He cried out, "Rocks —steep—" and the grandmother put her hand on the rock and steadied it and he stopped dreaming.

But when he woke up he knew that his father was dead.

9

The rocks with their steepness

The sudden shrilling of the telephone woke Meg with a jolt of terror. Her heart began to thud, and she pushed out of bed, hardly aware of Ananda. Her feet half in and half out of her slippers, one arm shoved into her robe, she stumbled downstairs and into her parents' bedroom, but they were not there, so she hurried on down to the kitchen.

Her father was on the phone, and she heard him saying, "Very well, Mrs. O'Keefe. One of us will be right over for you."

It was not the President.

But Mrs. O'Keefe? In the middle of the night?

The twins, too, were in the doorway.

"What was that about?" Mrs. Murry asked.

"As you gathered, it was Mrs. O'Keefe."

"At this time of night!" Sandy exclaimed.

"She's never called us before," Dennys said, "at any time."

Meg breathed a sigh of relief. "At least it wasn't the President. What did she want?"

"She said she's found something she wants me to see, and ordered me to go for her at once."

"I'll go," Sandy said. "You can't leave the phone, Dad."

"You've got the weirdest mother-in-law in the world," Dennys told Meg.

Mrs. Murry opened the oven door and the fragrance of hot bread wafted out. "How about some bread and butter?"

"Meg, put your bathrobe on properly," Dennys ordered.

"Yes, doc." She put her left arm into the sleeve and tied the belt. If she stayed in the kitchen with the family, then time would pass with its normal inevitability. The kythe which had been broken by the jangling of the telephone was lost somewhere in her unconscious mind. She hated alarm clocks, because they woke her so abruptly out of sleep that she forgot her dreams.

In the kything was something to do with Mrs. O'Keefe. But what? She searched her mind. Fireflies. Something to do with fireflies. And a girl and a boy, and the smell of fear. She shook her head.

"What's the matter, Meg?" her mother asked.

"Nothing. I'm trying to remember something."

"Sit down. A warm drink won't hurt you."

It was important that she see Mrs. O'Keefe, but she couldn't remember why, because the kythe was gone.

"I'll be right back," Sandy assured them, and went out the pantry door.

"What on earth . . ." Dennys said. "Mrs. O'Keefe is beyond me. I'm glad I'm not going in for psychiatry."

Their mother set a plateful of fragrant bread on the table, then turned to put the kettle on. "Look!"

Meg followed her gaze. Coming into the kitchen were the kitten and Ananda, single file, the kitten with its tail straight up in the air, mincing along as though leading the big dog, whose massive tail was wagging wildly. They all laughed, and the laughter froze as the two creatures came past the table with the telephone. Twice since the President's call the phone had rung, first Calvin, then his mother. When would it ring again, and who would call?

It surprised Meg that the warm bread tasted marvelous, and the tea warmed her, and she was able, at least for the moment, to relax. Ananda whined beseechingly, and Meg gave her a small piece of toast.

Outside came the sound of a car, the slamming of a door, and then Sandy came in with Mrs. O'Keefe. The old woman had cobwebs in her hair, and smudges of dirt on her face. In her hand she held some scraps of paper.

"Something in me told me to go to the attic," she announced triumphantly. "That name—Mad Dog Branzillo —it rang a bell in me."

Meg looked at her mother-in-law and suddenly the kythe flooded back. "Beezie!" She cried.

Mrs. O'Keefe lunged toward her as though to strike her. "What's that?"

Meg caught the old woman's hands. "Beezie, Mom. You used to be called Beezie."

"How'd you know?" the old woman demanded fiercely. "You couldn't know! Nobody's called me Beezie since Chuck."

Tears filled Meg's eyes. "Oh, Beezie, Beezie, I'm so sorry."

The family looked at her in astonishment. Mr. Murry asked, "What is this, Meg?"

Still holding her mother-in-law's hands, Meg replied, "Mrs. O'Keefe used to be called Beezie when she was a girl. Didn't you, Mom?"

"It's best forgotten," the old woman said heavily.

"And you called Charles Wallace *Chuck*," Meg persisted, "and Chuck was your little brother and you loved him very much."

"I want to sit down," Mrs. O'Keefe said. "Leave the past be. I want to show you something." She handed a yellowed envelope to Mr. Murry. "Look at that."

Mr. Murry pushed his glasses up his nose. "It's a letter from a Bran Maddox in Vespugia to a Matthew Maddox right here."

The twins looked at each other. Sandy said, "We were just talking about Matthew Maddox tonight when we were looking something up for Meg. He was a nineteenth-century novelist. Is there a date on the letter?"

Mr. Murry carefully drew a yellowed sheet of paper from the old envelope. "November 1865."

"So the Matthew Maddox could be the one whose book Dennys studied in college!"

"Let Father read the letter," Dennys stopped his twin.

My beloved brother, Matthew, greetings, on this warm November day in Vespugia. Is there snow at home? I am settling in well with the group from Wales, and feel that I have known most of them all our lives. What an adventure this is, to start a colony in this arid country where the children can be taught Welsh in school, and where we can sing together as we work.

The strangest thing of all is that our family legend was here to meet me. Papa and Dr. Llawcae will be wild with excitement. We grew up on the legend of Madoc leaving Wales and coming to the New World, the way other children grew up on George Washington and the cherry tree. Believe it or not—but I know you'll believe it, because it's absolutely true—there is an Indian here with blue eyes who says he is descended from a Welsh prince who came to America long before any other white men. He does not know how his forebears got to South America, but he swears that his mother sang songs to him about being the blue-eyed descendant of a Welsh prince. He is called Gedder, though that is not his real name. His mother died when he and his sister were small, and they were brought up by an English sheep rancher who couldn't pronounce his Welsh name, and called him Gedder. And his sister's name—that is perhaps the most amazing of all: Zillie. She does not have the blue eyes, but she is quite beauti-

ful, with very fine features, and shining straight black
hair, which she wears in a long braid. She reminds me
of my beloved Zillah.

Gedder has been extraordinarily helpful in many
ways, though he has a good deal of arrogance and a
tendency to want to be the leader which has already
caused trouble in this community where no man is expected to set himself above his brothers. .

But how wonderful that the old legend should be
here to greet me! As for our sister Gwen, she shrugs and
says, "What difference does a silly old story make?" She
is determined not to like it here, though she's obviously
pleased when all the young men follow her around.

Has Dr. Llawcae decided to let Zillah come and join
me in the spring? The other women would welcome
her, and she would be a touch of home for Gwen. I'm
happy here, Matthew, and I know that Zillah would be
happy with me, as my wife and life's companion.
Women are not looked down on here—Gwen has to admit that much. Perhaps you could come, and bring Zillah with you? The community is settled enough so that
I think we could take care of you, and this dry climate
would be better for you than the dampness at home.
Please come, I need you both.

                              Your affectionate brother,
                                        Bran

Mr. Murry stopped. "It's very interesting, Mrs. O'Keefe,
but why is it so important for me to see it?"—that you
called in the middle of the night, he seemed to be adding
silently.

"Don't you see?"

"No, sorry."

"Thought you was supposed to be so brilliant."

Mrs. Murry said, "The letter was mailed from Vespugia. That's strange enough, that you should have a letter which was mailed from Vespugia."

"Right," the old woman said triumphantly.

Mr. Murry asked, "Where did you find this letter, Mrs. O'Keefe?"

"Told you. In the attic."

"And your maiden name was Maddox." Meg smiled at the old woman. "So they were forebears of yours, this Bran Maddox, and his brother, Matthew, and his sister, Gwen."

She nodded. "Yes, and likely his girlfriend, Zillah, too. Maddoxes and Llawcaes in my family all the way back."

Dennys looked at his sister's mother-in-law with new respect. "Sandy was looking up about Vespugia tonight, and he told us about a Welsh colony in Vespugia in 1865. So one of your ancestors went to join it?"

"Looks like it, don't it? And that Branzillo, he's from Vespugia."

Mr. Murry said, "It's a remarkable coincidence—" He stopped as his wife glanced at him. "I still don't see how it can have any connection with Branzillo, or what it would mean if it did."

"Don't you?" Mrs. O'Keefe demanded.

"Please tell us," Mrs. Murry suggested gently.

"The names. Bran. Zillah. Zillie. Put them together and they aren't far from Branzillo."

Mrs. Murry looked at her with surprised admiration. "How amazing!"

Mr. Murry asked, "Are there other letters?"

"Were. Once."

"Where are they?"

"Gone. Went to look. Began thinking about this Branzillo when I went home. Remembered Chuck and me—"

"Chuck and you what, Mom?" Meg probed.

Mrs. O'Keefe pushed her cobwebby hair away from her eyes. "We used to read the letters. Made up stories about Bran and Zillah and all. Played games of Let's Pretend. Then, when Chuck—didn't have the heart for Let's Pretend any more, forgot it all. Made myself forget. But that name, Branzillo, struck me. Bran. Zillah. Peculiar."

Mr. Murry looked bemusedly at the yellowed paper. "Peculiar, indeed."

"Where's your little boy?" Mrs. O'Keefe demanded.

Mr. Murry looked at his watch. "He went for a walk."

"When?"

"About an hour ago."

"In the middle of the night, and at his age?"

"He's fifteen."

"No. Twelve. Chuck was twelve."

"Charles Wallace is fifteen, Mrs. O'Keefe."

"A runt, then."

"Give him time."

"And you don't take care of him. Chuck needs special care. And people criticize me for not taking care of my kids!"

Dennys, too, looked at his watch. "Want me to go after him, Dad?"

Mr. Murry shook his head. "No. I think we have to

trust Charles Wallace tonight. Mrs. O'Keefe, you'll stay awhile?"

"Yes. Need to see Chuck."

Meg said, "Please excuse me, everybody. I want to go back to bed." She tried to keep the urgency from her voice. She felt a panicky need to get back to the attic with Ananda. "Chuck *was* twelve," Mrs. O'Keefe had said. Chuck was twelve when what? Anything that happened to Chuck was happening to Charles Wallace.

Mrs. Murry suggested, "Would you like to take a cup of tea with you?"

"No, thanks, I'm fine. Someone call me when Charles gets in?"

Ananda followed her upstairs, contentedly licking her lips for the last buttery crumbs.

The attic felt cold and she got quickly into bed and wrapped the quilt around herself and the dog. —Charles Wallace wanted me to find a connection between Wales and Vespugia, and Dennys found one in his reference books. But it's a much closer connection than that. The letter Mrs. O'Keefe brought was from 1865, and from Vespugia, so the connection is as close as her attic.

Despite the warm glow of the electric heater, she shivered.

—Those people in the letter must be important, she thought, —and the Bran who wrote the letter, and his sister Gwen. Certainly the name Zillie must have some connection with Madoc's Zyll, and Ritchie Llawcae's Zylle, who was nearly burned for witchcraft.

—And then, the Matthew he wrote to must be the Matthew Maddox who wrote the books. There's something in that second book that matters, and the Echthroi don't want us to know about it. It's all interconnected, and we still don't know what the connections mean.

—And what happened to Beezie, that she should end up as Mom O'Keefe? Oh, Ananda, Ananda, whatever happened?

She lay back against the pillows and rubbed her hand slowly back and forth over the dog's soft fur, until the tingling warmth moved up her arm and all through her.

"But why Pa?" Beezie demanded over and over again. "Why did Pa have to die?"

"There's never an answer to that question, my Beezie," the grandmother replied patiently. "It's not a question to be asking."

"But I do ask it!"

The grandmother looked tired, and old. Chuck had never before thought of her as old, as being any age at all. She was simply Grandma, always there for them. Now she asked, not the children, but the heavens, "And why my Patrick, and him even younger than your father. Why anything?" A tear slid down her cheek, and Beezie and Chuck put their arms around her to comfort her.

Mrs. Maddox went over the ledgers so patiently kept up to date by her husband. The more she looked, the more slowly her hands turned the pages. "I knew it was bad, but I didn't know it was this bad. I should have realized when he sold Matthew Maddox's book . . ."

Chuck crawled up into the dark storage spaces under the eaves, looking for treasure. He found a bottle full of pennies, but no gold or jewels to give his mother. He found an old *Encyclopaedia Britannica*, the pages yellow, the bindings cracked, but still useful. He found a set of china wrapped in old newspapers dated long before he and Beezie were born, which he hoped they might be able to sell. He found a strongbox, locked.

He brought his findings to the living room. His mother was in the store, but Beezie and the grandmother were there, doing the week's baking.

"The pennies are old. They may be worth something. The china's good. It may pay for our fuel for a month or so. What's in the box?"

"There isn't a key. I'm going to break it." He took hammer and screwdriver and wrench, and the old lock gave way and he was able to lift the lid. In the box was a sheaf of letters and a large notebook with a crumbling blue leather binding. He opened the book to the first page, and there was a watercolor sketch, faded only slightly, of the spring countryside.

"Grandma! It's our rock, our picnic rock!"

The old woman clucked. "And so it is."

The rock was shaded in soft blues and lavenders merging into grey. Behind it the trees were lush with spring green. Above it flew a flock of butterflies, the soft blues of the spring azures complemented by the gold and black of the tiger swallowtails. Around the rock were the familiar spring flowers, dappling the grass like the background of a tapestry.

Chuck exclaimed in delight, "Oh, Beezie, oh, Grandma!" Reverently he turned the page. In beautiful script was written, *Madrun, 1864, Zillah Llawcae.*

The grandmother wiped her floury hands carefully and put on her spectacles, bending over the book. Together they read the first page.

Madrun.

Past ten o'clock. Through my bedroom window I can look down the hill to the Maddoxes' house. Mr. and Mrs. Maddox will be asleep. They get up at five in the morning. Gwen Maddox—who knows? Gwen has always considered herself a grownup and me a child, though we're separated by only two years.

The twins, my dear twins, Bran and Matthew. Are they awake? When Bran lied about his age, so afraid was he he'd miss the war, and went to join the cavalry, I feared he might be killed in battle. When I dreamed of his homecoming, as I did each night when I looked at his diamond on my finger and prayed for his safety, I never thought it could be like this, with Bran withdrawn and refusing to communicate with anyone, even his twin. If I try to speak to him about our marriage, he cuts me short, or turns away without a word. Matthew says there have been others who have suffered this sickness of spirit because of the horrors of war.

I am, and have been for nearly seventeen years, Zillah Llawcae. Will I ever be Zillah Maddox?

They continued to turn the pages, more quickly now, not pausing to read the journal entries, but looking at the delicate paintings of birds and butterflies, flowers and trees, squirrels and wood mice and tree toads, all meticulously observed and accurately reproduced.

A shiver ran up and down Chuck's spine. "Pa's mother was a Llawcae. This Zillah could be one of our ancestors . . . and she was alive when she painted all this, and it's just the way it is now, just exactly the same."

He turned another page; his eye was caught, and he read:

This is my seventeenth birthday, and a sorry one it has been, though Father and I were invited to the Maddoxes' for dinner. But Bran was there and yet he wasn't there. He sat at the table, but he hardly ate the delicious dishes which had been especially prepared, to tempt him as much as in honor of me, and if anyone asked him a question he answered in monosyllables.

He turned the page and paused again.

Matthew says Bran almost had a conversation with him last night, and he is hopeful that the ghastly war wounds of his mind and spirit are beginning to heal. I wear his ring with its circle of hope, and I will not give up hoping. What would I do without Matthew's friendship to comfort and sustain me? Had it not been for Matthew's accident, I wonder which twin would have asked for my hand? A question better not raised, since I love them both so tenderly.

The grandmother took the top letter from the packet. "It's from Bran Maddox, the one Zillah's talking about, but it's from some foreign place, Vespugia? Now where would that be?"

"It's part of what used to be Patagonia."

"Pata—?"

"In South America."

"Oh, then." She drew the letter out of its envelope.

My beloved brother, Matthew, greetings, on this warm
November day in Vespugia. It there snow at home? I
am settling in well with the group from Wales, and feel
that I have known most of them all our lives . . .

When she finished reading the letter, she said, "Your
poor pa would have been thrilled at all this."

Chuck, nodding, continued to turn the pages, reading
a line here and there. As well as the nature pictures, the
young Zillah Llawcae had many sketches of people, some
in ink, some in watercolor. There was an ink drawing of a
tall man in a stovepipe hat, carrying a black bag and
looking not unlike Lincoln, standing by a horse and
buggy. Underneath was written, "Father, about to drive
off to deliver a baby."

There were many sketches of a young man, just beyond boyhood, with fair hair, a clear, beardless complex-
ion, and wide-apart, far-seeing eyes. These were labeled,
"My beloved Bran," "My dearest Bran," "My heart's
love." And there were sketches of someone who looked
like Bran and yet not like Bran, for the face was etched
with lines of pain. "My dear Matthew," Zillah had
written.

"It's so beautiful," Beezie said. "I wish I could paint
like that."

But the old woman's thoughts had shifted to practicality. "I wonder, would this notebook bring a few dollars?"

"Grandma, you wouldn't sell it!" Chuck was horrified.

"We need money, lad, if we're to keep a roof over our heads. Your ma'll sell anything she can sell."

The antiques dealer who bought the pennies and the set of china for what seemed to Chuck and Beezie a staggering sum was not interested in Zillah's notebook.

Mrs. Maddox looked at it sadly. "I know it's worth something. Your father would know where I should take it. If only I could remember the name of the person who bought Matthew Maddox's book."

But Chuck could not feel it in his heart to wish the beautiful journal sold. His grandmother took an old linen pillowcase and made a cover to protect the crumbling leather binding, and on it Beezie embroidered two butterflies, in blue and gold. She was as entranced with the journal as was Chuck.

They shared the notebook and the letters with the grandmother, reading aloud to her while she did the ironing or mending, until they had her as involved as they were. The present was so bleak that all three found relief in living the long past.

Beezie and Chuck looked at the old foundation behind the store. "That's where the Maddoxes' house must have been. They didn't live above the store, the way we do."

"Our apartment was all part of the store."

"I wonder what happened to the house?"

"We'll never know," Beezie said drearily.

"I tried to check one of Matthew Maddox's books out

of the library," Chuck said. "But the librarian said they haven't been around in a long time. She thinks somebody must have lifted them. But I did get some books on Vespugia. Let's go upstairs and look at them."

They compared the photographs in the books with the watercolors in the final pages of the journal, where Zillah had tried to reproduce in ink and paint what Bran had described in his letters. Zillah's painting of vast plains rising terrace-fashion up to the foot of the Andes gave them a feeling of a world so different it might have been another planet.

Beezie had turned back to Zillah's notebook, to a painting of a tall and handsome Indian, with strange blue eyes set rather too close to his aquiline nose. The caption read: "This is how I think Gedder must look, the Indian who Bran writes is descended from Madoc's brother."

Chuck reached for one of Bran's letters and read:

I wish I was more drawn to Gedder, who is so obviously drawn to Gwen. I feel an ingrate when I think of all he has done for us. Building is completely different in Vespugian weather than at home—or in Wales, and I shudder to think what kind of houses we might have built had Gedder not shown us how to construct dwellings to let the wind in, rather than to keep it out. And he showed us what crops to plant, hardy things like cabbage and carrots, and how to make windbreaks for them. All the Indians have helped us, but Gedder more than the others, and more visibly. But he never laughs.

"I don't trust people who don't laugh." He put the letter down.

Beezie got a baby-sitting job that began right after school, so Chuck took her place at the cash register, pretending that he was Matthew Maddox and that the store was big and flourishing. The grandmother took in ironing and sewing, and her old hands were constantly busy. There was no time for leisurely cups of tea and the telling of tales. Chuck moved more and more deeply into his games of Let's Pretend. Matthew and Zillah, Bran and Gwen, Gedder and Zillie, all were more alive for him than anyone except Beezie and the grandmother.

One evening Mrs. Maddox stayed late downstairs in the store. When Chuck came home from chopping wood for one of their neighbors, he found Beezie and his grandmother drinking herb tea. "Grandma, I'm hungry." He could feel his belly growling. Supper had been soup and dry toast.

Seeming to ignore his words, the old woman looked at him. "Duthbert Mortmain's been calling on your ma. He's downstairs now."

"I don't like him," Beezie said.

"You may have to," the grandmother told her.

"Why?" Chuck asked. He remembered Duthbert Mortmain as a lumbering, scowling man who did small plumbing jobs. How did he smell? Not a pleasant smell. Hard, like a lump of coal.

"He's offered to marry your ma and take over the store."

"But Pa—"

"The funeral baked meats are long cold. Duthbert

Mortmain's got a shrewd business head, and no one's bought the store, nor likely to. Your ma's not got much choice. And for all her hard work and heavy heart, she's still a pretty woman. Not surprising Duthbert Mortmain should fall for her."

"But she's our *mother*," Beezie protested.

"Not to Duthbert Mortmain. To him she's a desirable woman. And to your mother, he's a way out."

"Out of what?" Chuck asked.

"Your mother's about to lose the store and the roof over our heads. Another few weeks and we'll be out on the street."

Chuck's face lit up. "We could go to Vespugia!"

"Going anywhere takes money, Chuck, and money's what we don't have. You and Beezie'd be put in foster homes, and as to your ma and me . . ."

"Grandma!" Beezie clutched the old woman's sleeve. "You don't want Ma to marry him, do you?"

"I don't know what I want. I'd like to know that she was taken care of, and you and Chuck, before I die."

Beezie flung her arms about the old woman. "You're not going to die, Grandma, not ever!"

Chuck's nostrils twitched slightly. The scent of dandelion spore was strong.

The old woman untangled herself. "You've seen how death takes the ready and unready, my Beezie. Except for my concern about your future, and your mother's, I'm ready to go home. It's been a long time I've been separated from my Patrick. He's waiting for me. The last few days I've kept looking over my shoulder, expecting to see him."

"Grandma"—Beezie pushed her fingers through her curls—"Ma doesn't *love* Duthbert Mortmain. She can't! I hate him!"

"Hate hurts the hater more'n the hated."

"Didn't Branwen?"

"Branwen hated not. Branwen loved, and was betrayed, and cried the rune for help, and not for hate or revenge. And the sun melted the white snow so that she could sleep warm at night, and the fire in her little stove did not burn out but flickered merrily to keep her toasty, and the lightning carried her message to her brother, Bran, and her Irish king fled to his ship and the wind blew him across the sea and his ship sank in its depths and Bran came to his sister Branwen and blessed the stark earth so that it turned green and flowering once more."

Beezie asked, "Did she ever love anybody again, after the Irish king?"

"I've forgotten," the old woman said.

"Grandma! Why don't we use the rune? Then maybe Ma won't have to marry Duthbert Mortmain."

"The rune is not to be used lightly."

"This wouldn't be lightly."

"I don't know, my Beezie. Patterns have to be worked out, and only the very brash tamper with them. The rune is only for the most dire emergency."

"Isn't this an emergency?"

"Perhaps not the right one." The old woman closed her eyes and rocked back and forth in silence, and when she spoke it was in a rhythmic singsong, much as when she intoned the words of the rune. "You will use the rune, my lamb, you will use the rune, but not before the time is ripe." She opened her eyes and fixed Beezie with a piercing gaze which seemed to go right through her.

"But how will I know when the time is ripe? Why isn't it ripe now?"

The old woman shook her head and closed her eyes and rocked again. "This moment is not the moment. The night is coming and the clouds are gathering. We can do nothing before they are all assembled. When the time is ripe, Chuck will let you know. From the other side of darkness, Chuck will let you know, will let you know, will let . . ." Her words trailed off, and she opened her eyes and spoke in her natural voice. "To bed with both of you. It's late."

"Horrid old Duthbert Mortmain," Beezie said to Chuck one fine summer's day. "I won't call him Pa."

"Nor I."

Duthbert Mortmain seemed quite content to have them call him Mr. Mortmain.

He ran the store with stern efficiency. With their mother he was gentle, occasionally caressing her soft hair. People remarked on how he doted on her.

A sign over the cash register read NO CREDIT. Beezie and Chuck helped out in the afternoons and on Saturdays as usual. And their mother still did not smile, not even

when Duthbert Mortmain brought her a box of choc-
olates tied with a lavender ribbon.

She no longer smelled of fear, Chuck thought, but
neither did she smell of the blue sky of early morning.
Now it was the evening sky, with a thin covering of cloud
dimming the blue.

Duthbert Mortmain saved his pleasantries for the customers. He laughed and made jokes and gave every ap-
pearance of being a hearty, kindly fellow. But upstairs
in the evenings his face was sour.

"Don't be noisy, children," their mother warned. "Your
—my husband is tired."

Beezie whispered to Chuck, "Pa was tired, too, but he
liked to hear us laugh."

"We were his own children," Chuck replied. "We don't
belong to Duthbert Mortmain, and he doesn't like what
doesn't belong to him."

Duthbert Mortmain did not show his vicious temper
until the following spring. There was never a sign of it in
the store, even with the most difficult customers or sales-
men, but upstairs he began to let it have its way. One
morning his wife ("I hate it when people call her
Mrs. Mortmain!" Beezie exploded) came to breakfast
with a black eye, explaining that she had bumped into a
door in the dark. The grandmother, Beezie, and Chuck
looked at her, but said nothing.

And it became very clear that Duthbert Mortmain did
not like children, even when they were quiet. Whenever
Chuck did anything which displeased his stepfather,

which was at least once a day, Mortmain boxed his ears, so that at last they rang constantly.

When Beezie sat at the cash register, her stepfather pinched her arm every time he passed, as though in affection. But her arms were so full of black and blue marks that she kept her sweater on all the time to hide the bruises.

One day at recess in the schoolyard, Chuck saw Paddy O'Keefe come up to Beezie, and hurried over to them to hear Paddy asking, "Old Mortmain after you?"

"What do you mean?"

"You know what I mean."

"No. I don't." But she shivered.

Chuck intervened, "You leave my sister alone."

"Better tell old Mortmain to leave her alone, runt. You ever need any help, Beezie, you just let me know. Li'l ole Paddy'll take care of you."

That night Duthbert Mortmain's temper flared totally out of control.

They had finished the evening meal, and when Beezie was clearing the table, her stepfather reached out and pinched her bottom, and Chuck saw the look of cold hatred she turned on him.

"Duthbert—" their mother protested.

"Duthbert Mortmain, take care." The grandmother gave him a long, level gaze. She spoke not another word, but warning was clear in her eyes. She put cups and glasses on a tray, and started for the sink.

Mortmain, too, left the table, and as the old woman neared the stairway he raised his arm to strike her.

"No!" Beezie screamed.

Chuck thrust himself between his grandmother and stepfather and took the full force of Mortmain's blow.

Again Beezie screamed, as Chuck fell, fell down the steep stairs in a shower of broken china and glass. Then she rushed after him.

Chuck lay in a distorted position at the foot of the stairs, looking up at her with eyes that did not see. "Gedder pushed me. He pushed me. Don't let him marry Gwen. Zillah, don't let Gedder, don't let . . ."

10

The earth with its starkness

A field of dandelions. Yellow. Yellow. Exploding into white, into a blizzard of white, a terror of white. Green stems, sickly trickling ooze.

Grandma.

Grandma.

Grandma, you're not going to die. Not ever.

Gedder.

Smell. Bad smell.

Gun. Gedder's gun. Stop him

terrible fall

Gwen   Zillah

head hurts
hurts

crystal horn heals
Matthew's unicorn comes
tip touches head with light   heals

Beezie! Grandma! Ma! Pa!

Two stones in the cemetery.
A fight at the edge of the cliff, like Gwydyr and Madoc
at the edge of the lake. Bad. Bad.
Beezie, never let him touch you.

From inside himself Charles Wallace watched as the
unicorn lowered his head and the blazing tip of the horn
touched Chuck's head, pouring light into it. He kept the
horn there until the light had poured itself out, and the
spasms of pain subsided and the boy stopped babbling
and slept.

"Charles Wallace!"
He listened. The voice sounded like Gaudior, and yet
it was not Gaudior, and he no longer saw the silver
beauty of the unicorn nor the light of the horn. Nothing
was visible, not even darkness. Something was happening, and he did not know what. He was still Within
Chuck, and yet he was intensely conscious of himself as
Charles Wallace, and something was pulling him.

Meg sat up, blinking and rubbing her hand against
Ananda's fur. The kitten had returned and was sleeping

on the pillow. At first Meg did not know why there were tears on her cheeks, or why she was frightened.

She closed her eyes in sadness and saw the unicorn standing motionless by the star-watching rock. A pear-shaped drop of crystal slid from Gaudior's eye and shattered into a thousand fragments on the stone. The unicorn looked up at the sky. The stars were sparkling brilliantly. Small wisps of starlit cloud moved in the rapid north wind. She thought she heard Gaudior saying, 'The Old Music was in them once. That was a victory for the Echthroi.'

Meg thought of Mrs. O'Keefe waiting downstairs. Yes. That was a victory for the enemy, indeed. That Beezie, the golden child, should have become the old hag with missing teeth and resentful eyes was unbearable.

There's more to her than meets the eye.

Infinitely more.

And what now? What's going to happen?

To Chuck?

To Charles Wallace?

"Charles Wallace!"

He listened. Was it Gaudior? He could hear, but he could not see, and the voice echoed as though coming from a great distance.

"Charles Wallace." The voice was compassionate. "You don't have to stay Within Chuck now that this has happened. We did not expect this."

Charles Wallace felt cold and confused and therefore cross. "But I *am* Within Chuck."

"Yes. And Chuck is unconscious, and when he comes to, he will not be the same. His skull has been fractured. Although the healing of the horn has taken away the worst of the pain it could not repair the brain damage. And so there have been instructions that you are to be released now if you so desire."

Charles Wallace felt weighed down by darkness and pain.

The almost-Gaudior voice continued. "Within Chuck as he is now, you will have no control over his actions. His brain is short-circuited. If there is a Might-Have-Been which you should alter in order to avert disaster, you will have no ability either to recognize it or to change it."

"If you release me from Within Chuck, then what?"

"You will be sent Within someone else, and then you will be better able to accomplish your mission. Time is of the essence, as you understand. And we do not know what may happen while you are trapped Within this injured child."

"Who are you?" Charles Wallace asked the invisible voice. "You sound like Gaudior, but you aren't Gaudior."

The voice laughed gently. "No, I am not Gaudior. All the healing light went from his horn, but he could not cure Chuck, though he kept him from dying—and that may not have been a kindness. He has gone home to dip his horn in the pools of healing to replenish it."

"Then who are you?"

Again the voice laughed. "You saw me when Gaudior took you home after you nearly drowned in the Ice Age sea. I am the unicorn you saw come forth from the shell."

"Why can't I see you? Why can't I see anything?" The words of the voice had reassured him, and yet he still felt foreboding.

"While you are in Chuck, you see only what Chuck sees, and he is unconscious, and will be for several days. Come, Charles Wallace, there's no time to be lost. Let us help you out of Chuck. If Mad Dog Branzillo is to be prevented from starting a holocaust you must not dally."

"I have to think—" Something was wrong, and he did not know what.

"Charles Wallace. Gaudior will corroborate what I have told you. Chuck's brain has been damaged. He's little better than an idiot. Come out."

"If I come out, will I see you?" There was something about the voice which was inconsistent with the visual image of the baby unicorn; but of course it would no longer be a baby.

"Of course you'll see me. Hurry. There's a terrible urgency about what you are to accomplish."

"I?"

"Of course, you. You were selected, weren't you?"

"No. Beezie—Mrs. O'Keefe—laid a charge on me."

"Because you're the only one who can prevent Branzillo."

"But I can't—"

"Of course you can." The voice was tenderly patient. "Why do you think you were chosen?"

"Well—Gaudior seemed to think it was that I might

be able to go Within people, because of the way Meg and I kythe."

"Exactly. You were chosen because of your special gifts, and your unusual intelligence. You know that yourself, don't you?"

"Well—I can kythe. And I know my I.Q.'s high, as far as that goes. But that's not enough—"

"Of course it is. And you have the ability to see the difference between right and wrong, and to make the correct decisions. You were selected because you are an extraordinary young man and your gifts and your brains qualify you. You are the only one who can control the Might-Have-Been."

Charles Wallace's stomach was churning.

"Come, Charles Wallace. You have been chosen. You are in control of what is going to happen. You are needed. We must go."

Charles Wallace began to throw up. Was it in reaction to the tempting words, or because Chuck, with his bashed-in skull, was vomiting? But he knew that whatever the voice looked like, it was not a unicorn. When he had stopped retching he said, "I don't know who you are, but you're not like Gaudior. Gaudior would never say what you've just said. It was trying to use my high I.Q. and trying to control things that got us into trouble in the first place. I don't know what I'm supposed to use, but it's not my intellect or strength. For better or worse, I'm Within Chuck. And I've never come out of Within on my own. It's always happened to me. I'm staying Within."

Meg let out a long sigh. "He made the right choice, didn't he?"

Ananda's warm tongue gently touched Meg's hand.

Meg closed her eyes, listening. She thought she heard a howl of defeat, and she whiffed the ugly stench of Echthroi.

So they had been trying to get at Charles Wallace in a much more subtle way than by trying to snatch him from Gaudior's back or throw him into Projections.

Duthbert Mortmain had nearly killed Chuck. Nothing went in straight lines for him any more, not time, not distance. His mind was like the unstable earth, full of faults, so that layers shifted and slid. It was like being in a nightmare from which there was no possibility of waking. She ached for him, and for Charles Wallace Within him.

Pain and panic
the world tilting
twirling on its axis, out of control
spinning off   away from the sun   into the dark
light bursting against his eyes, an explosion of light
a kaleidoscope of brilliant colors   assailing his nostrils
"Chuck!" The voice came echoing from a vast distance, echoing along the unseen walls of a dark tunnel.

"Chuck! It's Beezie, your sister. Chuck, can you hear me?"

He was weighted down by the vast heaviness of the atmosphere, but he managed to lift one finger in response to Beezie's calling, afraid, as he did so, that if the weight lifted he would fall off the wildly tilting earth . . .

"He hears me! Ma, Chuck moved his finger!"

Slowly the rampant, out-of-control speed lessened, and the planet resumed its normal pace. Colors stopped their kaleidoscopic dance and stayed in place. Smells became identifiable once more: coffee; bread; apples. Beezie: the gold was not as brilliant as it had been, but it was still Beezie. And their mother. the blue was cloudy now, hardly blue at all, closer to the grey of rain clouds. Grandma: where is Grandma's smell? Why is there emptiness? Where is the green?

"Grandma!"

"She's dead, Chuck. Her heart gave out."

"Gedder pushed her. He killed her."

"No, Chuck." Beezie's voice was bitter, and the bitterness further muted the gold. "Duthbert Mortmain. He was furious with her, and he was going to strike her, but you saved her, and he hit you instead, and you fell all the way down the stairs and fractured your skull. And Grandma—she just . . ."

"What? Did Gedder—"

"No, no, not Gedder, Chuck, Duthbert Mortmain. He felt as awful as he's capable of feeling. He and Ma drove you to the hospital, and I stayed home with Grandma, and she looked at me and said, 'I'm sorry, Beezie, I can't wait any longer. My Patrick's come for me.' And she gave a little gasp, and that was all."

He heard her, but between the stark words came other sounds and the smell of a hot and alien wind. Time's layers slipped and slid under him. "But Gwen shouldn't marry Gedder. Gwydyr's children shouldn't marry Madoc's."

There was panic in Beezie's voice. "What are you talking about? Chuck, please don't. You scare me. I want you to get all the way well."

"Not Let's Pretend. Real. Gwen and Gedder—it would be bad, bad . . ."

The cliff loomed high over him, dark, shadowing. Gedder was at the top of the cliff, waiting, waiting . . . who was he waiting for?

Chuck slowly improved, until he could put cans and boxes on the store shelves. Even though he could not manage school, he recovered enough to mark the prices on the store's stock. He seldom made a mistake, and when he did, Duthbert Mortmain did not box his ears.

Sometimes Chuck saw him as Mortmain, sometimes as Gedder, when his worlds warped. "Gedder is nicer than he used to be," he reported to Beezie. "He's nicer to Ma. And to Grandma and me."

"Grandma—" A sob choked Beezie's voice. "Chuck, how can you! How can you play Let's Pretend about that?" Her voice rose with outrage. "How can you go away from me like this when I need you? Don't leave me!"

He heard and he did not hear. He was caught between

the layers and he could not get into the right layer so that he could be with Beezie. "Grandma says I'm not to let him hear me call him Gedder, because that's not his real name, so I won't." He had intended to say, he thought he was saying, 'I'll never leave you, Beezie,' but the words of the other layer came out of his mouth. "Where's Matthew? I want to talk to him. He has to get Zillah to Vespugia."

Sometimes the earth started to tilt again and he could not stand upright against the velocity. Then he had to stay in bed until the tilting steadied.

He climbed the attic stairs one day when the earth was firm under his feet, and crawled into all the dimmest and most cobwebby corners, until his hands felt a packet. At first he thought it was an old tobacco pouch, but then he saw that it was oilskin wrapped about some papers. Letters. And newspaper clippings.

Letters from Bran to Zillah, to Matthew. Urgent letters.

He looked at them and the words danced and flickered. Sometimes they seemed to say one thing, sometimes another. He could not read the small print. He pushed the heels of his hands against his eyeballs and everything sparkled like fireworks. He sobbed with frustration, and took the letters and clippings downstairs and put them under his pillow.

—I'll tell Grandma. She'll help me read them.

The kythe came to Meg in distorting waves.

One minute she understood, and the next she was

caught up in Chuck's shifting universe. She pulled herself away from the kythe to try to think.

—What's coming clear, she thought, —is that it's important to know whether Mad Dog Branzillo is from Madoc's or Gwydyr's line. Somehow or other, it's between the two babies in the scry, the scry which both Madoc and Brandon Llawcae saw.

We don't know much about Gwydyr's line. He was disgraced, and he went to Vespugia eventually, and we think Gedder is his descendant.

We know a little more about Madoc's line. From each time Charles Wallace has gone Within, we know that most of Madoc's ancestors stayed around here.

So Branzillo's ancestors matter. And it's all in Matthew Maddox's book that Charles Wallace can't get at because the Echthroi are blocking him. But what can Charles Wallace do about it, even if he and Gaudior ever do get to Patagonia?

Slowly, she moved back into the kythe.

"Chuck." It was Beezie's voice.

"Here I am."

"How do you feel?"

"Dizzy. The earth's spinning, like the night we saw the fireflies."

"The night Pa died."

"Yes. Like then."

"You remember?" she asked in surprise.

"Of course."

"Lots of things you don't remember. That's why you can't go to school any more. Chuck—"

"What?"

"Ma's going to have a baby."

"She can't. Pa's dead."

"She's married again."

"She and Gedder can't have a baby. It would be bad."

"I thought you were talking the way you used to. I thought you were all right!" Her voice rose in frustration and outrage. "Not Gedder! Mortmain!"

He tried to come back to her, but he could not. "Same difference. Same smell. The baby has to come from Madoc. Bran and Zillah have to have the baby because of the prayer."

"What prayer?" she shouted.

> "*Lords of blue and Lords of gold,*
> *Lords of winds and waters wild,*
> *Lords of time that's growing old,*
> *When will come the season mild?*
> *When will come blue Madoc's child?*"

"Where'd you learn that?"

"The letters."

"What letters?"

He became impatient. "Bran's letters, of course."

"But we've read them all. There wasn't anything like that in them."

"Found some more."

"When? Where?"

"In the attic. Grandma helps me read them."

"Where are they?" she demanded.

He fumbled under his pillow. "Here."

Chuck walked through a spring evening, smelling of growing grass, and blossoms drifting from the trees. He walked over the fields, over the brook, drinking the water rushing with melting snow, lifting his head, clambering to his feet, going on to the flat rock. Pain walked with him, and there was a dark veil of cloud between his eyes and the world. If a chair was pulled out of place he walked into it. Trees and rocks did not move; he felt safer at the rock than anywhere else.

He did not tell anybody about the veil.

He began to make mistakes in stamping the prices on the stock, but Duthbert Mortmain assumed it was because the fall had made him half-witted.

The baby came, a boy, and the mother no longer worked in the store. Paddy O'Keefe had dropped out of school and came in to help. Chuck followed Paddy's instructions, marking the cans with the stamp which Paddy set for him. He heard Paddy say, "He's more trouble than he's worth. Whyn't you send him to the nuthouse?"

Mortmain muttered something about his wife.

"Aren't you afraid he'll hurt the baby?" Paddy asked.

After that, Chuck stayed out of the way as much as possible, spending the warm days at the flat rock, the cold ones curled up in the attic. He saw Beezie to talk to only in the evenings, and Sunday afternoons.

"Chuck, what's wrong with your eyes?"

"Nothing."

"You're not seeing properly."

"It's all right."

"Ma—"

"Don't tell Ma!"

"But you ought to see a doctor."

"No! All they want is any excuse to put me away. You must have heard them, Paddy and Duthbert. They want to put me in an institution. For my own good, Mortmain said to Ma. He said I'm an idiot and I might hurt the baby."

Beezie burst into tears and flung her arms around her brother. "You wouldn't!"

"I know I wouldn't. But it's the one thing Ma might listen to."

"And you're not an idiot!"

His cheeks were wet with Beezie's tears. "If you tell them about my eyes they'll put me in an insane asylum for my own good and the baby's. I'm trying to keep out of the way."

"I'll help you, oh, Chuck, I'll help you," Beezie promised.

"I have to stay long enough to make sure Matthew sends Zillah to Vespugia. He's saving the money."

"Oh, Chuck," Beezie groaned. "Don't let them hear you talk like this."

As the veil deepened and darkened, his inner vision lightened. When the weather was fine he lay out on the flat rock all day, looking up toward the sky and seeing

pictures, pictures more vivid than anything he had seen
with unveiled eyes. His concentration was so intense that
he became part of all that was happening in the pictures.
Sometimes in the evenings he told Beezie about them,
pretending they were dreams, in order not to upset
her.

"I dreamed about riding a unicorn. He was like moonlight, and so tall I had to climb a tree to get on his back,
and we flew among the fireflies, and the unicorn and I
sang together."

"That's a lovely dream. Tell me more."

"I dreamed that the valley was a lake, and I rode a
beautiful fish sort of like a porpoise."

"Pa said the valley was a lake, way back in prehistory.
Archaeologists have found fish fossils in the glacial rocks.
Maybe that's why you dreamed it."

"Grandma told us about the lake, the day we blew
dandelion clocks."

"Oh, Chuck, you're so strange, the way you remember
some things . . ."

"And I dreamed about a fire of roses, and—" He
reached gropingly for her hand. "I can move in and out
of time."

"Oh, Chuck!"

"I can, Beezie."

"Please—please stop."

"It's only dreams," he comforted.

"Well, then. But don't tell Ma."

"Only you and Grandma."

"Oh, Chuck."

He knew the route to the rock so well that it was easier for him to go in the dark, when he could see nothing, than in sunlight when shafts of brilliance penetrated the veil like spears and hurt his eyes and confused his sense of direction.

Time. Time. There wasn't much time.

Time. Time was as fluid as water.

He stood by Matthew's couch. "You can't wait any longer. You have to get Zillah to Vespugia now, or it will be too late."

Matthew is writing, writing against time. It's all in the book Pa talked about. They don't want me to see the book.

Ritchie is cutting a window in Brandon's room, before leaving for Wales . . .

But Zillah isn't there . . . Why is there an Indian girl instead?

Because it isn't Zillah's time. She comes later, in Matthew's time

Unicorns can move in time

and idiots

space is more difficult

Paddy wants me out of the way. Paddy and Mortmain. Not much time

> *Lords of space and Lords of time,*
> *Lords of blessing, Lords of grace,*
> *Who is in the warmer clime?*
> *Who will follow Madoc's rhyme?*
> *Blue will alter time and space.*

Did you not learn in Gwynedd that there is room for one king only?

You will be great, little Madog, and call the world your own, to keep or destroy as you will. It is an evil world, little Madog.

You will do good for your people, El Zarco, little Blue Eyes. The prayer has been answered in you, blue for birth, blue for mirth

Which blue will it be

They are fighting
up on the cliff
on the steep rock

the world
it's tilting
it's going too fast
I'm going to fall

11

All these I place

The light came back slowly. There had been shadows, nothing but deepening shadows, and pain, and slowly the pain began to leave and healing light touched his closed lids. He opened them. He was on the star-watching rock with Gaudior.

"The wind brought you out of Chuck."

"What happened to him?"

"Mortmain had him institutionalized. Are you ready? It's time—" A ripple of tension moved along the unicorn's flanks.

Charles Wallace felt the wind all about them, cold,

and yet strengthening. "What Chuck saw—two men fighting—was it real?"

"What is real?" Gaudior replied infuriatingly.

"It's important!"

"We do not always know what is important and what is not. The wind sends a warning to hurry, hurry. Climb up, and hold very tight."

"Should I bind myself to you again?"

"The wind says there's no time. We'll fly out of time and through galaxies the Echthroi do not know. But the wind says it may be difficult to send you Within, even so. Hold on, and try not to be afraid."

Charles Wallace felt the wind beneath them as Gaudior spread his wings. The flight at first was serene. Then he began to feel cold, a deep, penetrating cold far worse than the cold of the Ice Age sea. This was a cold of the spirit as well as the body. He did not fall off the unicorn because he was frozen to him; his hands were congealed in their clenched grasp on the frozen mane.

Gaudior's hoofs touched something solid, and the cold lifted just enough so that the boy was able to unclench his hands and open his frozen lids. They were in an open square in a frozen city of tall, windowless buildings. There was no sign of tree, of grass. The blind cement was cracked, and there were great chunks of fallen masonry on the street.

"Where—" Charles Wallace started, and stopped.

The unicorn turned his head slowly. "A Projection—" Charles Wallace followed his gaze and saw two men in gas masks patrolling the square with machine guns. "Do they see us?"

The question was answered by the two men pausing, turning, looking through the round black eyes of their gas masks directly at unicorn and boy, and raising their guns.

With a tremendous leap Gaudior launched upward, wings straining. Charles Wallace pressed close to the neck, hands twined in the mane. But for the moment they had escaped the Echthroi, and when Gaudior's hoofs touched the ground, the Projection was gone.

"Those men with guns—" Charles Wallace started. "In a Projection, could they have killed us?"

"I don't know," Gaudior said, "and I didn't want to wait to find out."

Charles Wallace looked around in relief. When he had left Chuck, it was autumn, the cold wind stripping the trees. Now it was high spring, the old apple and pear trees in full blossom, and the smell of lilac on the breeze. All about them, the birds were in full song.

"What should we do now?" Charles Wallace asked.

"At least you're asking, not telling." Gaudior sounded unusually cross, so the boy knew he was unusually anxious.

Meg shivered. Within the kythe she saw the star-watching rock and a golden summer's day. There were two people on the rock, a young woman, and a young man—or a boy? She was not sure, because there was something wrong with the boy. But from their dress she was positive that it was the time of the Civil War— around 1865.

The Within-ing was long and agonizing, instead of immediate, as it had always been before. Charles Wallace felt intolerable pain in his back, and a crushing of his legs. He could hear himself screaming. His body was being forced into another body, and at the same time something was struggling to pull him out. He was being torn apart in a battle between two opposing forces. Sun blazed, followed by a blizzard of snow, snow melted by raging fire, and violent flashings of lightning, driven by a mighty wind, which whipped across sea and land . . .

His body was gone and he was Within, Within a crippled body, the body of a young man with useless legs like a shriveled child's . . . Matthew Maddox.

From the waist up he looked not unlike Madoc, and about the same age, with a proud head and a lion's mane of fair hair. But the body was nothing like Madoc's strong and virile one. And the eyes were grey, grey as the ocean before rain.

Matthew was looking somberly at the girl, who appeared to be about his age, though her eyes were far younger than his. "Croeso f'annwyl, Zillah." He spoke the Welsh words of endearment lovingly. "Thank you for coming."

"You knew I would. As soon as Jack O'Keefe brought your note, I set off. How did you get here?"

He indicated a low wagon which stood a little way from the rock.

She looked at the powerful torso, and deeply muscled shoulders and arms. "By yourself, all the way?"

"No. I can do it, but it takes me a long time, and I had to go over the store ledgers this morning. When I went to the stables to find Jack to deliver the note, I swallowed my pride and asked him to bring me."

Zillah spread her billowing white skirts about her on the rock. She wore a wide-brimmed leghorn hat with blue ribbons, which brought out the highlights in her straight, shining black hair, and a locket on a blue ribbon at her throat. To Matthew Maddox she was the most beautiful, and desirable, and—to him—the most unattainable woman in the world.

"Matt, what's wrong?" she asked.

"Something's happened to Bran."

She paled. "How do you know? Are you sure?"

"Last night I woke out of a sound sleep with an incredibly sharp pain in my leg. Not my own familiar pain, Bran's pain. And he was calling out to me to help him."

"O dear Lord. Is he going to be all right?"

"He's alive. He's been reaching out to me all day."

She buried her face in her hands, so that her words were muffled. "Thank you for telling me. You and Bran—you've always been so close, even closer than most twins."

He acknowledged this with a nod. "We were always close, but it was after my accident that—it was Bran who brought me back into life, Zillah, you know that."

She dropped her hand lightly on his shoulder. "If Bran is badly wounded, we're going to need you. As once you needed Bran."

After the accident, five years earlier, when his horse had crashed into a fence and rolled over on him, crushing his pelvis and legs and fracturing his spine, Bran had shown him no pity; instead, had fiercely tried to push his twin brother into as much independence as possible, and refused to allow him to feel sorry for himself.

'But Rollo jumps fences twice as high with ease.'

'He didn't jump that one.'

'Bran, just before he crashed, there was a horrible, putrid stink—'

'Stop going back over things. Get on with it.'

They continued to go everywhere together—until the war. Unlike Bran, Matthew could not lie about his age and join the cavalry.

"I lived my life through Bran, vicariously," Matthew told Zillah. "When he went to war, it was the first time he ever left me out." Then: "When you and Bran fell in love, I knew that I had to start letting him go, to try to find some kind of life of my own, so that he'd be free. And it was easier to let go with you than with anyone else in the world, because you've always treated me like a complete human being, and I knew that the two of you would not exclude me from your lives."

"Dear Matt. Never. And you are making your own life. You're selling your stories and poems, and I think they're as good as anything by Mark Twain."

Matthew laughed, a warm laugh that lightened the

pain lines in his face. "They're only a beginner's work."

"But editors think they're good, too, and so does my father."

"I'm glad. I value Dr. Llawcae's opinion as much as anybody's in the world."

"And he loves you and Bran and Gwen as though you were my brothers and sister. And your mother has been a second mother to me since my own dear mama died. As for our fathers—they may be only distant kin, but they're like as two peas in a pod with their passion for Wales. Matt, have you said anything about Bran to Gwen or your parents?"

"No. They don't like the idea that Bran and I can communicate without speech or letters the way we do. They pretend it's some kind of trick we've worked out, the way we used to change places with each other when we were little, to fool people. They think what we do isn't real."

"It's real, I don't doubt that." Zillah smiled. "Dear Matt, I think I love you nearly as much as Bran does."

A week later, Mr. Maddox received official news that his son had been wounded in battle and would be invalided home. He called the family into the dark, book-lined library to inform them.

Mrs. Maddox fanned herself with her black lace fan. "Thank God."

"You're glad Bran's been wounded!" Gwen cried indignantly.

Mrs. Maddox continued to fan herself. "Of course not, child. But I'm grateful to God that he's alive, and that he's coming home before something worse than a bullet in the leg happens to him."

—It *is* worse, Mama, Matthew thought silently. —Bran has been shutting me out of his thoughts and he's never done that before. All I get from him is a dull, deadening pain. Gwen is more right than she knows, not to be glad.

He looked thoughtfully at his sister. She was dark of hair and blue of eye like Zillah, making them appear more like sisters than distant cousins. But her face did not have Zillah's openness, and her eyes were a colder blue and glittered when she was angry. After Matthew's accident she had pitied him, but had not translated her pity into compassion. Matthew did not want pity.

Gwen returned his gaze. "And how do you feel about your twin's coming home, Matthew?"

"He's been badly hurt, Gwen," he said. "He's not going to be the same debonair Bran who left us."

"He's still only a child." Mrs. Maddox turned toward her husband, who was sitting behind the long oak library table.

"He's a man, and when he comes home the store will become Maddox and Son," her husband said.

—Maddox and Son, Matthew thought without bitterness —not Maddox and Sons.

He turned his wheelchair slightly away. He was totally committed to his writing; he had no wish to be a partner in Maddox's General Store, which was a large and prosperous establishment in the center of the village, and had the trade of the surrounding countryside for many miles.

The first story of the rambling frame building was filled with all the foodstuffs needed for the village. Upstairs were saddles and harnesses, guns, plows, and even a large quantity of oars, as though Mr. Maddox remembered a time when nearly all of the valley had been a great lake. A few ponds were all that remained of the original body of water. Matthew spent most mornings in the store, taking care of the ledgers and all the accounts.

Behind the store was the house, named Merioneth. The Llawcae home, Madrun, stood beyond Merioneth, slightly more ostentatious, with white pillars and pink-brick façade. Merioneth was the typical three-storied white frame farmhouse with dark shutters which had replaced the original log cabins.

'People think we're putting on airs, giving our houses names,' Bran had complained one day, before the accident, as he and Matthew were walking home from school.

Matthew did a cartwheel. 'I like it,' he said as he came right side up. 'Merioneth is named in honor of a distant cousin of ours in Wales.'

'Yah, I know, Michael Jones, a congregational minister of Bala in Merioneth.'

'Cousin Michael's pleased that we've given the house that name. He mentions it almost every time he writes to Papa. Weren't you listening yesterday when he was telling us about Love Jones Parry, the squire of Madrun, and his plan to take a trip to Patagonia to inspect the land and see if it might be suitable for a colony from Wales?'

'That's the only interesting bit,' Bran had said. 'I love
to travel, even just to go with Papa to get supplies. Maybe
if the squire of Madrun really does take that trip, we
could go with him.'

It was not long after this that the accident happened,
and Matthew remembered how Bran had tried to rouse
him from despair by telling him that Love Jones Parry
had actually gone to Patagonia, and reported that although the land was wild and desolate, he thought that
the formation of a Welsh colony where the colonists
would be allowed to teach their native tongue in school
might be possible. The Spanish government paid scant
attention to that section of Patagonia, where there were
only a few Indians and a handful of Spaniards.

But Matthew refused to be roused. 'Exciting for you.
I'm not going to get very far from Merioneth ever again.'

Bran had scowled at him ferociously. 'You cannot afford the luxury of self-pity.'

—It is still an expensive luxury, Matthew thought,
—and one I can ill afford.

"Matt!" It was Gwen. "A penny for your thoughts."

He had been writing when his father had summoned
them, and still had his note pad on his lap. "Just thinking
out the plot for another story."

She smiled at him brightly. "You're going to make the
name of Maddox famous!"

"My brave baby," Mrs. Maddox said. "How proud I am
of you! That was the third story you've sold to *Harper's
Monthly*, wasn't it?"

"The fourth—Mama, Papa, Gwen: I think I must warn

you that Bran is going to need all our love and help when
he comes home."

"Well, of course—" Gwen started indignantly.

"No, Gwen," he said quietly. "Bran is hurt much more
than just the leg wound."

"What are you talking about?" his father demanded.

"You might call it Bran's soul. It's sick."

Bran returned, limping and withdrawn. He shut Matthew out as effectively as though he had slammed a door
in his twin's face.

Once again Matthew sent a note to Zillah to meet him
at the flat rock. This time he did not ask Jack O'Keefe for
help, but lying on the wagon, he pulled himself over the
rough ground. It was arduous work, even with his powerful arms, and he was exhausted when he arrived. But he
had allowed more than enough time. He heaved himself
off the wagon and dragged over to the rock, stretched
out, and slept under the warm autumn sun.

"Matt—"

He woke up. Zillah was smiling down at him.
"F'annwyl." He pushed the fair hair back from his eyes
and sat up. "Thanks for coming."

"How is he today?"

Matthew shook his head. "No change. It's hard on Papa
to have another crippled son."

"Hush. Bran's not a cripple!"

"He'll limp from that leg wound for the rest of his life.
And whether or not his spirit will heal is anybody's
guess."

"Give him time, Matt . . ."

"Time!" Matthew pushed the word away impatiently. "That's what Mama keeps saying. But we've given him time. It's three months since he came home. He sleeps half the day and reads half the night. And he's still keeping himself closed to me. If he'd talk about his experiences it might help him, but he won't."

"Not even to you?"

"He seems to feel he has to protect me," Matthew said bitterly, "and one of the things I've always loved most in Bran was his refusal to protect or mollycoddle me in any way."

"Bran, Bran," Zillah murmured, "the knight in shining armor who went so bravely to join the cavalry and save the country and free the slaves . . ." She glanced at the ring on her finger. "He asked me to return his ring. To set me free, he said."

Matthew stretched out his hand to her, then drew it back.

"There has to be time for me as well as for Bran. When he gave me this ring I promised I'd be here for him when he returned, no matter what, and I intend to keep that promise. What can we do to bring him out of the slough of despond?"

Matthew ached to reach out to touch her fair skin, to stroke her hair as black as the night and as beautiful. He spread his hand on the warm rock. "I tried to get him to take me riding. I haven't ridden since he went away."

"And?"

"He said it was too dangerous."

"For you? Or for him?"

"That's what I asked him. And he just said, 'Leave me alone. My leg pains me.' And I said, 'You never used to let me talk about it when my legs and back hurt.' And he just looked at me and said, 'I didn't understand pain then.' And I said, 'I think you understood it better then than you do now.' And we stopped talking because we weren't getting anywhere, and he wouldn't open an inch to let me near him."

"Father says his pain should be tolerable by now, and the physical wound is not the problem."

"That's right. We've got to get him out of himself somehow. And Zillah, something else happened that I need to talk to you about. Yesterday when I hoped I could get Bran to take me riding I wheeled out to the stable to check on my saddle, and when I pushed open the stable door there were Jack and—and—"

"Gwen?"

"How did you guess?"

"I've noticed him looking at her. And she's looked right back."

"They were doing more than looking. They were kissing."

"Merchant's daughter and hired hand. Your parents would not approve. How about you?"

"Zillah, that's not what I mind about Jack O'Keefe. He's a big and powerful man and he has nothing but scorn for me—or anything with a physical imperfection. I saw him take a homeless puppy and kill it by flinging it against the wall of the barn."

She put her hands over her eyes. "Matt! Stop!"

"I think it's his enormous physical healthiness that attracts Gwen. I'm a total cripple, and Bran's half a one, at least for now. And Jack is life. She doesn't see the cruelty behind the wide smile and loud laugh."

"What are you going to do about it?"

"Nothing. For now. Mama and Papa have enough on their minds, worrying their hearts out over Bran. And if I warn Gwen, she'll just think I'm jealous of all that Jack can do and all that I cannot. I'll try to talk to Bran, but I doubt he'll hear."

"Dear Matt. It comforts me that you and I can talk like this." Her voice was compassionate, but it held none of the pity he loathed. "My true and good friend."

One night after dinner, while the men lingered over the port, Mr. Maddox looked at Bran over the ruby liquid in his glass. "Matthew and Zillah would like you to join them in their Welsh lesson this week."

"Not yet, Papa."

"Not yet, not yet, that's all you've been saying for the past three months. Will Llawcae says your wound is healed now, and there's no reason for your malingering."

To try to stop his father, Matthew said, "I was remarking today that Gwen looks more Indian than Welsh, with her high cheekbones."

Mr. Maddox poured himself a second glass of port, then stoppered the cut-glass decanter. "Your mother does not like to be reminded that I have Indian blood, though it's generations back. The Llawcaes have it, too, through our common forebears, Brandon Llawcae and Maddok of the People of the Wind, whose children intermarried. Maddok was so named because he had the blue eyes of Welsh Madoc—but then, I don't need to repeat the story."

"True," Bran agreed.

"I like it." Matthew sipped his wine.

"You're a romanticizer," Bran said. "Keep it for your writing."

Mr. Maddox said stiffly, "As your mother has frequently pointed out, black hair and blue eyes are far more common in people of Welsh descent than Indian, and Welsh we indubitably are. And hard-working." He looked pointedly at Bran.

Later in the evening Matthew wheeled himself into Bran's room. His twin was standing by the window, holding the velveteen curtains aside to look across the lawn to the woods. He turned on Matthew with a growl. "Go away."

"No, Bran. When I was hurt I told you to go away, and you wouldn't. Nor will I." Matthew wheeled closer to his brother. "Gwen's in love with Jack O'Keefe."

"Not surprised. Jack's a handsome brute."

"He's not the right man for Gwen."

"Because he's our hired hand? Don't be such a snob."

"No. Because he is, as you said, a brute."

"Gwen can take care of herself. She always has. Anyhow, Papa would put his foot down."

There was an empty silence which Matthew broke. "Don't cut Zillah out of your life."

"If I love Zillah, that's the only thing to do. Free her."

"She doesn't want to be free. She loves you."

Bran walked over to his bed with the high oak bedstead and flung himself down. "I'm out of love with everything and everybody. Out of love with life."

"Why?"

"Do you have to ask me?"

"Yes, I do. Because you aren't telling me."

"You used to know without my having to tell you."

"I still would, if you weren't shutting me out."

Bran moved his head restlessly back and forth on the pillow. "Don't you be impatient with me, twin. Papa's bad enough."

Matthew wheeled over to the bed. "You know Papa."

"I'm no more cut out to be a storekeeper than you are. Gwen's the one who has Papa's hard business sense. But I don't have a talent like yours to offer Papa as an alternative. And he's always counted on me to take over the business. And I don't want to. I never did."

"What, then?" Matthew asked.

"I'm not sure. The only positive thing the war did for me was confirm my enjoyment of travel. I like adventure—but not killing. And it seems the two are seldom separated."

It was the nearest they had come to a conversation since Bran's return, and Matthew felt hopeful.

Matthew was writing on his lap desk in a sunny corner of the seldom-used parlor.

There Bran found him. "Twin, I need you."

"I'm here," Matthew said.

Bran straddled a small gilt chair and leaned his arms on the back. "Matt, nothing is the way I thought it was. I went to war thinking of myself as Galahad, out to free fellow human beings from the intolerable bondage of slavery. But it wasn't as simple as that. There were other, less pure issues being fought over, with little concern for the souls which would perish for nothing more grand than political greed, corruption, and conniving for power. Matt, I saw a man with his face blown off and no mouth to scream with, and yet he screamed and could not die. I saw two brothers, and one was in blue and one was in grey, and I will not tell you which one took his saber and ran it through the other. Oh God, it was brother against brother, Cain and Abel all over again. And I was turned into Cain. What would God have to do with a nation where brothers can turn against each other with such brutality?" Bran stopped speaking as his voice broke on a sob.

Matthew put down his lap desk and drew his twin to him, and together they wept, as Bran poured out all the anguish and terror and nightmare he had lived through. And Matthew held him and drew the pain out and into his own heart.

When the torrent was spent, Bran looked at his twin. "Thank you."

Matthew held him close. "You're back, Bran. We're together again."

"Yes. Forever."

"It's good to have you coming back to life."

"Coming back to life hurts. I need to take my pain away."

Matthew asked, startled, "What?"

"Matt, twin, I'm going away."

"What!" Matthew looked at Bran standing straight and strong before him. The yellow satin curtains warmed the light and brightened Bran's hair. "Where?"

"You'll never guess."

Matthew waited.

"Papa had a letter from Wales, from Cousin Michael. A group left for Patagonia to start a colony. They're there by now. I'm going to join them. How's that for an old dream come true?"

"We were going together . . ."

"Dear my twin, you're making a name for yourself here with your pen. I know that the creation of a story is work, even if Papa doesn't. But you couldn't manage a life of physical hardship such as I'll be having in the Welsh colony."

"You're right," Matthew acknowledged. "I'd be a burden."

"I won't be far from you, ever again," Bran assured him, "even in Patagonia. I promise to share it with you, and you'll be able to write stories about it as vividly as though you'd been there in body. Cousin Michael writes that the colony is settling in well, in a small section known as Vespugia, and I'll tell you everything about it, and describe a grand cast of characters for you."

"Have you told Zillah?"

Bran shook his head.

"Twin, this affects Zillah too, you know. She wears your ring."

"I'll tell everyone tonight at dinner. I'll get Mama to ask the Llawcaes."

Dinner was served in the dining room, a large, dark, oak-paneled chamber that seemed to drink in the light from the crystal chandelier. Heavy brown curtains like the ones in the library were drawn against the cold night. The fire burning brightly did little to warm the vast cavern.

During the meal, conversation was largely about the Welsh expedition to Patagonia, with both Mr. Maddox and Dr. Llawcae getting vicarious excitement out of the adventure.

"What fun," Gwen said. "Why don't you go, Papa? If I were a man, I would."

Matthew and Bran looked at each other across the table, but Bran shook his head slightly.

After dessert, when Mrs. Maddox pushed back her chair, nodding to Gwen and Zillah to follow her, Bran stopped them. "Wait, please, Mama. I have something to tell everybody. We've all enjoyed discussing the Patagonian expedition, and the founding of the colony in Vespugia. Years ago, before Matt's accident, we dreamed of joining the squire of Madrun when he made his journey to see if it would be a suitable place for a colony. So perhaps it won't surprise you that I have decided to join the colonists and make a new life for myself in Vespugia. Today I've written Cousin Michael and Mr. Parry in Wales, and sent letters to Vespugia."

For a moment there was stunned silence.

Bran broke it, smiling. "Dr. Llawcae says a warmer climate will be better for me."

Mr. Maddox asked, "Isn't going to Patagonia rather an excessive way to find a warmer climate? You could go south, to South Carolina or Georgia."

Bran's lips shut in a rigid expression of pain. "Papa, do you forget where I've come from and what I've been doing?"

Mrs. Maddox said, "No, son, your father does not forget. But the war is over, and you must put it behind you."

"In the South? I doubt I would be welcome in the Confederate states."

"But Vespugia—so far away—" Tears filled Mrs. Maddox's eyes. Zillah, her face pale but resolute, drew a fresh handkerchief from her reticule and handed it to her. "If you'd just continue to regain your strength, and go on studying Welsh with Matthew, and come into the business with your father—"

Bran shook his head. "Mama, you know that I cannot go into the business with Papa. And I have no talent, like Matthew's, which I could use here. It seems that the best way to pull myself together is to get out, and what better way to learn Welsh than to be with people who speak it all the time?"

Mr. Maddox spoke slowly, "You took me by surprise, son, but it does seem to be a reasonable solution for you, eh, Will?" He looked at the doctor, who was tamping his pipe.

"In a way, I identify with Madoc, Papa," Bran said. "Matt and I were reroading T. Gwynn Jones's poem about him this evening." He looked at Gwen. "Remember it?"

She sniffled. "I never read Welsh unless Papa forces me."

"Madoc left Wales in deep despair because brother was fighting against brother, just as we did in this ghastly war, 'until it seemed as if God himself had withdrawn his care from the sons of men.' . . . *ymdroi gyda diflastod as anobaith Madog wrth ystried cyflwr gwlad ei ededigaeth, lle'r oedd brawd un ymladd yn erbyn brawd hyd nes yr oedd petal Duw ei hun wedi peidio â gofalu am feibion dynion.*"

Mr. Maddox drew on his pipe. "You do remember."

"Good lad," Dr. Llawcae approved.

"I remember, and too well I understand, for there were many nights during the war when God withdrew from our battlefields. When the sons of men fight against each other in hardness of heart, why should God not withdraw? Slavery is evil, God knows, but war is evil, too, evil, evil."

Zillah pushed her empty dessert plate away and went

to kneel by Bran, impulsively taking his hand and pressing it against her cheek.

He took her hand in his. "I went to war thinking that mankind is reasonable, and found that it is not. But it has always been so, and at last I am growing up, as Matthew grew up long before me. I know that he would give a great deal to come to Vespugia with me, and I to have him, but we both know that it cannot be."

Mrs. Maddox was still weeping into the handkerchief Zillah had given her. "Never again can there be a war that can do such terrible things to people."

Mr. Maddox said, "My dear, it is not good for us to keep reminding Bran of the war. Perhaps getting away from Merioneth and going to Vespugia will be the best way for him to forget."

Matthew looked at his father and saw him letting his dream of *Maddox and Son* disappear into the wilderness of Vespugia.

"Bran." Zillah rose and looked down at him.

"Little Zillah."

"I'm not little Zillah any more, Bran. You changed that the night before you went to war when you put this ring on my finger."

"Child," Dr. Llawcae remonstrated, "it is the dearest wish of my heart that Llawcaes and Maddoxes be once more united in marriage. I gave Bran my blessing when he came to me to ask for your hand. But not yet. You're only seventeen."

"Many women are married and mothers at seventeen. I want to go to Vespugia with Bran, as his wife."

"Zillah," Dr. Llawcae said, "you will wait. When Bran is settled, in a year or two, he can send for you."

Bran pressed Zillah's hand. "It needn't all be decided tonight."

In the end, Bran went with Gwen, not with Zillah. Mr. Maddox caught Gwen and Jack O'Keefe kissing behind the stable door, and announced flatly that she was to accompany her brother to Vespugia. No amount of tears, of hysterics from Gwen, of pleading from Mrs. Maddox, could change his stand.

Gwen and Zillah wept together. "It's not fair," Gwen sobbed. "A woman has no say in her own life. I hate men!"

Matthew tried to intercede with Dr. Llawcae for Zillah, but the doctor was adamant that she should wait at least until she was eighteen, and until Bran had suitable living arrangements.

Store and house were empty after they left. Matthew spent the morning working on accounts, and in the afternoon and evenings he stayed in his corner of the empty parlor, writing. His first novel was published and well received and he was hard at work on his second. It was this, and conversations with Zillah, who came frequently to Merioneth from Madrun, which kept him going.

"Bran's all right," he assured Zillah. "He sends love."

"They can't even have reached Vespugia yet," Zillah protested. "And there's certainly been no chance for him to send a letter."

"You know Bran and I don't need letters."

She sighed. "I know. Will Bran and I ever be like that?"

"Yours will be a different kind of unity. Better, maybe, but different."

"Will he send for me?"

"You must give him time, Zillah—time once again. Time to settle into a new world and a new way of life. And time for your father to get used to the idea of having his only child go half the way across the world from him."

"How's Gwen?"

"Part sulking and feeling sorry for herself, and part enjoying all the sailors on the ship making cow's eyes at her and running to do her bidding. But she's not going to be happy in Vespugia. She's always hated hot weather, and she's never liked roughing it."

"No, she wasn't a tomboy, like me. She thought Father was terrible to let me run wild and play rough games with you and Bran. Will your father relent and let her come home?"

"Not while Jack's around. There's no second-guessing Papa, though, when he latches on to an unreasonable notion." He paused. "Remember the old Indian verses, Zillah?"

"About black hair and blue eyes?"

"Yes. They've been singing around in my head, and I can't get them out, especially one verse:

"*Lords of spirit, Lords of breath,*
Lords of fireflies, stars, and light,

> Who will keep the world from death?
> Who will stop the coming night?
> Blue eyes, blue eyes, have the sight."

"It's beautiful," Zillah said, "but I don't really know what it means."

"It's not to be taken literally. The Indians believed that as long as there was one blue-eyed child in each generation, all would be well."

"But it wasn't, was it? They've been long gone from around here."

"I think it was a bigger all rightness than just for their tribe. Anyhow, both you and Gwen have at least a drop of Indian blood, and you both have the blue eyes of the song."

"So, in a way," Zillah said dreamily, "we're the last of the People of the Wind. Unless—"

Matthew smiled at her. "I think you're meant to have a black-haired, blue-eyed baby."

"When?" Zillah demanded. "Bran's a world away from me. And I'll be old and white-haired and wrinkled before Papa realizes I'm grown up and lets me go." She looked at him anxiously.

Matthew's work began to receive more and more critical acclaim, and Mr. Maddox began thinking of it as something 'real,' rather than fanciful scribbling not to be taken seriously. One of the unused downstairs rooms was fixed up as a study, and Dr. Llawcae designed a larger and more efficient lap desk.

The study was at the back of the house and looked across the lawn to the woods, and in the autumn Matthew feasted on the glory of the foilage. The room was sparsely furnished, at his request, with a black leather couch on which he could rest when sitting became too painful. As the cold weather set in, he began more and more often to spend the nights there. In front of the fireplace was a butler's table and a comfortable lady chair upholstered in blue, the color of Zillah's eyes: Zillah's chair, he thought of it.

It was midsummer before letters began to arrive on a regular basis. True to his promise, Bran sent Matthew vivid descriptions:

How amazingly interconnected everything is, at least to us who have Welsh blood in our veins. My closest friends here are Richard Llawcae, his wife, and his son Rich. They must be at least distant kin to all of us, for Llawcae is not a common name, even in Wales. Richard says they have forebears who emigrated to the New World in the very early days, and then went back to Wales, for nothing there was as bad as the witch-hunting in the Pilgrim villages and towns. One of their ancestors was burned, they think, or nearly so. They don't know exactly where they came from, but probably around Salem.

Rich has eyes for no one but Gwen, and I wish she would see and return his love, for I can think of no one I'd rather have as a brother-in-law. But Gwen sees Gedder before Rich. Gedder is taller and bigger and stronger—perhaps—and certainly more flamboyant. He worries me. Zillie has told me of his fierce ambitions, and his manner toward all of us becomes a little more

lordly every day. God knows he is helpful—if it weren't
for the Indians, I'm not sure the colony would have
survived, for everything is different from at home—
times for planting, what to plant, how to irrigate, etc.
We are grateful indeed that the Indians not only have
been friendly but have given us all the help they could.
Yet I could wish Gedder had been more like his brethren and not so pushy and bossy. None of us likes the
way Gedder treats his sister, as though she were his
slave and inferior.

It is astounding how Zillie has the same features as
Gwen and Zillah, the wide-apart eyes with the faintest
suggestion of a tilt—though hers are a warm brown, and
not blue—and the high cheekbones and delicate nose.
And, of course, the straight, shining black hair. People
have remarked on the likeness between Gwen and
Zillie. I haven't talked with anyone except the Llawcaes
about the Madoc legend following us to Vespugia, and
they don't laugh it away. Truly, truth is stranger than
fiction. Put it into a story for me, Matt.

—I will, Matthew promised silently. —I will. But you
must tell me more.

My house is nearly finished, large and airy, with
verandas. Everyone knows that it is being built for my
bride, and for our children. Zillie often comes and
stands, just out of the way, and looks, and that makes
me uncomfortable. I don't think she comes of her own
volition. I think Gedder sends her. I talk much about
my Zillah, and how I long for the day when she will arrive. Matthew, twin, use your influence on Dr. Llawcae
to let her come soon. Why is he keeping her with him?
I need her, now.

As winter closed in and Matthew could not go out of doors, Zillah began to come from Madrun to Merioneth nearly every day at teatime, and Matthew missed her more than he liked to admit when she did not appear. He was hurrying to finish his second novel, considerably more ambitious than the first, but he tired quickly, and lay on the black couch, reaching out to Bran and Vespugia, all through the winter, the summer, and into a second winter. He felt closer to his twin than ever, and when he neared the shallows of sleep he felt that he actually was in arid Vespugia, part of all that was happening in the tight-knit colony.

In the mornings, when he worked with his soft, dark pencil and large note pad, it was as though he were setting down what he had seen and heard the night before.

"You're pale, Matt," Zillah said one afternoon as she sat in the lady chair and poured his tea.

"It's this bitter cold. Even with the fire going constantly, the damp seeps into my bones."

He turned away from her concern and looked out the window at the night drawing in. "I have to get my book finished, and there's not much time. I have a large canvas, going all the way back to the Welsh brothers who fought over Owain of Gwynedd's throne. Madoc and his brother, Gwydyr, left Wales, and came to a place which I figure to have been somewhere near here, when the valley was still a lake left from the melting of the ice. And once again brothers fought. Gwydyr wanted power, wanted adulation. Over and over again we get caught in fratricide, as Bran was in that ghastly war. We're still bleeding from the wounds. It's a primordial pattern, left us from Cain and Abel, a net we can't seem to break out of. And unless it is checked it will destroy us entirely."

She clasped her hands. "Will it be checked?"

He turned back toward her. "I don't know, Zillah. When I sleep I have dreams, and I see dark and evil things, children being killed by hundreds and thousands in terrible wars which sweep over them." He reached for her hand. "I do not croak doom casually, f'annwyl. I do not know what is going to happen. And irrationally, perhaps, I am positive that what happens in Vespugia is going to make a difference. Read me the letter from Bran that came today once more, please."

She took the letter from the tea table and held it to the lamp.

Dear my twin, and dear my Zillah, when are you coming? Matthew, if you cannot bring Zillah to me, then Zillah must bring you. She writes that the winter is hard on you, and she is worried. There would be much to hold your attention here. Llewellyn Pugh languishes for love of Zillie, and I think she would turn to him did Gedder not keep forcing her on me, no matter how loudly I say that I am betrothed, and that my Zillah is coming to join us any day now. Do not make me a liar!

We have had our first death, and a sad one it was, too. The children are forbidden to climb up onto the cliff which protects the colony from the winds, but somehow or other, one of them managed the steep climb, and fell. We all grieve. It may be a good thing

that there is so much work for everybody that there is
little idle time, and this helps us all, particularly the
parents of the little one. Rich has been a tower of
strength. He was the one of us who was able to bring
tears from the mother, partly because he was not
ashamed to weep himself.

"He is a good man, that Rich," Matthew said. "He'd
do anything in the world for Gwen."

"You talk as though you know him."

Matthew smiled at her. "I do. I know him through
Bran. And through my novel. What happens with Rich,
with Bran, with Gwen, with Zillie—it matters to my
story. It could even change it." She looked at him questioningly. "This book is pushing me, Zillah, making me
write it. It excites me, and it drives me. In its pages,
myth and matter merge. What happens in one time can
make a difference in what happens in another time, far
more than we realize. What Gedder does is going to
make a difference, to the book, perhaps to the world.
Nothing, no one, is too small to matter. What *you* do is
going to make a difference."

In the early winter Matthew caught a heavy chest
cold, which weakened him, and Dr. Llawcae came daily.
Matthew spent the days on the black leather couch,
wrapped in blankets. He continued to work on his novel
and sold several more stories. He kept his earnings,
which were considerable, in a small safe in his study.
And now he left the study not at all.

When he was too exhausted to write, he slid into a shallow sleep, filled with vivid dreams in which Bran and the Vespugian colony were more real than chilly Merioneth.

He was at the flat rock in his dream, the rock where he used to meet Zillah when he sought privacy. But instead of Zillah there was a boy, perhaps twelve years old, dressed in strange, shabby clothes. The boy was lying on the rock, and he, too, was dreaming, and his dream and Matthew's merged.

Gedder is after Gwen. Stop him. The baby must come from Madoc. Gwydyr's line is tainted. There is nothing left but pride and greed for power and revenge. Stop him, Matthew.

He saw his twin, but this was not Bran in Vespugia . . . Was it Bran? It was a young man, about their age, standing by a lake. Behind him stood another, a little older, who looked like Bran and yet not like Bran, for there was resentment behind the eyes. Like Gedder. The two began to wrestle, to engage in mortal combat.

At the edge of the lake a huge pile of flowers smoldered, with little red tongues of flame licking the petals of the roses—

"Matthew!"

He opened his eyes and his mother was hovering over him with a cup of camomile tea.

Beside the growing pages of the manuscript lay a genealogy which he had carefully worked out, a genealogy which could go in two different directions, like a double helix. In one direction there was hope; in the other, disaster. And the book and Bran and the Vespugian colony were intertwined in his mind and heart.

The winter was bitter cold.

"As the days begin to lengthen, the cold begins to strengthen," Matthew said to Dr. Llawcae, who listened gravely to Matthew's heart and his chest.

He leaned back and looked at the young man. "Matthew, you are encouraging Zillah."

Matthew smiled. "I've always encouraged Zillah, from the days when we were all children and she wanted to climb trees as high as Bran and I did."

"That's not what I mean. You're encouraging her in this wild-goose chase to go to Vespugia and join Bran."

"When Bran asked you for Zillah's hand, you gave him your blessing," Matthew reminded the doctor.

"That was with the understanding that Bran would stay here and become his father's partner."

"Once a blessing is given, Dr. Llawcae, it cannot be withdrawn." Matthew urged, "Zillah's heart is in Vespugia with Bran. I understand how she has taken her mother's place in your house and at your table. But she is your daughter, Dr. Llawcae, and not your wife, and you must not keep her tied to you."

The doctor's face flushed darkly with anger. "How dare you!"

"Because I love Zillah with all my heart, and I always have. I will miss her as much as you. Without Zillah, without Bran, I would be bereft of all that makes life worthwhile. But I will not hold them back out of selfishness."

The doctor's face grew darker. "You are accusing me of selfishness?"

"Inadvertent, perhaps, but selfishness, nonetheless."

"You—you—if you weren't a cripple, I'd—" Dr. Llawcao dropped his raised hand, turned, and left the room.

One afternoon in March, with occasional splatters of rain coming down the chimney and hissing out in the fire, Matthew looked intensely at Zillah, presiding over the tea tray. "Zillah. It's time. You must go to Vespugia."

"You know I want to." She reached out to hold his thin fingers. "Father says maybe next year."

"Next year's too late. Bran needs you now. What are you going to do about your father? Next year will always be next year. He'll not let you go."

She stared into the fire. "I'd rather go with Father's blessing, but I'm afraid you're right, and he's not going to give it. The problem is money, and finding a ship, and booking passage—all the things that are difficult, if not impossible, for a girl."

"You must go, this spring as soon as the ice breaks and ships can sail."

"Why, Matt, such urgency, all of a sudden?"

"Bran reached out to me last night—"

"Is something wrong?"

"Not with Bran. But Gedder—Rich—" He was seized

with a fit of coughing, and when he leaned back he was
too weak to talk.

Zillah continued to come daily to sit in the lady chair
by the fire, to preside over the tea tray, and warm him
with her smile. For the next few weeks he did not mention her going to Vespugia. Then one day, when the bare
outlines of the trees were softened with coming buds, he
greeted her impatiently.

He could hardly wait for her to sit down behind the
tea tray. "Zillah, open the safe." Carefully, he gave her
the combination, watching her fingers twirl the dial as
she listened. "All right. Good. Bring out that big manila
envelope. It's for you."

She looked at him in surprise. "For me?"

"I've been busy these last weeks."

"Father says you're pushing yourself too hard. Is the
book done?"

"To all intents and purposes. There's some deepening
to do, and a certain amount of revision. But I've been
busy in other ways. Open the envelope."

She did so. "Money, and—what's this, Matt?"

"A ticket. There's a ship sailing for South America in
four days. You must be on it."

"But, Matthew, I can't let you—"

"I've earned the money by my writing. It's mine to do
with what I will. Zillah, Bran needs you. You must go.
You will swing the balance."

"What balance?"

"The line must be Madoc's and not Gwydyr's—"

"I don't understand. You're flushed. Are you—"

"I'm not feverish. It's part of the book . . . You do love Bran?"

"With all my heart."

"Enough to leave Madrun without your father's blessing, and secretly?"

She held the manila envelope to her breast.

"You'll go?"

"I'll go." She took his cold hand and held it to her cheek.

"All will be well," he promised. "When thou passest through the waters, I will be with thee; and through the rivers, they shall not overflow thee: when thou walkest through the fire, thou shalt not be burned; neither shall the flame kindle upon thee. For the fire is roses, roses . . ."

He did not see her again. Neither could bear the pain of parting.

Dr. Llawcae came storming over to Merioneth. Matthew could hear him shouting, "Where did she get the money? How did she get the passage?"

Matthew smiled, fleetingly grateful that Dr. Llawcae considered him such a cripple that he could not possibly have made the necessary arrangements.

When the doctor came into the study to check Matthew's heart, his temper had cooled enough so that he was no longer shouting. "I suppose you're pleased about this?"

"Zillah and Bran love each other," Matthew replied quietly. "It is right that they be together. And you have always been so interested in your Welsh heritage, and in this colony, that you will end up feeling differently. You can visit them—"

"Easy enough to say. What about my practice?"

"You haven't taken a vacation in years. You've earned a few weeks away."

Dr. Llawcae gave him only a cursory examination, saying, "You'll feel better when warmer weather comes."

Summer was slow in coming.

Matthew sent the book off to his publisher. The pain in his back was worse each day, and his heart skipped and galloped out of control. In his dreams he was with Bran, waiting for Zillah. He was with Gwen, still resentful, but beginning to laugh again with Rich, to respond to his steadfast love, his outgoing ways. At the same time she was still intrigued by Gedder, by his fierce dark looks and the hiddenness behind his eyes, so unlike Rich's candid ones. She knew that Rich loved her, but Gedder's strangeness fascinated her.

She's playing with Rich and Gedder and it will make trouble, the boy on the rock told Matthew as he slipped deeper into the dream.

Gedder and Bran. Standing on the cliff and looking down at the houses of the settlement. Gedder urging Bran to marry Zillie, to give Gwen in marriage to him, in order to secure the future.

"What future?" Bran asked.

Gedder looked appraisingly down at the prospering colony. "Ours."

And Zillie came and looked adoringly at Bran, Zillie so like and so unlike Zillah.

Wait, twin! Wait for Zillah! Do not trust Gedder—

Matthew was jolted out of the dream as his supper tray was brought. He ate a few bites, then pushed the tray away and slid back into the dream

Felt the Vespugian heat, warming his chilled bones

Bran, if only I could have come with Zillah

Gedder again. Gedder in his favorite place up on the cliff's lip, looking down on the colony, the colony he wants for his own.

Someone's with him. Not Bran. Rich.

Quarreling. Quarreling over Gwen, over the colony. Quarreling at the cliff's edge.

Danger.

Matthew stirred restlessly on the couch, his eyes tightly closed. The boy was there, the child from another time, urging him. "Matthew, you must help Rich. Please . . ."

Once upon a time and long ago, men did not quarrel in this way, when the morning stars sang together and the children of men shouted for joy

But dissonance came

Madoc and Gwydyr fought

Gedder and Rich

Rich, watch out! Gedder has a knife—

Rich sees, sees in time, grasps the knife hand, twists it, so that the knife drops. Gedder reaches after it, snarling with anger, reaching for the knife so that he loses his balance and falls—falls after the knife, over the edge of the cliff, falls, falls . . .

Zillie screams and cannot stop screaming.

Matthew waited for the next letter from Bran, but it did not come until the lilac bushes were in full bloom.

My very dear twin,

Zillah is here, at last she is here, but my dearest heart has arrived to a community in confusion and desolation. Gwen weeps and will not stop. Zillie's tears no longer flow, but her eyes hold anguish. Gedder is dead, and— inadvertently—by Rich's hand. Gedder provoked a quarrel, and drew a knife. Rich took the knife from him, and Gedder, lunging after it, lost his balance and fell from the cliff to his death. It was an accident; nobody blames Rich, even Zillie. But Rich feels he cannot stay here with us, not with blood on his hands.

Will it ever cease, the turning of brother against brother? Gedder wanted power, and I cannot grieve for his death, only for his life, with its inordinate lust and pride. Why does Gwen weep? I do not think she knows. 'I am homesick,' she cries, 'I want to go home.' So Rich will take her home. And what will happen then, who knows?

Gwydyr fought Madoc and lost and the battle continued through to Gedder, brother against brother

And the ship which brought Zillah carried Gwen and Rich to the Northern continent, to lilies of the valley and lilacs in the dooryard, to Merioneth and the store, and Papa will at last have his partner, and the store will be Maddox and Llawcae

Oh, Zillah, my Zillah

> *Lords of melody and song,*
> *Lords of roses burning bright,*
> *Blue will right the ancient wrong,*
> *Though the way is dark and long,*
> *Blue will shine with loving light.*

A coughing fit jerked Matthew awake, away from Vespugia, from Bran and Zillah.

"Gwen—" he gasped, "Rich— Can't wait—sorry—"

Then the coughing took him, and when the racking had passed, there was nothing but agony. His back was an explosion of pain and the room began to get dark, and a rank stink like spoiling flowers choked him. There was no longer any light or warmth in the crackling flames . . .

"Matthew!" Meg opened her eyes, and she was calling the name aloud. The kitten, disturbed, jumped down from the bed. Ananda did not move.

—What happened? What happened to Matthew? to Charles Wallace? Is Charles Wallace all right?

—Strange, she thought, —the kythe with Matthew was clearer than any since Harcels. Maybe because Matthew and Bran were kythers.

She reached out to Charles Wallace, and felt only absence. Nor did she sense Gaudior. Always, when Charles Wallace was brought out of Within, she could see him, could see the unicorn.

"I'm going downstairs," she said aloud, and pushed her feet into her slippers.

Ananda followed her downstairs, stepping on the seventh step so that it let out a loud groan, and the dog yelped in surprise. Behind them the kitten padded softly, so light that the seventh step made the merest sigh.

The kitchen fire was blazing, the kettle humming. Everything looked warm and comfortable and normal, except for Mrs. O'Keefe in the rocking chair. The kitten padded across to her and jumped up on her lap, purring, and flexing its sharp little claws.

Meg asked, "Charles Wallace isn't back yet?"

"Not yet. Are you all right, Meg?" her mother asked.

"I'm fine."

"You look pale."

"Maybe I'll take Sandy and Dennys up on their offer of bouillon, if it's still good."

"Sure, Sis," Sandy said. "I'll make it. Chicken or beef?"

"Half a spoon of each, please, and a slosh of lemon juice." She looked at the twins with fresh comprehension. Was she closer to Charles Wallace than to the twins because they were twins, sufficient unto themselves? She glanced at the phone, then at her mother-in-law. "Mom—Beezie, do you remember Zillah?"

Mrs. O'Keefe looked at Meg, nodded her head, shook it, closed her eyes.

"Mom, Zillah really did get to Vespugia, didn't she?" Meg looked at the old woman, needing reassurance.

Mrs. O'Keefe huddled her arms about herself and rocked. "I forget. I forget."

Mrs. Murry looked anxiously at her daughter. "Meg, what is this?"

"It makes all the difference who Branzillo's forebears were."

Sandy handed Meg a steaming cup. "Sis, the past has happened. Knowing who Branzillo's ancestors were can't change anything."

"There was a time when it hadn't happened yet," Meg tried to explain, realizing how strange she sounded. "It's the Might-Have-Been Charles Wallace was to change, and I think he's changed it. It's the charge Mom O'Keefe laid on him when she gave him the rune."

"Stop talking!" Mrs. O'Keefe pushed herself up out of the rocking chair. "Take me to Chuck. Quickly. Before it's too late."

12

Between myself and the powers of darkness

They ran, pelting across the frozen ground, which crunched under their feet, Meg and the twins and Mrs. O'Keefe. They ran across the rimed lawn and through the aisles of the twins' Christmas trees to the stone wall.

Meg held her hand out to Mrs. O'Keefe and helped her over the low wall. Then, still holding her mother-in-law's hand, pulling her along, she ran down the path, past the two large glacial rocks, to the star-watching rock.

Charles Wallace was lying there, eyes closed, white as death.

"Beezie!" Meg cried. "The rune! Quickly!"

Mrs. O'Keefe was panting, her hand pressed to her side. "With me . . ." She gasped. "Grandma . . ."

Dennys knelt on the rock, bending over Charles Wallace, feeling for his pulse.

"With Chuck in this fateful hour," Mrs. O'Keefe gasped, and Meg joined in, her voice clear and strong:

> *"I place all Heaven with its power*
> *And the sun with its brightness,*
> *And the snow with its whiteness,*
> *And the fire with all the strength it hath,*
> *And the lightning with its rapid wrath,*
> *And the winds with their swiftness along their path,*
> *And the sea with its deepness,*
> *And the rocks with their steepness,*
> *And the earth with its starkness,*
> *All these I place*
> *By God's almighty help and grace*
> *Between myself and the powers of darkness!"*

Light returned slowly. There had been pain, and darkness, and all at once the pain was relieved, and light touched his lids. He opened them, to the sharpness of starlight. He was lying on the star-watching rock, with Gaudior anxiously bending over him, tickling his cheek with the curly silver beard.

"Gaudior, what happened?"

"We barely got you out in time."

"Did Matthew—"

"He died. We didn't expect it quite so soon. The Echthroi—"

"I guess we got to 1865 after all." Charles Wallace looked up at the stars.

"Stand up." Gaudior sounded cross. "I don't like to see you lying there. I thought you were never going to open your eyes."

Charles Wallace scrambled to his feet, lifted one leg, then the other. "How strange to be able to use my legs again—how wonderful."

Gaudior knelt beside him. "Climb."

Charles Wallace, legs shaky as though from long disuse, clambered onto the great back.

He rode a Gaudior who had become as tiny as a dragonfly, rode among the fireflies, joining their brilliant dance, twinkling, blinking, shooting over the star-watching rock, over the valley, singing their song, and he was singing, too, and he was himself, and yet he was all he had learned, he carried within himself Brandon and Chuck and their song and the song was glory . . .

And he rode a Gaudior who had become as large as a constellation, rode among the galaxies, and he was himself, and he was also Madoc, and he was Matthew, Matthew flying through showers of stars, caught up in the joy of the music of the spheres . . .

part of the harmony, part of the joy

The silver neigh of the unicorn sounded all about the star-watching rock, rippling over Meg and the twins, Mrs. O'Keefe and Charles, and the night was illumined by the flash of the horn, blinding them with oblivion as it pointed at each of them in turn.

Meg thought she heard Charles Wallace call, "Gaudior, goodbye—oh, Gaudior, goodbye . . ."

Who was Gaudior?

She knew once who Gaudior was.

Again she heard his silver knell ringing in farewell.

Sandy asked, "Hey, did you see lightning?"

Dennys looked bewildered. "It's too cold. And look at all the stars."

"What was that flash, then?"

"Beats me. Like everything else tonight. Charles, what was with you? I couldn't find a pulse and then suddenly it throbbed under my fingers."

Slowly, color was returning to the boy's cheeks. "You came just in time." He looked at Mrs. O'Keefe, who still had her hand to her side and was breathing with painful gasps. "Beezie. Thank you." There was infinite sadness in his voice.

"That's what Meg called her," Sandy said. "What is all this?"

"Mom O'Keefe laid a charge on me . . ."

Dennys said, "We told you it was nuts for you to think you could stop Branzillo single-handed. Did you fall asleep or something? You could have got frostbite." He sounded concerned and uncertain.

"Come on in, now," Sandy added, "and no more of this nonsense."

"After the President's call, you call it nonsense?" Meg demanded fiercely.

"Meg, you shouldn't be out in the cold," Dennys objected.

"I'm all right."

Charles Wallace took Mrs. O'Keefe's hands in his. "Thank you."

"Chuck's no idiot." Mrs. O'Keefe thumped Charles Wallace on the shoulder.

"Come on," Sandy urged. "Let's get moving."

Dennys held Mrs. O'Keefe's arm. "We'll help you."

They returned to the house, Sandy and Dennys supporting Mrs. O'Keefe; Meg holding Charles Wallace's hand as though they were both small children once more.

Ananda greeted them ecstatically.

Mrs. Murry hurried to her youngest son, but refrained from touching him. "She's really adopted us, hasn't she? You'd think she'd been with us forever."

"Watch out for that tail." Mr. Murry moved between the dog and the model of the tesseract. "A couple of indiscriminate wags and you could undo years of work." He turned to his daughter. "Meg, you shouldn't have gone out in this weather with your cold."

"It's all right, Father. My cold's better and I didn't get chilled. Did the President—"

"No. Nothing yet."

Meg tried to think. What did she remember? The President's call, of course. Mrs. O'Keefe's rune, and the response of the weather. The coming of Ananda. Kything with Charles Wallace in the attic, kything through aeons of time, kything which had faded to dreams because the unicorn—

A unicorn. That was absurd.

There was Mrs. O'Keefe's phone call in the middle of the night. Sandy went for her and brought her back to the house, and she had an old letter—who was it from? What did it say?

"Well, Charles." Mr. Murry regarded his son gravely. "How about the charge?"

Charles Wallace did not reply immediately. He was studying the model of the tesseract, and he touched one of the Lucite rods carefully, so that the entire model began to vibrate, to hum softly, throwing off sparkles of brilliance. "We still don't know much about time, do we? I think—" He looked bewildered. "Father, I think it's going to be all right. But not because I was intelligent, or brave, or in control. Meg was right, earlier this evening, when she talked about everything, everywhere, interreacting."

"You were gone longer than we expected."

"I was gone a long time. An incredibly long time."

"But what did you do?" Sandy asked.

"And where did you go?" Dennys added.

"Mostly I stayed right by the star-watching rock—"

"Father!" Meg exclaimed. "The letter Mom O'Keefe brought. Charles hasn't seen it."

Mrs. O'Keefe held out the yellowed paper to Mr. Murry.

"Please read it to me, Father." Charles Wallace looked pale and exhausted.

"My dear Gwen and Rich," Mr. Murry read,

Thank you for writing us so promptly of Papa's death. Zillah and I are grateful that he died peacefully in his sleep, with none of the suffering he feared. I know that you both, and little Zillah, are a consolation for Mama. And Papa had the satisfaction of having Rich for his partner, and of knowing that the name of Maddox and Llawcae will not be lost, for our young Rich talks with great enthusiasm about going to Merioneth when he is old enough.

Our little Matthew is a rapidly growing boy. I had hoped that as he grew out of babyhood he would be called Matthew, but he keeps the nickname given him by the Indian children, Branzillo, a combination of my name and Zillah's. Little Rich tries to keep up with his big brother in every way . . .

Mr. Murry looked up. "The letter breaks off there. Strange—it seems diff—is that what I read before?"

Mrs. Murry frowned slightly. "I'm not sure. It didn't sound quite—but we're all exhausted with strain and lack of sleep. Memory plays queer tricks at times like this."

"It has to be what Father read before," Sandy said flatly. "It offends my reasonable mind, but it really does seem possible that Branzillo's forebears came from around here."

"The letter did come from Mrs. O'Keefe's attic," Dennys said. "So it's even likely that he's distantly descended from her forebears, and that would make them ump-teenth cousins."

Sandy protested, "But what effect could that have on his starting a nuclear war? Or—we hope—on not starting one?"

Charles Wallace turned away from the argument, looked once more at the tesseract, then went to Mrs. O'Keefe, who was once again huddled in the rocking chair in front of the fire. Meg left the twins and followed Charles Wallace.

"Beezie," he asked softly, "what happened to Chuck?"

—Beezie, Chuck. They were in the vanishing kythe. Meg stepped closer to the rocker to hear Mrs. O'Keefe's reply.

"He died," she said bleakly.

"How?"

"They took him away and put him in an institution. He died there, six months later."

Charles Wallace expelled a long, sad breath. "Oh, Beezie, Beezie. And the baby?"

"Took after Duthbert Mortmain. Died in the State Penitentiary. Embezzlement. Let it be. What's done's done. What's gone's gone."

Ananda pressed against Meg, and she stroked the raised head.

Beezie. Chuck. Paddy O'Keefe. The kythe flickered briefly in Meg's mind. Beezie must have married Paddy for more or less the same reasons that her mother had married Duthbert Mortmain. And she learned not to feel, not to love, not even her children, not even Calvin.

Not to be hurt. But she gave Charles Wallace the rune, and told him to use it to stop Mad Dog Branzillo. So there must be a little of the Old Music left in her.

"Matthew's book," Charles Wallace said. "It's happening, all that he wrote."

The phone rang.

Mrs. Murry looked toward her husband, but did not speak.

They waited tensely.

"Yes, Mr. President?" Mr. Murry listened, and as he listened, he smiled. "El Zarco is setting up a Congress for the working out of peace plans and the equitable distribution and preservation of the earth's resources. What's that, Mr. President? He wants me to come as an advisor on the use of space for peace? Well, yes, of course, for a few weeks . . . This is splendid news. Thank you for calling." He put down the receiver and turned to his family.

"El Zarco—" Meg whispered.

"Madog Branzillo's favorite nickname, you know that," her father said. "The Blue-eyed."

"But his threats—"

Her father looked at her in surprise. "Threats?"

"Of war—"

Everybody except Charles Wallace and Mrs. O'Keefe was looking at her.

"The phone call before dinner—" she said. "Wasn't the President afraid of war?"

"El Zarco has put down the militant members of his cabinet. He's always been known as a man of peace."

Charles Wallace spoke softly, so only Meg could hear. "They haven't traveled with a unicorn, Meg. There was no El Rabioso for them. When Matthew sent Zillah to marry Bran, and when Gedder was killed, that was the Might-Have-Been. El Rabioso was never born. It's always been El Zarco." He held her hand so tightly that it hurt.

Mrs. O'Keefe looked at Meg, nodding. "Baby will be born."

"Oh, Mom," Meg cried. "Will you be glad to be a grandmother?"

"Too late," the old woman said. "Take me home. Chuck and Grandma are waiting for me."

"What's that?" Mr. Murry asked.

"Chuck and Grandma—never mind. Just take me home."

"I'll drive you," Mr. Murry said.

Meg kissed her mother-in-law good night. It was the first time she had ever kissed her. "See you, Mom. See you soon."

When the car drove off, Dennys turned to his sister. "I'm not sure she'll make it to be a grandmother, Meg. I think her heart's running out."

"Why?"

"Badly swollen ankles. Blue tinge to her fingernails and lips. Shortness of breath."

"She ran all the way to the star-watching rock."

"She was short of breath before then. It's a wonder it didn't kill her. And what all that was about I'll never know."

"This whole evening's confusing," Sandy agreed. "I

suggest we just forget it and go to bed. And Mrs. O'Keefe would never have made it back without Dennys and me, Meg. But you're right, Mother, she's quite an old girl."

"She is, indeed," Mrs. Murry agreed. "And I agree with you, Sandy, about getting to bed. Meg, you need your sleep."

The baby within Meg stirred. "You're more than right about Mom O'Keefe, Mother, more right than any of us could possibly have imagined. There's much much more to her than meets the eye. I hate the thought of losing her, just as we're discovering her."

Charles Wallace had once again been contemplating the intricate model of the tesseract. He spoke softly to his sister. "Meg, no matter what happens, even if Dennys is right about her heart, remember that it was herself she placed, for the baby's sake, and yours, and Calvin's, and all of us—"

Meg looked at him questioningly.

Charles Wallace's eyes as he returned her gaze were the blue of light as it glances off a unicorn's horn, pure and clear and infinitely deep. "In this fateful hour, it was herself she placed between us and the powers of darkness."